"Are you offering your resignation, Miss Bryant?"

"My lord, if you wish it, I will leave my post straightaway."

"You must agree that I've no reason to be impressed so far." James saw that she was now very pale, though her gaze was still steadfast. "But it probably didn't help," he went on, "that I gave no warning of my arrival today. I feel it would be easier for us all if you stayed on in your post, at least for a while."

She widened her eyes slightly. Perhaps she thought him a fool for giving her another chance. Maybe he was a fool, but he was also curious, because she puzzled him.

She was far too well-bred to be a housekeeper. She was also too young. He could see little of her figure under that hideous dress, but there was nothing particularly wrong with her face. Though that big cap canceled out any feminine appeal.

"And there's one more thing, Miss Bryant. You'll doubtless have heard stories about me."

She blinked. "My lord?"

"You must have heard that my reputation has been somewhat damaged of late. But absolutely none of the things that are said about me is true."

He thought that perhaps she said, very softly, "Of course." And then she departed. There was no doubt about it—the woman was ridiculously out of place here and would certainly have to go, sooner rather than later. So why hadn't he accepted the resignation she'd so swiftly volunteered?

Author Note

When I was a student, I used to work in a busy seaside café during the summer holidays. Most customers were lovely, but some could be difficult—and to make matters worse, the full-time staff used to relish playing tricks on the new staff members!

So I felt the utmost sympathy for the heroine of this story, Emma Bryant, who out of financial necessity takes on the role of housekeeper at a large country mansion. Not only does Emma have the mischievous footmen to deal with, but she also has to cope with Viscount Grayford, who has problems of his own—until he realizes that the young Miss Bryant could be his salvation.

No handsome viscount ever turned up at my café. But even then, I used to love dreaming up happy-ever-afters.

LUCY ASHFORD

———

The Viscount's
New Housekeeper

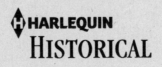

HARLEQUIN®
HISTORICAL™

Recycling programs
for this product may
not exist in your area.

ISBN-13: 978-1-335-40756-6

The Viscount's New Housekeeper

Copyright © 2021 by Lucy Ashford

This edition published by arrangement with Harlequin Books S.A.

For questions and comments about the quality of this book,
please contact us at CustomerService@Harlequin.com.

Harlequin Enterprises ULC
22 Adelaide St. West, 41st Floor
Toronto, Ontario M5H 4E3, Canada
www.Harlequin.com

Printed in U.S.A.

Lucy Ashford studied English and history at Nottingham University, and the Regency era is her favorite period. She lives with her husband in an old stone cottage in the Derbyshire Peak District in the UK, close to beautiful Chatsworth House, and she loves to walk in the surrounding hills while letting her imagination go to work on her latest story. You can contact Lucy via her website, lucyashford.com.

Books by Lucy Ashford

Harlequin Historical

Visit the Author Profile page
at Harlequin.com.

Chapter One

April 1816—Oxfordshire

There was mud. There was rain, hurling itself across the hills and fields, turning the road into a quagmire. James Brandon, the Seventh Viscount Grayford, pulled up his big horse on the crest of a hill and gazed around. The black gelding—ugly but strong as an ox—pawed the ground.

'Eager for more, Goliath?' said the Viscount. 'You're a glutton for punishment, like me. Well, then. On we go.'

He was heading home at last. But he'd never wanted to return like this. Never.

For five long years he'd been an officer in Wellington's army, fighting in the battles of the Peninsular War. But now the war was over; indeed, life as he'd known it was over, because early in March his older brother Simon, the Sixth Viscount Grayford, had died, leaving James not only with the title, but with the responsibilities that went with it.

By all that was holy, he didn't want to be a viscount!

He wanted neither Simon's grand Mayfair house, nor the sprawling Oxfordshire mansion to which he was heading on this rain-soaked spring evening. He wanted his old life again. But that was impossible.

Goliath whinnied and shook his head, as if to remind him there was no going back. Sighing, James turned up the collar of his long grey riding coat and cantered onwards. There was no doubt about it, he told himself grimly—his army career was finished. What was more, his reputation as a trusted servant of Crown and country had gone too.

'We can find,' the government enquiry had concluded in London last week, *'no evidence that Viscount Grayford has committed any wrongdoing.'*

In other words, there was no proof of his guilt—but neither was there proof of his innocence. As the old saying went, mud tended to well and truly stick, just as it did now to Goliath's hooves and fetlocks. Back in London he'd heard the whispers everywhere, observed too the sheer relish with which people muttered that James Brandon wouldn't have escaped nearly so lightly if it weren't for that new title of his.

'Maybe it's best to face your enemies out,' his cousin Theo Exton had advised as they sat till late in a Strand tavern some days ago.

'I've been fighting my country's enemies for years,' James had answered. His mood had been bleak and too much ale hadn't cheered him, rather the opposite. 'I've been a fool, Theo, not to realise I have so many enemies here. I'm planning on leaving London for Oxfordshire just as soon as I can.'

'But what about the house in Mayfair?'

'The staff are capable enough. Anyway, for them I

imagine my absence will be a considerable relief after all the parties my brother used to hold.'

Theo nodded. 'I can see you've made up your mind. But don't forget that hiding away when the world's treated you badly doesn't get you anywhere.'

James silently acknowledged the warning. Theo was not only his cousin but his oldest friend, who'd once longed to join the army too. But a childhood illness had left Theo lame and his widowed mother had no wealth, so while James pursued military splendour, Theo had resigned himself to a desk job in the Home Office.

'Let's say,' replied James at last, 'that I need a little breathing space away from London society. I also ought to take a good look around the Oxfordshire estate, now that I'm responsible for it all, God help me. But after the army I'm going to find it devilishly quiet.' He glanced at his cousin. 'I've an idea. Why don't you visit me there?'

Theo looked startled. 'You mean it? You want me to come to Oxfordshire?'

'I do, and the sooner the better. You told me you were due some leave and I'm sure to need your sound advice, especially since it's over three years since I set eyes on the place!'

Theo was nodding slowly. 'It could take me a day or two to make all the arrangements. But, yes, I really think I can manage it.' He grinned and raised his glass. 'Well, Major Brandon—here's to your new life as the Seventh Viscount Grayford!'

Already James was aware that he was starting off on the wrong foot, because the new Viscount should be arriving at Grayford Hall with pomp and ceremony, accompanied by servants and luggage. But coming here as a solitary traveller—journeying to Oxford by overnight mail, then riding the remainder of the way— had given him plenty of time to reflect on how his life had changed. Hell, he still found it hard to believe that his brother had been thrown from his horse in some midnight adventure and killed instantly! All right, so the two of them had never been close, but James had assumed Simon would always be there. Would marry and produce heirs, leaving James free to pursue his army career.

Years ago, James had imagined in his vanity that he could help his country in its hour of need. He'd even imagined himself coming home a hero... *Ha!* Another bitter exclamation escaped his lips. Theo had advised him to move on with his life, but this, he reflected as he looked around the dismal landscape, was more like hiding himself away at the back of beyond. In the dark recesses of Grayford Hall, to be precise, because now he could see the stern façade of his ancestral home looming through the trees.

It still looked just as he remembered, its turrets black with age and its gaunt stone walls draped with great clumps of tangled ivy. Visitors used to joke that there really ought to be a ghost here and indeed, as James rode up the familiar driveway, he noticed that the old oaks around him were stretching out gaunt fingers as if...

As if to welcome him? Or to warn him?

There would certainly be nobody here to make him welcome. How could there be, when he'd not sent word he was coming? He was also noticing signs of neglect:

fallen branches left to rot on the lawns, flower beds strewn with last year's dead growth, tiles missing from the roof of the pavilion where his mother and father used to entertain in the summer. No groundsmen or grooms busied themselves around the outbuildings. No smoke rose from any of the chimneys. He could almost have believed the vast building to be abandoned.

Then James reminded himself that his brother spent very little time here, so he never employed the number of staff a place of this size demanded. In fact Simon once told him that he left most of the management of the household to the steward, Francis Rowley; James had met him once and considered him a shifty character. Would Rowley be pleased to see him? He doubted it.

By now Goliath's hooves were clattering loudly over the cobbles of the Hall's forecourt, but still no one appeared. Frowning now, James dismounted and was about to loop the reins over a metal post when a skinny lad came hurrying out of the stables.

'Are you one of the grooms?' James spoke brusquely.

'Y-yes sir. I'm the only groom. My name's Gregory, if you p-please, sir!'

The lad was thin as a rake with wild, spiky hair. 'Take this horse,' James instructed, 'and see that he's well cared for. I'm the new Viscount Grayford.'

The lad's mouth fell open as James thrust the reins at him. 'You're the—the...'

'I am.' This nervous youngster was the only groom? But then, he noticed how the lad had moved to stroke Goliath's neck and was assessing his strong forequarters and that scar on his right flank.

'Is he an old army horse, m-my lord?'

'He is indeed. I bought him yesterday at a horse fair in Oxford, where he was destined for the knacker's yard. He's not pretty, but he's strong and willing, so take good care of him, won't you? His name's Goliath.'

'I'll look after him well, my lord, I promise!' Gregory began to coax Goliath towards the stables while James strode up the great stone steps with the rain dripping from his coat and pulled open the mighty oak doors.

Only to step back in shock.

What in hell's name...?

Straight away a powerful smell invaded his nostrils, catching at his throat and eyes like the acrid smoke of cannon fire. Blinking hard to clear his vision, he saw three housemaids on their knees in the vast hall, scrubbing away at the stone-flagged floor. Two were in grey dresses, one in brown. On seeing him standing in the doorway, the two in grey simultaneously gave faint screams and dropped their brushes with a clatter.

The third rose to her feet. Like the other two she wore an unflattering white cap that completely concealed her hair, while soap suds stained the skirt of her brown gown. 'Sir,' she began, 'may I ask—?'

She broke off as one of the older housemaids hissed to her, 'Miss. It's His Lordship. It's the new Viscount!'

He saw the younger woman's eyes widen in mingled shock and dismay. 'My lord,' she said, with an ill-balanced attempt at a curtsy. 'Welcome to Grayford Hall. We had no idea you were returning today. I am so sorry...'

She sounded shaken and confused and looked years younger than her fellow housemaids. The other two were curtsying also, their heads bowed low.

He frowned and was about to speak, but at that very moment a footman walked in with a pail of water. At the sight of James he dropped the thing and it landed with a crash, sending yet more water swirling over the already soaking floor. 'My lord!' he gasped.

James's brow was dark. 'What,' he pronounced, 'in the name of God, is going on here?'

The footman answered promptly. 'It was pickles, my lord.'

'Pickles?'

'Yes. It was her idea, my lord—Miss Bryant's.' The footman was pointing an accusing finger at the maid in the brown dress.

Why the deuce, thought James, was the footman referring to a housemaid in such a formal manner? But the footman was still talking, so he listened.

'She ordered Robert and me to lift the pickle vats from the cellars and carry them outside, my lord. She said they were starting to leak. But once we got them up here, they exploded. There were bits of pickle everywhere—cauliflower, beetroot, the lot.'

Exploding pickles? James listened in stupefaction. 'Where is the steward? Why isn't he taking care of this? And where on earth is Mrs Padgett, the housekeeper?'

At first he thought no one was going to answer him, but once more it was the young housemaid in the brown dress who spoke up. 'It's me,' she said. Her voice shook a little, though she did manage to meet his icy gaze. 'I'm your housekeeper, my lord.'

For a moment he was unable to speak. Good God, she could be no more than nineteen or twenty! Then he said, in a dangerously soft voice, 'Do you seriously expect me to believe that?'

'My name,' she said, 'is Miss Bryant. Miss Emma Bryant.' This time she spoke more steadily. 'I'm very sorry there are pickles everywhere, but those casks had been in the cellar for far too long and they were fermenting. Besides, as I said, we did not know you were coming.'

He was staring at her with incredulity. He said at last, keeping his voice calm with an effort, 'What has happened to Rowley and Mrs Padgett?'

'They've gone, both of them, my lord. Mr Rowley appointed me three months ago after Mrs Padgett's departure, then in March Mr Rowley himself left.'

Good God. So this inept young creature was currently in charge of the Hall? James said at last, 'What did my brother think of these extraordinary changes? What did he think of *your* appointment, Miss Bryant?' The stink of pickles was making him quite dizzy.

She said, 'I'm not even sure he knew of it all. You see, your brother has not visited the Hall since I arrived.'

He realised she'd folded her hands in front of her and was speaking again, this time even more quietly. 'We were all shocked to hear of Lord Grayford's death. I am most sorry for your loss, my lord.'

He nodded curtly. 'Thank you.'

She cleared her throat. 'Have you any luggage?'

'I travelled without,' he told her. 'It will be arriving tomorrow.'

'Very good, my lord. I'll ensure that your bedroom is immediately prepared. In the meantime, might I suggest that you wait in the front parlour? The fire in there can be lit straight away. Perhaps I can offer you refreshment of some kind?'

He frowned again, puzzled because she was so damned well spoken! He pulled off his dripping greatcoat and one of the footmen hurried to take it. 'I'll go to the parlour,' he said. 'Bring me some brandy. And at some point this evening, Miss Bryant, I'd like a private word with you.'

'You would, my lord?' She said it a little tremulously.

'Yes. I'd like a full explanation as to what, exactly, has been going on here in the last few months. I'll send for you when I'm ready.'

She bowed her head then turned to the footmen. 'Robert, please light the fire in the parlour. Thomas, you see to the fires in His Lordship's suite upstairs.'

The footmen set off. The two housemaids, he realised, were still staring at him, mouths agape. Shaking his head, he set off in the direction of the parlour, pausing only to call over his shoulder, 'And don't forget the brandy!'

If Miss Bryant answered, he didn't hear it. James wasn't normally a heavy drinker, but it struck him that over the next few days, he might be indulging a little more frequently than usual.

Chapter Two

As silence descended upon the remaining occupants of the hallway, Emma Bryant—who at twenty-one was surely the youngest ever housekeeper at Grayford Hall—remembered that there had been two entries in her diary for today. The first one was:

Confirm the household menus for the coming week with Cook.

The second?

Investigate the pickle casks in the cellar.

Oh, dear. If she'd possessed magical powers of fore-sight, she would have added a third instruction. *Do not, on any account, let the new Viscount arrive to see you on your knees, scrubbing a floor that reeks of vinegar.*

'He's a real good-looker, isn't he, miss?'

Emma jumped as one of the housemaids, Betsey, sidled close. 'His brother,' Betsey was murmuring, 'was handsome enough, but this one's something else altogether. He'll have all the fine ladies chasing him now he's a viscount. They won't care if it's whispered that he's let down his country, oh, no. They'll just be after his kisses—'

'Betsey!' Emma interrupted sharply. 'I want you and Moll to get rid of all traces of this vinegar, while I go upstairs to inspect His Lordship's rooms.'

'Yes, miss. Certainly, miss,' Betsey replied, with a mock civility that was even more galling than disobedience. 'But first, hadn't you better check that Cook knows she'll need to prepare an evening meal for His Lordship? He won't expect common servants' fare, you know.'

You should have thought of that yourself, Emma.

Taking a deep breath, she headed along the corridor towards the vast kitchen area. Lord Grayford wouldn't be used to servants' fare indeed, but no one had known he was coming, so how could Cook prepare a meal fit for a viscount?

On reaching the kitchen, though, she realised with relief that two scullery maids were already busy peeling and chopping vegetables and Mrs Clegg the cook was rolling out pastry so vigorously that Emma had to call out to be heard above the noise of clattering implements.

'Mrs Clegg!' Emma stepped closer. 'Clearly you've heard that His Lordship has unexpectedly arrived.'

'My goodness, yes.' Mrs Clegg turned to face Emma, rolling pin in hand as if ready for battle. 'But who would have guessed he'd turn up like this, without the slightest bit of warning!'

Emma tried her very best to look calm and collected. 'It is indeed a surprise, but you look as if you've already made a splendid start on his evening meal. Can I do anything to help?'

'We've got everything in hand.' Mrs Clegg pointed her rolling pin triumphantly at the large stove. 'I've a fine saddle of mutton roasting in there, my girls are preparing the vegetables and there's already some pea soup on the hob. So Major Brandon—His Lordship, I must call him now!—will be getting as hearty a meal as he'd find anywhere.'

She peered more closely at Emma. 'Now, don't you fret. You look a mite worried, but from what I remember of him as a youngster, our new Viscount is a good man. A *fair* man. Though you'll have to be even more careful than ever that those cheeky maids and the footmen don't give you trouble.'

Mrs Clegg had been here for years and once boasted to Emma that she'd never taken a bit of notice of Steward Rowley. 'The kitchen and storerooms are my domain!' she liked to declare. 'I'll have no interference from anyone else, thank you!'

Fortunately she'd taken Emma to her heart and was a useful ally, though now Emma had a sinking feeling that she was going to need her support more than ever.

Leaving the kitchen with the knowledge that at least she could be sure Lord Grayford would receive a good meal, she climbed the stairs to inspect the Viscount's private quarters, which consisted of a bedroom, dressing room and sitting room, all furnished by the last Viscount with no expense spared.

Indeed, Emma had to blink every time she entered, such was the opulence. The gilded furniture and crystal chandeliers positively sparkled, the curtains of thick French velvet swathed the windows luxuriously and marble statues lurked in every corner. Even though Lord Grayford hadn't visited for months, Emma had always told the maids to dust and air the rooms each day. Now, with a fire blazing in the sitting room and candles lit everywhere, she couldn't help but be pleased with the result.

Thomas the footman was lounging by the fireplace waiting for her verdict. 'Good enough for His Lordship, do you think, miss?'

'I hope so, Thomas. Would you go downstairs and tell the Viscount that everything is ready up here?'

Thomas had the same look of sly insolence as those ornate Chinese dogs that sat on the mantelshelf. 'Are you sure you don't want to tell him yourself, miss?'

Emma spoke in a crisper tone. 'As you'll have noticed, he's arrived with no valet. So I'm hoping you may make yourself useful in that respect, if His Lordship requires it.'

'I'll do that,' Thomas answered cheerfully. He set off, then paused by the door. 'By the way. Our new Viscount didn't half look mad when he arrived to see the hallway in such a mess.'

'Then we'll all have to make sure that he forms a better opinion of us very quickly. Won't we?'

Thomas grinned and sauntered off.

Useless, Emma. Quite useless. You sound like a peevish scold.

Taking one last, almost despairing look around, she made some completely unnecessary adjustments to the curtains and the garishly patterned counterpane then headed downstairs again to her housekeeper's quarters, which contained a small parlour and an even smaller bedroom. She drew a deep breath to steady herself, then swiftly changed her vinegar-stained gown and apron and inspected herself in her mirror.

She might be twenty-one, but with her petite figure she was often told she looked nineteen at the most. Her long hair was tightly pinned up beneath her big cap; her brown eyes, which had occasionally been admired, were at the moment full of anxiety. The stink of those pickle casks still haunted her. As did the look on Viscount Grayford's face, when she'd told him she was his housekeeper.

Oh, goodness. She'd heard a good deal of gossip about his older brother—that he was a much-admired member of the fashionable set in London and had enjoyed a luxurious lifestyle. She'd heard rather less about Major James Brandon. 'He went off to join the army when he was nineteen,' Cook had once told her. 'He was a bit of a rebel who didn't get on with his family and he left as soon as he could. They say he was one of Lord Wellington's bravest officers during the war.'

Recently, however, there had been rumours of a different kind—that he'd been accused of somehow letting down his country. Emma had listened carefully, knowing that some day soon he would turn up here—but what she'd not expected was for him to arrive without a word of warning. Neither had she expected him to be so dangerous-looking as he stood there in the doorway and surveyed the scene before him with increasing anger.

Oh, goodness. The footmen were tall, but he'd simply towered over them. His black hair, flattened by the rain, had emphasised the harshness of his expression. His dark blue eyes had almost pierced her and his mouth had curled with disbelief at the thought that she, Emma Bryant, could possibly be his housekeeper.

And his ominous words still rang in her head like peals of doom. *'At some point this evening, Miss Bryant, I'd like a private word with you.'*

Suddenly aware that her legs were wobbling slightly, Emma instructed herself to breathe deeply. The man had every reason to be astonished at her position in the household and he wasn't the only one. All the maids and footmen had reacted to her appointment with outright disbelief and who could blame them? She was young. She had no experience and when she applied for the job she'd not even expected to be granted an interview. She'd arrived at the Hall one frosty afternoon in early January to be met by Mr Rowley, who'd appeared to be already rather drunk.

'You're on the young side, Miss Bryant,' the steward had pronounced, lounging back in the chair behind his desk. 'And you've no record of domestic service. Why on earth do you think you can do this job?'

Though she was shrouded in a winter cloak and bonnet, she'd been acutely conscious of his sharp eyes roving her face and figure. 'I've kept house for my father for some time now, Mr Rowley. I believe that has given me some knowledge of running a household.'

He'd almost sneered. 'A household like this one?'

'I was going to add, sir, that of course our small house is nothing like Grayford Hall. I only wished to point out that I do have some practical experience.'

'Experience, eh?' His gaze now was a downright leer. 'You do know that Lord Grayford is away most of the year?'

'I realise that.' Everyone in the neighbourhood knew that the Sixth Viscount, like most of his fellow peers, far preferred London to the seclusion of his country home. She asked, 'What happened to the previous housekeeper, Mr Rowley?'

'Mrs Padgett? She left before Christmas to live with her daughter and grandchildren. We've managed, because it's pretty quiet here most of the year. Lord Grayford's unlikely to arrive any time soon and as for his brother, Major Brandon, he's been in the army for years, playing at being a hero. All of which means that you've plenty of time to learn the ropes.' He leaned back in his chair. 'Very well. You've got the job, Miss Bryant. Good luck. You'll maybe need it.'

And he'd been right. Since Mrs Padgett had left, it was plain that discipline among the staff had all but vanished. There was no butler to keep the footmen in order—the last one had apparently walked out after a huge argument with Mr Rowley in the summer—and Emma's attempts to restore routine had been a disaster. The maids resented her, the footmen laughed at her and as for Rowley, well, he just *leered.* Mrs Clegg the cook was her sole ally, and that was only because the kind woman pitied her.

It was a relief when Steward Rowley disappeared. He rode off one morning in early March without a word and the reason soon became clear enough, for the day after his departure the news arrived that Lord Grayford had died in a riding accident and his younger brother, the army officer, had inherited everything. Clearly Rowley had heard already and had no intention of facing the new Lord Grayford. Emma had felt a similar apprehension. Rather desperately, she'd renewed her efforts to put the house in order, labouring alongside the maids in clearing out the attics and dusty guestrooms, giving the footmen firm instructions to sweep a multitude of cobwebs from the lofty ceilings and chandeliers.

And yesterday, she'd decided to explore the cellars.

The maids had already informed her that Rowley had been drinking his way through the Sixth Viscount's wine stores and indeed the empty spaces in the wine racks told their own story. That would be another tricky subject to broach when the new heir eventually put in his appearance. What was more, as she ventured further into the labyrinth of underground rooms, she'd detected a strong smell of vinegar coming from some old wooden casks.

'That'll be the pickles, miss,' Moll, the oldest of the housemaids, had told her. 'They've been in those casks for years. I doubt there's any point trying to do anything with them.'

'But they're leaking!'

Moll had shrugged. 'Leave well alone, miss, that's my advice.'

But on returning to her room, Emma had consulted the book she'd been given by her father's elderly housemaid, Biddy. It was called *The Good Housekeeper's Daily Deeds* and it offered advice on every topic from dealing with the junior staff to making table decorations for grand dinner parties.

'You study this, Miss Emma,' kind Biddy had urged as she pressed it on her. 'You'll find all you need to know!'

Almost feverishly, Emma had looked up the section on pickled items and read:

*On no account should the meticulous house-
keeper leave any pickles in storage if the con-
tainers are found to be unsound.*

Right. Time to exert her authority. On finding the
two senior footmen playing dominoes in the staff dining room, she'd said, 'Thomas and Robert, I'd like
you to bring up the casks of pickles from the cellar.'

They hadn't been impressed. 'Why is that, miss?'

'Because they're no longer fit to be eaten. Besides,
they're taking up space down there.'

Thomas had yawned. 'Does it matter? It's not as if
the new Viscount's likely to be back any time soon.
We've heard he's in a spot of hot water in London, so
that's going to keep him busy. Isn't it, Robert?'

'Oh, definitely,' Robert agreed. He tapped a domino
on the table. 'Your turn to play, Thomas.'

Emma felt her breath coming a little faster because
she'd heard the rumours too. She looked steadily at
Thomas and said, 'I very much hope that you're not
adding to the gossip about His Lordship?'

Thomas returned her gaze, all innocence. 'Oh, no,
miss. Loyal as anything, I am. All us footmen are, as
long as he pays our wages. As for the maids, they'll
make no trouble, since they always were a bit sweet
on the Major—gallant army officer and all that.' He
wagged a finger. 'Make sure you don't go the same
way, miss. He's quite a handful in the bedroom department, or so I've heard tell.'

One of the maids had come in and was openly
laughing. 'Thomas, you leave Miss Bryant alone, poor,
innocent lamb that she is.'

Emma pretended not to have heard. 'Thomas and

Robert, I'd like those casks brought from the cellar now, if you please!' Oh, lord, she was useless at giving orders—she sounded either prim or stupid.

'Upstairs, miss? Through the main hall?'

'Yes. Of course. They'll be too big to manage any other way.'

That was the plan, but out in the hallway, one of the casks had either fallen or was dropped, it was impossible to say which. The result was that the blessed thing had split open, the contents spilled all over the floor and it was then, just when they'd swept up the bits and begun to mop up the vinegary mess, that the new Viscount had arrived.

His face had been as black as thunder, his voice as cold as ice. And very soon now, he would summon her. To dismiss her? She wouldn't be surprised. Well, it was no use hiding in her housekeeper's quarters any longer. Standing up from her desk, Emma pushed *The Good Housekeeper's Daily Deeds* aside and looked in her mirror again to make sure her cap was straight and every strand of hair pinned out of sight. The cap was huge and hideous. Her cheeks were pale with worry, making quite obvious the faint dusting of freckles across her unfashionably short nose.

There was a loud knock just then at her door. She went to open it and saw Thomas standing in the doorway.

'You wanted me, Thomas?'

'It's not me that wants you, miss, but His Lordship.'

Emma's spirits sank once more.

'And,' continued Thomas, 'here's a word of warning, miss. He's in a *furious* temper.' He winked. 'Just saying.' And off he went, whistling under his breath.

Emma forced herself to stay calm. After all, what was the worst he could do? Dismiss her? At that moment, she thought that she honestly wouldn't mind. Glancing round, she grabbed a small notebook and pencil from her desk, recalling more of the manual's advice.

Lists are an essential aid to a housekeeper's efficiency. Carry a notebook somewhere about your person at all times.

Taking a deep breath, she headed upstairs to the Viscount's private quarters on the second floor, remembering yet again the unpleasant rumour that in London he had been investigated for some kind of fraud—treachery, even—and the servants were buzzing with it. What a homecoming.

By now she'd reached the door of his rooms and, after fighting a strong impulse to run, she knocked. 'My lord?' she called. 'It's Miss Bryant. Your housekeeper.'

There was no reply, so after a moment's hesitation she went in. The parlour was empty and the bedroom door was shut, but she thought she heard some movement from the dressing room.

'My lord?' she repeated, stepping carefully over the Persian rug and blinking, as she always did, at the gaudy colours in here. 'I believe you sent word you were ready to see me?'

She gasped, because Lord Grayford was emerging from his dressing room—and he was most definitely *not* ready to see her. He wasn't even clothed. Well, he did have a large white towel slung around his hips, but the upper half of his torso was stark naked and glistening with drops of water.

He must have just emerged from his bath. Oh, goodness. She'd never seen anything like it.

The Viscount looked at first bewildered then just plain furious. 'What the devil,' he said, 'are you doing in here, Miss Bryant?'

Wishing myself dead, thought Emma.

'My lord,' she began, 'I am most sorry to intrude. But I was told you wished to speak to me—'

'I wished to speak to you at seven o'clock! Those were my precise instructions to the footman, whatever his name was. And that's not for another half an hour!'

She could hardly speak. Could hardly think. *Look away*, her brain said, but her eyes weren't obeying her brain and remained totally fixed on his shoulders and chest. Those muscles. The power in them. The strength. She glimpsed an old scar—from a sword, or a dagger?—curling under his armpit like a badly stitched seam and then, what was even worse, her gaze was straying downwards to the totally forbidden zone that was concealed by nothing but the white towel.

'I—I'll go,' she stammered at last. 'I'm extremely sorry to have intruded, my lord. I must have misunderstood the message. I really cannot apologise enough. It will not happen again…'

She was backing clumsily towards the door, but the Viscount, still firmly gripping that towel around his middle, rapped out, 'You are not leaving. I have no desire to be disturbed by you later on, Miss Bryant, so let's get this conversation over with here and now.'

The conversation about dismissing her, did he mean? Yes. She had no difficulty appreciating that.

Through a fog of misery, she realised he was still talking.

'Wait there a moment,' he ordered. 'I'm going to dress myself and I won't be long. Do you understand?'

'I understand, my lord.' She clasped her hands to steady herself as he turned to go into his dressing room, giving her this time a view of his powerful shoulders, as well as the way the damp towel clung to his hips... Too much, all of it. Once he'd shut the door of his dressing room, she sank down rather weakly on the nearest chair.

Of course Thomas had done this deliberately. He must have known the Viscount was taking a bath, since he and Robert would have brought up his hot water. Doubtless at this very moment, Thomas would be telling the other staff about the trick he'd played on their foolish young housekeeper and they would all be almost crying with laughter. Every part of her positively ached with shame.

But then she was jumping to her feet again, because far sooner than she'd expected the Viscount was emerging, rubbing his hair dry with a towel. From somewhere he'd found a clean white shirt, buckskin breeches and glossy boots—yet he'd brought nothing with him, so where had he found them?

He answered her unvoiced question immediately. 'No doubt you're wondering where these clothes came from, since I brought no luggage.' He cast the towel on the nearest chair. 'The answer is that I've always kept plenty of spare garments in my old bedroom here.'

Of course. She should have remembered that, since she and the maids had spring-cleaned that room only weeks ago.

'So.' He was speaking again in his deep, sonorous voice. 'Miss Bryant, I think you have some explaining to do. Tell me, if you will, how you come to find yourself the housekeeper of Grayford Hall.'

Emma's brain still refused to work properly. She'd just seen him naked—well, half of him anyway—and she still wanted to sink through the floor. He'd looked so very *dangerous* with scarcely anything on and even now, his narrowed blue eyes and his curling mouth made her feel quite shaky. Her thoughts turned rather desperately to the housekeeping manual lying on her desk—but what possible answer could it have to a situation like this?

Chapter Three

James had expected to find Grayford Hall in a state of moderate neglect, since his brother visited it so rarely. But he had not expected to find that his new housekeeper was…what exactly were the words he was looking for? Gauche. Naive. Completely out of place in her role.

He had wondered if she was going to faint after the shock of seeing him half-dressed. If she'd been less innocent-looking, he might have suspected her of intruding on his bath in an attempt to show her wealthy master that she was available for his pleasure. Clearly, however, there was no danger of that in her case.

'You'd better sit down,' he said with something of a sigh, pointing to a chair as he settled in another and poured himself brandy from the decanter close by. 'You know, Miss Bryant, you could always start by telling me exactly why Rowley and Mrs Padgett left the Hall.'

She met his gaze steadily—he'd give her credit for that. 'My lord,' she began, 'Mrs Padgett retired, I believe, to live with her family in Reading.'

'So you took over her job? How on earth did you come to be appointed?'

He saw her colour heighten. 'Mr Rowley inter-viewed me for the post. He informed me there were no other applicants.'

He regarded her steadily. *Either that, or old Rowley decided you'd be mighty convenient one way or another.* Aloud he said, 'Did Rowley make advances, Miss Bryant? Did he let you know he expected certain, shall we say, favours in return for appointing you?'

That provoked an unexpected glint of anger. 'He did not, my lord! And if he had given any indication of such expectations, I would have let him know my feelings on the matter!'

Yes, she was innocent indeed—and puritanical too, James guessed. He knew he should have apologised for his callous comment, but because his stubborn streak got the better of him he forged on relentlessly. 'So what happened to Rowley, then? Did he decide he'd had enough of the Hall?'

Her eyes glinted, bringing another touch of rebel-lion to her otherwise constrained expression. 'Mr Rowley, my lord, was a thief. And I told him so!'

Well. That was quite a declaration. 'Do you have evidence, for that rather bold accusation?'

'Yes, I do! I discovered that during your brother's frequent absences, he had been steadily disposing of the wine in the cellar.'

'Drinking it, you mean?'

'Not only was he drinking it, he was selling off the most valuable bottles.'

'You sound quite certain of this, Miss Bryant. Yet you didn't think to inform my brother?'

'I was considering it, when the sad news came that the Viscount had died.' She let the silence lie a moment before saying, 'Mr Rowley vanished the very next day.'

Hmm. James twirled his brandy glass. 'Do you think he was afraid of facing me?'

'That is not for me to say, my lord. But of course, his departure meant that the Hall has been without a steward for some weeks. Presumably, now that you're here, you'll no doubt be eager to appoint someone in his place.' She raised her eyes to meet his. 'You will also, of course, require a new housekeeper.'

He studied her for a moment, noting those rather vivid brown eyes that were almost defiant. 'Am I to understand that you're offering your resignation, Miss Bryant?'

'My lord, if you wish it I will leave my post straight away. I can only apologise for the state in which you've found us all on your arrival.'

James said, 'You can't help but agree that I've no reason to be impressed so far.' He saw that she was now very pale, though her gaze was still steadfast. 'But it probably didn't help,' he went on, 'that I gave no warning of my arrival today. In conclusion, Miss Bryant, I feel it would be easier for us all if you stayed on in your post, at least for a while.'

She widened her eyes slightly, but otherwise she looked—deuce take it—she didn't look pleased or even a little relieved. Perhaps she thought him a fool for giving her another chance. James frowned. Well, maybe he was a fool, but he was also curious, because she puzzled him.

She was far too well bred both in her voice and

her deportment to be a housekeeper. She was also too young. He could see little of her figure under that hideous dress and apron, but there was nothing particularly wrong with her face. Though that big cap cancelled out any feminine appeal, especially since it completely hid her hair—which was probably cut short, he told himself, and mousy too.

He realised she was speaking again. She said, a little incredulously, 'So you're not dismissing me?'

'Not yet.' His eyes never left her face. 'There's a saying in the army that a quick decision can lead to bad results.' He rose to his feet. 'And that,' he added, 'is all I have to say for the time being. I imagine your routine will be rather busier now that I've taken up residence, so you'll have to let me know if you need more staff.'

She had risen to her feet also. 'Of course. My lord, will it suit you if your evening meal is served in the dining hall at eight?'

'Indeed. And there's one more thing, Miss Bryant. You'll doubtless have heard stories about me.'

She blinked. 'My lord?'

'Don't try to tell me you don't know.' He spoke curtly because he had no time for pretence. 'You must have heard that my reputation has been somewhat damaged of late. But absolutely none of the things that are said about me are true.'

She curtsied. He thought that perhaps she said, very softly, 'Of course.' That was all. And then she departed, leaving James feeling frustrated and confused. There was no doubt about it—the woman was ridiculously out of place here and would certainly have to go, sooner rather than later. So why hadn't he accepted the resignation she'd so swiftly volunteered?

Because he already had enough to deal with, that was the answer. He needed to sort out the aftermath of his brother Simon's unexpected death. He needed to assess all his new responsibilities. He also had to decide how on God's earth he was going to redeem his reputation—and that would be the hardest thing of all.

He suddenly realised he hadn't fastened the top few buttons of his shirt, but what the devil did it matter when Miss Bryant had seen rather a lot more of him than that? And the sight certainly hadn't pleased her; indeed, he suspected from her reaction that she must have some antipathy to men in general. Once she'd recovered from the shock of finding him wrapped only in a towel, she'd pursed her mouth as primly as a middle-aged dowager encountering one of London's rakehells.

But really, for a moment or so he'd also thought she was rather pretty, despite that awful cap. And her eyes were a distractingly unusual shade of brown, with hints of gold almost...

Finding your housekeeper attractive? Your wits have gone wandering, man.

Pressing his lips together, he walked to the mirror and started putting on one of the neckcloths he'd fetched from his old room. The mirror was as ornate as the rest of his brother's furnishings, gilded and scrolled in a manner he found quite ridiculous. He scowled at the two Chinese dogs on the mantelshelf and shook his head. He had hoped life would be quiet at Grayford Hall, but his first few hours here had proved to be just the opposite—and not in a good way.

* * *

Emma walked away so quickly from the Viscount's rooms that she found herself heading in completely the wrong direction. The house was huge and many of the corridors were still a maze to her.

Even so, you foolish creature.

Just for a moment, she felt a threatening ache at the back of her throat. That horrifying fiasco of the bath was her own fault—yes, Thomas the footman had played his part, but she should have known better than to go blundering into Lord Grayford's private chamber!

Lord Grayford, with nothing but a towel round his waist—she'd never seen a sight like it. Were all men so daunting without their clothes on? Did they all make you feel exceedingly weak at the knees and melt your brain at the same time?

Still half-dazed, she retraced her footsteps to the servants' stairs. She could, she supposed, have tried to explain to the Viscount that Thomas had tricked her, but what was the point? How she wished she was home again in the cottage two miles from here, where her father would be settled in his armchair poring over some learned book and quite possibly forgetting to eat the supper that kind Biddy would have prepared for him.

He had never wanted her to take this job. On their last evening together he'd watched her packing her bags and said sadly, 'My dearest girl. You should have been looking forward to marriage and children, instead of going off alone to that big, half-empty house. I'm so sorry.'

She'd hugged him hard. 'Marriage, Papa? I've met no one who's tempted me in the slightest, I assure you!

And I can visit you often—Steward Rowley said so. As for my being lonely, you mustn't worry, because I'll have all the other staff for company.'

'Maybe so,' her father had replied. 'But I fear you won't have any friends.'

Her father had been right, of course. It was hard to believe now that at her interview, she'd practically begged for the post. Emma had resolved that by the time the new Viscount made his appearance the Hall would be immaculate, but instead he had arrived to chaos—and she'd made an utter fool of herself by walking in on him almost naked.

Her cheeks burned anew.

She tried telling herself it was really exceedingly stupid of her to be so embarrassed, when everyone knew that servants were all but invisible to their lofty employers. But the trouble for Emma was that she hadn't been born into poverty. Her mother had died when Emma was an infant, but her father, who'd been a well-known scholar, had both money and connections and when Emma was nineteen her mother's spinster aunt, Lady Lydia Dunstable, had offered her a London Season.

Lady Lydia, who lived then in Hanover Square, had doted on her great-niece and Emma dutifully attended routs and parties with her for three months. But then the news came that her father had lost nearly all of his money through bad investments and Emma had seen him age overnight. It was she who'd had to organise their return to Oxford; she who had to arrange the sale of their spacious house there and find them a rented cottage in the village of Hawthorne, which lay just beyond the boundary of the Grayford estate.

Poor Lady Lydia had bewailed their fate and offered financial help, but Emma had declared she was
quite happy to return to Oxfordshire with her father.
For she hadn't enjoyed her brief Season. She'd guessed
that most of her suitors were after her father's money;
certainly most had vanished into thin air when the
news broke that he was ruined.

I can cope with being poor, Emma had told herself fiercely.

Indeed, she'd seen her job here as a way of proving her independence. But if she had to leave straight
away, without references—what then?

She walked on to the dining room, determined to
ensure that all was ready for the Viscount's evening
meal. But on reaching the doorway she halted, because Thomas and Betsey were in there and clearly
they hadn't heard her approach.

'I reckon His Lordship's come to the Hall to lick
his wounds,' Thomas was saying with relish. 'Obvi-
ously he can't stand the heat in London.'

'Is it true then?' Betsey's eyes were wide. 'Is he really in disgrace?'

'Why else would he hide away here, if he has nothing to be ashamed of? It all looks mighty suspicious,
if you ask me. And—' He broke off as Emma entered
the room. 'Ah, miss,' said Thomas. He kept his face
straight, but she could see the laughter lurking in his
eyes. 'I gather His Lordship wasn't quite ready for
you after all.'

Betsey smothered a giggle and Emma felt her chest
grow tight. 'Thomas,' she said, 'I find it astonishing
that you're talking so maliciously about a man who
has given so much service to his country.'

'But miss, haven't you heard?' protested Betsey. 'They're saying in Oxford—'

'I don't care what they're saying in Oxford! Yes, there has been gossip about him, but no proof of his wrongdoing has been established. And I will not allow those false rumours to be repeated here. Do you understand? Now, is everything ready? Have you polished the silver and the wine glasses?'

'We're just about to do that,' said Thomas woodenly.

'Then I suggest you carry on.' But as Emma turned to go, she heard Betsey murmur, 'She won't forget His Lordship's bathtime in a hurry. I'll bet she's never seen a sight like that in her life.'

No, thought Emma as she hurried away. Betsey was right. Still somewhat dazed by the recollection, she went next to the kitchen, where the two scullery maids stood at the range watching over a variety of bubbling pots and pans. On the centre table Mrs Clegg was about to tackle the roasted haunch of mutton with a huge carving knife, while on a sideboard stood a variety of tarts, creams and fruit jellies.

Emma's spirits rose a little. 'Mrs Clegg, you appear to have everything under control here.'

Mrs Clegg gave a satisfied nod. 'I remember His Lordship's hearty appetite from when he was a lad. You watch, my dear—he'll find his temper improving mightily once he's enjoyed a good meal!' She stuck a big fork into the mutton and the juices oozed as she prepared to carve the first slice. 'All you need to do is to make sure those idle servants have the dining room ready—oh, and why don't you pick some flow-

ers to put on the table? That'll make everything look
nice and welcoming.'

Of course! Her housekeeping manual's advice precisely.

*The sight of a pleasantly adorned table refreshes
the most jaded appetite.*

'What an excellent thought! Thank you, Cook.'

Emma went out by the side door to the garden. The
flowerbeds had been neglected over winter, but a few
days ago she'd noticed that some white tulips had burst
into bloom. She cut just a few and after carefully arranging them in a silver vase, she took them to the
dining room. Thomas and Betsey had vanished and
she saw with considerable relief that the table looked
perfect, laid with the best silver and a white damask
cloth. She reminded herself that she needed to check
the linen store, preferably tonight, because more ta-
blecloths and napkins would be in use now that the
Viscount was in residence.

*A well-kept home can be judged by the state of
its linen. Keep it pristine, always...*

She jumped when Thomas strolled in. 'Cook says
to tell you, miss,' he announced, 'that the food's all
done.' He glanced at the table. 'Nice flowers. Did you
put them there?'

'Yes,' she replied. 'Thomas, please go and inform
the Viscount that his meal is ready. You and Robert
will of course be serving him, so you must ensure that
nothing—absolutely nothing—goes wrong.'

'You can count on me, miss,' Thomas said with a grin.

If only.

Onwards, then, to the laundry store at the back of the house, where the linen lay folded on airy wooden shelves. Drawing her notebook from her apron pocket, she began to make a list. There appeared to be no cause for worry here, thank goodness; no need to be concerned about the Viscount's meal either, since Cook's food was always wonderful. So how could even the mischievous servants ruin it?

She dropped her pencil on hearing a roar of masculine anger coming from the direction of the dining room.

'What the *devil* is going on here?'

That was the Viscount's voice. It had the kind of force he must have used to his men on the battlefields of Europe. Lifting her skirts Emma ran to the dining room, heart thumping, to discover the Viscount on his feet and Thomas leaning across the table jabbing at something with a napkin, while Robert hovered in the background. The tulips lay scattered.

No one noticed her coming in, because all their attention was focused on two earwigs that were crawling purposefully across the damask cloth in the direction of the Viscount's plate of half-eaten mutton. Thomas was endeavouring to pick them up but was making a poor job of it, so much so that in the end the Viscount, using his own napkin, grabbed at both earwigs and thrust the bundle towards Robert.

'Here,' he ordered. 'Take the wretched things outside.' Robert scurried off, leaving Thomas to face the Viscount's wrath. 'Well?' His Lordship declared. 'And whose bright idea was it to bring in those flowers? Because that's where the damned creatures came from!'

He still hadn't registered Emma's arrival, but Thomas had and was already looking in her direction. Emma stepped forward. 'My lord, it was me.'

What else could she say? *There were no earwigs when I placed the flowers in the vase. Someone must have put them there...* Weak. Totally weak.

The Viscount turned his steely blue gaze on her and she felt herself wilting like those poor tulips. He said to Thomas, over his shoulder, 'Remove the flowers immediately.'

'Yes, my lord.' Emma saw the slight smirk on Thomas's face as he left.

Those flowers had looked so very pretty. 'My lord,' Emma began, 'I'm extremely sorry about the earwigs, but if you'd like to resume your meal, there are more savoury dishes to come—'

'No need,' the Viscount retorted. 'I find I've lost my appetite. I'm retiring to my room.' In moments he was gone.

Emma stood there on her own feeling sick with shame—anger too, because she knew who would have put the earwigs there. *Thomas.* He would have guessed that since the Viscount already thought her an incompetent fool, the finger of blame would point immediately to her. She stood gazing at the fine silverware glittering in the light of the beeswax candles and she felt cold with sudden misery.

She was still standing there when Thomas returned a few minutes later. He halted and look pointedly around the room. 'Oh,' he said. 'Isn't His Lordship coming back to finish his meal?'

'No,' she said. 'He isn't. And let me tell you that there'll be no more of this. Do you understand?'

He feigned innocence. 'I don't understand, miss, no, not really. What are you trying to accuse me of?'

'Of making trouble. For *me.* You know very well that you've been trying to destroy my authority here from the day I arrived. I want you to stop your tricks, or…'

'Or what?' He was starting to clear away the dishes. 'You'll tell the Viscount?' He carried on piling up the plates then left the room with them, not even waiting for her answer, because he knew there wasn't one.

Of course, she could complain to the Viscount about the servants and explain how they relished making a fool of her. But he might well reply, in that impatient way of his, 'Then I consider you are the fool, Miss Bryant, for allowing them to do so.'

She went back to her own room, closed the door and leaned wearily against it. He was hardly likely to take her complaint seriously when he'd arrived to see her on her knees scrubbing the floor, with the place looking like a wreck! And when she'd looked up and seen him towering over her, she'd felt—what exactly had she felt?

She dreaded to think.

In London during her ill-fated Season, Lady Lydia had introduced her to one gentleman after another. 'All of them,' Lady Lydia had whispered eagerly in her ear, 'are looking for a sweet girl like you, my dear.' Two years later Emma could hardly remember their names, let alone what they'd looked like. Yet she knew already that she would never forget Lord Grayford. The sight of him fresh from his bath had almost caused her heart to stop. She'd been utterly dismayed by the way strange tingling sensations had erupted in places she wasn't even supposed to think about, even as those blue eyes of his gazed at her almost in disbelief—and no wonder.

She caught sight of herself in the mirror and saw that her horrible cap had slipped sideways so she tugged it off. Really, dismissal would be almost a relief. But in the meantime she'd better turn to the paperwork on her desk, because thanks to the upheavals of the day she'd not yet investigated the post she was supposed to deal with. As usual there were several tradesmen's bills, which she put aside for tomorrow. There was a letter from Lady Lydia, who still wrote to her even though she'd now moved from London to Surrey.

> *Dear Emma,*
> *When are you coming to visit me? There are several very pleasant gentlemen in this neighbourhood who I'm sure would love to meet you...*

Poor Lady Lydia had never quite been able to absorb the fact that Emma was no longer a desirable match for any gentleman. Emma sighed and put the letter aside.

The next one caused her to frown because it was addressed to no one in particular and bore only the name of the Hall. Emma opened it and the paper fell to her desk as if it burned her fingers. It said,

> *Think you'll be welcome here? Think again.*

There was no signature, merely a tiny black drawing of a bird—a menacing-looking creature with narrowed eyes and a large, open beak. The note must be for her. But why the sinister-looking drawing?

She knew that by now the staff would be gathering in the servants' dining hall for their supper. One of them must have sent it, that was the only possible answer. Pushing it to the back of her desk, she drew out her diary to write down as she usually did the events of the day.

Today, Lord Grayford arrived. Today...

Today, quite simply, had been a disaster.

Chapter Four

James slept badly that night. *Give me an army tent any time*, he had muttered as he tried to get comfortable beneath the heavy counterpane—embroidered with gold Chinese dragons, for God's sake! At long last he'd drifted into sleep, but his dreams were odd indeed because earwigs kept appearing.

Maybe his reaction to the creatures had been a bit strong for a man used to the battlefield, but the episode had certainly put him off his dinner. Even more annoyingly, his dreams had ended with the arrival of a rather mousy little housekeeper whose brown eyes— the only striking thing about her— were full of dismay as she said, over and over, *'I really cannot apologise enough. It will not happen again.'*

Miss Bryant was damned right it wouldn't happen again. She'd offered to resign and he'd refused, but another day like the one just over and she would most definitely be packing her bags.

He rose at seven the next morning and, clad in a serviceable dressing gown that he'd retrieved from his old bedroom, he was pulling back the curtains to let in some light when a footman came in bearing a tray.

'I believe you like coffee in the morning, my lord?'

'I do indeed.' James watched somewhat warily as the servant placed the tray on his bedside table. Silver coffee pot, cream jug, porcelain cup and saucer. *Hmm*. No mishaps so far.

Then James realised a second footman had entered. 'My lord, here are your riding boots from yesterday. I polished them myself.' He spoke with a certain amount of pride, to which he was entitled; the boots positively gleamed.

'Thank you,' James said. 'My luggage should be arriving later today.'

Which indicated to them, of course, that he was staying, but if they were dismayed by the news they didn't show it. 'Do you require assistance in dressing, my lord?' the first one asked.

'No. I'll manage perfectly well.'

They bowed and retreated and James poured himself coffee. It was surprisingly good—strong and rich, just as he liked it. He added a little cream and after glowering at those two Chinese dogs over the hearth he went, cup in hand, to gaze out of the window again. Unlike yesterday, the sky was crystal blue and he could see beyond the wooded park to the hills where sheep grazed. Yesterday it had been almost dark when he arrived, but now was the time to remind himself that all of this was his responsibility now.

He'd registered yesterday that the estate had been neglected and no doubt a further inspection would reveal more problems.

Well. At least that will make a change from brooding over your ruined reputation.

Swigging down the last of his coffee, he resolved to ride out before breakfast and get a feeling for the lie of the land. Dressing and shaving didn't take him long, since the rigours of army life had encouraged speed, so only ten minutes later, clad in riding coat, breeches and boots, he set off downstairs intending to go straight out to the stables.

But his way through the main hall was halted by none other than Miss Bryant.

Inwardly he groaned. *Last night*... Doubtless she felt considerable embarrassment also, but she must have taken a good look at him because she'd realised he was in outdoor attire.

'Good morning, my lord,' she began. The colour was rising in her cheeks already, but she pressed on. 'I see that you are about to go out, so if you don't wish to take your breakfast yet, it can be easily delayed. I shall inform Cook straight away.'

'You mean that it's all prepared?' He added, maybe a little too sharply, 'Is it edible, I wonder?'

He felt a twinge of regret as he saw a flutter of fresh anxiety cross her face. She answered, 'I trust so, my lord, since I personally supervised it.'

He sighed. 'Very well, Miss Bryant. Since everything's ready, I'll take my meal now, but I often enjoy a ride before breakfast. Perhaps later today, I'll instruct you as to my usual routine.'

'Certainly, my lord.'

Watching her departing figure, he frowned over that grim brown dress and awful cap. But it struck him anew that her voice was pleasing on the ear, while she carried herself like a lady. God in heaven, why was she working here? Shaking his head, James strode on towards the breakfast parlour and began to examine the chafing dishes set out on the sideboard, finding bacon, kidneys and kedgeree as well as fresh-baked rolls and another steaming pot of coffee.

He realised just how ravenous he was and was helping himself to a large plateful when Cook came in. With a bob of a curtsy she beamed widely at him. 'My lord. It's truly good to have you back!'

'Mrs Clegg!' He smiled. 'How are you? Believe me, it was worth returning for your cooking alone.'

Although at least fifty, she blushed like a girl. 'Thank you, my lord!'

After that he was left in peace since Miss Bryant, thank goodness, appeared to have vanished. In fact she was an invisible sort of person, he decided as he helped himself to more bacon—invisible, that was, unless she was making a mess of something.

But his respite didn't last long. He was finishing off his third cup of coffee when Miss Bryant reappeared. 'My lord?'

'Yes?' He was a little annoyed at being interrupted, but tried to maintain civility. 'What is it now?'

'It's about your visitors, my lord.'

'Visitors?' He put down his cup sharply. 'Already? Surely not!'

'They are not here yet, but I think some may arrive very soon. Mr and Mrs Eldon have already sent word of their intention to call, and so have several others.' She put before him a silver salver containing some cards.

'The Eldons? Good God!' He remembered the Eldons all too well and a more tedious couple he could not imagine. 'I apologise for my language, Miss Bryant, but what I mean is—surely no one expects me to receive visitors so soon?'

He saw her blink at his forthrightness. 'My lord, I imagine they will all wish to express their gladness at seeing you home once more. But I know, of course, that you were hoping for a quiet ride around the estate this morning.'

'I was,' he agreed, reaching to wipe his fingers on a napkin.

He saw her take a deep breath. 'If you wish me to help—may I suggest something?'

Well. Here was a turn-up for the books. He, the Viscount, was being offered advice as to his actions by his novice housekeeper? He drawled, 'I'm always open to advice, from any quarter. It's one of my better points, I believe.'

He thought he saw her flinch slightly, but she said, calmly enough, 'I know it's presumptuous of me, my lord, and I apologise if I'm speaking out of turn. But my suggestion is that you go out now, before any of these people arrive. I will tell them you have urgent visits to make and won't be back until later this afternoon.'

James leaned back in his chair and folded his arms across his chest. 'So you'll tell lies for me, will you, Miss Bryant? I'm rather surprised at you.'

She was a little pink again but otherwise there was no emotion now in her impassive face. No capacity for it either, he guessed, beneath that tightly buttoned brown dress of hers. She replied, 'I'm thinking of your best interests, my lord. Your neighbours will naturally be eager to welcome you back, but their haste could be described as rather thoughtless considering your long journey yesterday. And—I'm afraid it's presumptuous of me again—I've asked the groom, Gregory, to have your horse ready. Because—'

She broke off as a footman hurried in. 'My lord, I was upstairs just now and I caught sight of Mr and Mrs Eldon's carriage approaching the park gates.'

'My God,' muttered James. He gulped down the last of his coffee and was on his feet instantly. 'I'm on my way,' he declared. 'I'm obliged to you, Miss Bryant.'

She bobbed a curtsy and began placing some plates on a tray. As James set off for the door he stopped and let his eyes briefly follow her.

He realised that her tightly tied apron strings laid an unexpected emphasis on her tiny waist. And he couldn't help but notice that even the full skirts of her hideous brown dress couldn't hide the fact that she had a very shapely derrière.

For God's sake, man, he rebuked himself. *What are you thinking?* All right, he acknowledged he'd been telling himself that Miss Bryant was entirely lacking in feminine appeal. But maybe he was wrong…

Pull yourself together.

Purposefully he set off again for the door, only to hear a loud crash behind him. Swinging round, he realised his young housekeeper had dropped the stacked tray and the plates were on the floor in pieces. Her face was a picture of dismay. Two footmen who'd darted in to see what was going on were barely suppressing their laughter.

He barked at them, 'Don't just stand there. Help Miss Bryant to clear up that mess!'

'Yes, my lord.' They bowed obediently. 'Of course, my lord.'

James left the scene shaking his head.

She is so hopelessly clumsy.

He had quite enough to endure without a housekeeper who was clearly intent on wrecking the place.

Emma was almost in despair as she went to fetch a brush and dustpan then came back to sweep up the residue. Robert and Thomas had gathered up the larger segments of crockery without a word, but there were smirks on both their faces. Emma said, 'I'll see to the rest of this. You may go.'

The simple truth was that the tray had been too heavy for her; she'd realised it as soon as she'd picked it up, but for that to have happened in front of the Viscount was excruciatingly awful. At least one thing was certain. Whatever mistakes she made from now on, the Viscount couldn't possibly think less of her than he did now. Could he?

Through the window she caught sight of a carriage drawing up in the courtyard. Mr and Mrs Eldon had called here at least twice since the news of Lord Grayford's death and she could see that Mr Eldon was already emerging, no doubt eager to ingratiate himself with the new Viscount.

Abandoning the mess in the breakfast parlour, Emma hurried out to forestall him. 'I'm so sorry, but His Lordship is out on estate business. Perhaps you could call again in a few days? Yes, I'm afraid he really is very busy...'

With obvious disappointment Mr Eldon ordered his driver to turn the carriage round and Emma heaved a sigh of relief before recalling there was something else she needed to deal with. She headed to the stables where Gregory was grooming one of the horses in its stall. Poor Gregory—she was aware that the other servants teased him over his shyness, but she was glad that he always seemed pleased to see her.

'Morning, Miss Bryant!' Gregory put down his brushes.

'Good morning, Gregory. I gather the Viscount's gone out for a morning ride. Did you find his horse easy to manage?'

'Gentle as a lamb, miss—though I was glad you warned me that His Lordship might be wanting to take Goliath out this morning, so I had him all ready. What a beauty of a horse he is—well, not a beauty, exactly.' Gregory scratched his spiky hair so it stood up more than ever. 'I suppose he's quite ugly, in fact, with that long nose and those battle scars on his chest.'

Emma was curious. 'Do you know if Goliath was with the Viscount in Spain?'

'No, miss, but His Lordship explained he was an army horse. He bought him only yesterday, in Oxford. Told me he'd meant to hire a horse for the last stage of his journey, but then he saw old Goliath about to be taken to the knacker's yard so he bought him. His Lordship said this morning that he was very pleased with the way I'd settled him in.' Gregory beamed.

So at least something had gone right. 'Gregory, there was something else I wanted to ask you. You know you told me you thought you'd seen Mr Rowley's dog, Jasper, in the stable yard last week?'

'That's right.' Gregory suddenly looked anxious. 'He came creeping into the yard at dusk, but as soon as I called to him he vanished. It's been weeks since he ran away from here and I don't b-blame him after the way old Rowley punished him. Beating poor Jasper because he was scared of rats! It was soon after you started work here, miss, that Jasper ran off.'

Rowley had treated the big but gentle dog with a casual cruelty that had horrified Emma. 'Gregory, listen. Jasper trusted you, didn't he? If he comes back, feed him and we'll find an outhouse for him to sleep in. But we must keep him away from the Viscount.'

'In case His Lordship doesn't like him? But he seems fond of animals, miss.'

Maybe so, but she'd realised Jasper had the knack of accidentally breaking most things in his path—and if he got into the house, his arrival might be the final straw for the Viscount. Aloud she said, 'We'd best be on the safe side, Gregory. Just in case.'

'Very well, miss. I'm glad, though, that the Viscount's here. Aren't you?'

To which Emma could not, at that moment, think of a suitable reply.

To make quite certain of escaping any more visitors, James had avoided the main drive and instead had taken one of the lesser-used paths through the wooded park. From there he headed up to higher land and paused to take in the views, but that was when his mood became sombre again because, as he'd registered on arriving yesterday, there were signs of neglect everywhere. Dead trees that should have been felled. Blocked ditches and badly rutted tracks.

But at least some of his tenants were hard at work, for ahead of him a group of men were repairing a hawthorn hedge, cutting and laying the overgrown branches with meticulous skill. As he drew nearer he recognised Farmer Hobday and his three sons, all full-grown since last he'd seen them. Peter Hobday had always been among the most loyal of the estate's tenants, but James was aware of his own unease as he approached. Was it possible men like these had heard the rumours besmirching his name?

Then he realised they'd all doffed their caps. 'My lord!' exclaimed Peter Hobday. 'It was a sad shock indeed to hear of your brother's death. But we're heartily glad to welcome you home.'

Relief swelled in James's heart. 'I'm glad to be back, Peter.' He steadied Goliath and gazed around. 'Your fields look well. Have the crop yields been decent of late?'

'We can't complain, my lord.' Hobday spoke with some satisfaction. 'Not a lot changes in these parts, as you know. We get snow in winter and too much rain in spring, but we're a hardy breed and as used to the weather as those sheep of mine.' He pointed to a flock of shaggy-coated ewes up on the hillside.

'Your sheep appear to be thriving. As do your strapping sons.' James nodded towards the three big lads, who blushed and grinned.

Peter beamed. 'My wife Alice—you remember her?—is doing a fine job feeding us all.'

'Of course I remember Alice. I also remember her excellent fruit cakes. I'll call at your house one day soon, to catch up with you all properly.'

'It will be an honour, my lord.' Hobday hesitated.

'Now, maybe it's not my place to say it, but we didn't see much of the last Viscount and some of the farms have lacked a firm hand—you'll see it for yourself soon enough. It brings bad luck to abandon the old ways. I don't mean just running the land, but following the traditions of our forefathers, passed on to us for hundreds of years. I hope I give no offence, my lord, by saying all this.'

'And none is taken,' said James, gathering up his reins. 'Good to see you, Peter.'

'There's just one more thing, my lord!'

James halted his horse. 'Yes?'

'My oldest lad, Robin, was at Oxford market yesterday. He said there was someone handing bits of paper around the crowd, all printed up, all exactly the same.'

'You mean broadsheets?'

'Aye, that's the word! Broadsheets. Anyhow, my Robin looked at one but couldn't read it proper, so he asked a fellow nearby what it said.'

'And?'

'It said—' Hobday hesitated '—that you are not welcome, my lord. I'm sorry, but I thought you ought to know.'

James felt his fists tighten on Goliath's reins. 'Very well,' he said. 'Thank you for telling me. I'll see you all again soon, I hope.'

James rode on, aware that the sun had vanished behind a cluster of clouds. So scurrilous scandal sheets were being handed round Oxford market. Even this far from London, the malice was spreading.

He suddenly remembered how his father used to lecture his two young sons about the ancestors whose portraits frowned down on them from the Hall's stately gallery. 'They all kept their inheritance in good order,' their father used to declare. 'They observed the customs of the past and were respected by their neighbours and tenants alike.'

James had once thought this a dull epitaph, since as far as he could tell there was not a hero among them. Now, though, he reflected that he would be content enough if such praise came his way. Dark of mood, he remembered how he used to dream as a boy of becoming a soldier and covering himself with glory. But what would future generations say about him? That he'd kept out of public life after being suspected of fraud at a high level?

He headed back to the Hall, hoping for maybe an hour or two of peace in which to take a look at the estate's accounts and record books he'd noticed piled up in the study. He was also hoping, most definitely, not to meet with Miss Bryant, though she had shown some presence of mind in alerting him to the fact that he faced a barrage of visitors that morning. She'd promised to turn them away and for that, at least, he was grateful.

But maybe he'd assumed too much.

He pulled up sharply as he approached the Hall because he could see an ostentatious carriage dominating the courtyard. Rather grimly he rode on to the stables where the young groom ran forward to hold his horse. 'Did you enjoy your ride, my lord?'

'I did.' James nodded as he dismounted. 'Goliath seems in fine fettle, but I didn't want to take him far until he's settled in.'

'A good idea, my lord. Sometimes your b-brother

rode his horses t-too hard—' The lad broke off in confusion, clearly worried he'd said too much.

'It's all right,' James said quietly. 'I know that my
brother was somewhat hot-headed where horses were
concerned.' He indicated the carriage in the courtyard.
'Tell me, has that vehicle been here long?'

'For a good half-hour now, my lord.'

Damn. James entered the Hall with a sense of
impending doom, not lessened by the fact that as a
footman came to take his riding coat, Miss Bryant
appeared.

'My lord...' she began.

Good grief. She looked even more flustered than
usual and if possible even more of a fright, with her
dress tightly buttoned and her big cap lopsided. He
sighed. 'Yes, Miss Bryant?'

'You have a visitor. Sir George Cartwright.'

He groaned inwardly because Sir George was a
pompous, jumped-up bore. He said abruptly, 'I thought
we agreed, Miss Bryant, that you would inform any
visitors I was occupied for the whole day with estate
business.'

She flinched slightly at his cool tone, but the look
in her eyes was steadfast. 'I have turned away a variety of well-wishers, my lord, from the Eldons and the
local vicar to someone representing the Committee
for the Welfare of Local Orphans.'

'Already?' He was astonished. 'These people have
been here already?'

'Word travels fast. I suggested they make appoint-
ments for a future date, but I'm afraid Sir George would
not be deterred. He is in the drawing room. And...'

'And?'

'His daughter is with him.'

Dear God, thought James. He braced himself. 'Bring us tea, will you?'

To his surprise, she hesitated slightly. 'I will send in one of the maids—'

'No! I'd like you to serve us, Miss Bryant. Now that I'm in residence, you must become used to dealing with visitors.'

He thought she was about to speak again, but instead she bowed her head briefly. 'As you wish, my lord.'

'Oh, and Miss Bryant?'

'My lord?'

'Straighten your cap, will you?'

And with that, James set off for the drawing room.

Chapter Five

Sir George Cartwright was full of the self-importance of a man who had made his own fortune thanks to extensive ship-building interests in the north of England. Over twenty years ago, he'd bought himself a mansion in the Oxfordshire countryside, not far from the Grayford estate.

He was married to a woman who was rarely seen in public and the couple had only one child, their daughter Belinda. Simon had once laughingly mentioned that Sir George harboured hopes of a match between himself and Belinda—and now the man had brought her here. Was it to meet *him*? Good grief, was the girl about to be pushed in his direction now?

Sighing, James walked into the drawing room where Belinda, dressed in something pink and flowery with a large matching bonnet, was perched nervously on the edge of a large sofa. Sir George had been gazing out of the window, but he turned as soon as he heard James enter.

'Lord Grayford!' He stepped forward and extended his hand, which James took warily. 'May I express my sincere condolences on the loss of your brother? I would also like to add how very glad I am to know that the Grayford estate is in your safe hands!'

James blinked. 'Thank you.'

'My dear daughter—' Sir George indicated Belinda '—shares my feelings, as does my wife, although unfortunately my wife's delicate state of health forbids her from telling you so in person. I hope that you and I will be good neighbours, my lord. And you may rest assured that during the past few weeks—which must have been difficult indeed for you!—I have been doing my utmost to defend you in the locality against the unfortunate slurs that have clouded your reputation. We all make mistakes, after all.'

James replied very softly. 'Do we, Sir George?'

'Of course,' answered that gentleman breezily. 'Whatever's in the past can be forgiven—and let me assure you that you will be welcome at my house any time! My wife and I will be delighted to see you, as will my beloved daughter.'

James felt his anger mounting. He'd much prefer out-and-out insults to this brazen condescension. He glanced at Belinda and noticed that her eyes were downcast—with utter mortification, he guessed. He thought she was trembling slightly.

He said to her quietly, 'Miss Cartwright, are you quite well? Can I get you anything?'

'The girl is perfectly well!' Sir George broke in. 'She's merely a little overcome at seeing you safely home after your exploits overseas, that's all! Now, my lord, shall we get back to business? It was mentioned some years ago between your father and myself that the union of our two families—in other words, marriage—would be a most desirable prospect. Your older brother—what a fine example of the aristocracy we had in him!—was not quite ready, I think, to settle down. But as for you, my lord, I think it would be a wise option for you to live well away from London, to make your home here and take a wife. And talking of marriage, well, look at my sweet daughter! You could fare far worse, couldn't you, hey? After all, you might find your choices rather limited in your present circumstances.'

James felt fresh anger ripping through him but before he could reply, he realised that Belinda had suddenly burst into tears.

Just at that moment, the door opened and Miss Bryant entered bearing a laden tea tray. She'd straightened her cap, but the thing still shadowed half her face while her gown was all but obscured by a huge apron. Dear God, thought James, acutely irritated. Did the woman *want* to look as unattractive as possible?

She settled the tray safely enough on a nearby table and if she'd noticed that Belinda Cartwright was in tears, she gave no hint of it. Sir George, who'd been watching Miss Bryant with narrowed eyes, said loudly to James, 'Well, my lord. You must have been mighty surprised by your new housekeeper? I've heard many a tale of her incompetence. Now, if you want me to recommend someone who actually has some idea of what the job is all about—'

'Excuse me a moment, Sir George.' James deliberately cut into his flow and turned to his housekeeper. He felt furious that Sir George had spoken like that in front of her because whatever his housekeeper's faults, they were none of this man's business. He said, 'Miss

Bryant, I suspect that Miss Cartwright is a little fatigued by her journey here and could do with a moment or two of rest. Would you guide her to another room and perhaps offer her some refreshment?' He drew closer and added in a low voice, 'She is upset. Please calm her if you can.'

Her clear brown eyes met his and for just a moment he saw some emotion in them that he didn't quite understand. Pity for Belinda? he wondered. But there was also, when she glanced over at Sir George, something that could have been a flash of anger. Then she answered quietly, 'Of course, my lord,' and went over to Belinda, ignoring Sir George's aggressive stare. 'I understand you're finding it a little uncomfortable in here, Miss Cartwright,' she said. 'No doubt that is due to the heat of the fire. May I take you to the front parlour, which has a little more air?'

Sir George looked thoroughly displeased but said nothing as she guided Belinda out. James remained silent also. But as soon as the door had closed behind them, then—then, James turned on his unwanted visitor. 'To do that, to your daughter. To force her into my presence and make ridiculous hints about a possible match that was neither in her head or mine, unless you, sir, quite falsely encouraged her expectations!'

Sir George was clearly struggling for words, but at last he barked out, 'Let me point out, my lord, that you will be lucky to find a better match, in this neighbourhood at least. You will find that not all your Oxfordshire neighbours are as willing to forgive your transgressions as I!'

James forced down his fury. 'What are my transgressions? Spell them out, if you please!'

'Well,' said Sir George. 'We all know that after the defeat of Bonaparte, the peace talks began. Bargaining over border treaties, that kind of thing, between all the countries who'd fought Old Boney for years. But the treaties were causing all sorts of arguments between the British and the rest of them—Austrians, Russians, the whole lot.'

'Go on,' said James with deceptive calm.

'You, I gather, were asked last winter to deliver a gift to the Archduke of Austria, because the fellow was proving a little slow to agree to the treaty. The gift was a bribe, in other words, to secure a settlement of European borders. Only something went wrong and the gift disappeared in rather odd circumstances. An unhappy business, eh? Especially for you.'

'Why is that, Sir George?' James's voice was still dangerously calm.

Sir George waved his hand impatiently. 'As I said, best to let all that be forgotten. Now, if you wish to visit my fair daughter at any time, you'll be more than welcome, believe me   '

He broke off because James was advancing on him with one fist clenched. 'Listen to me. If you choose to believe the downright lies that have been spread about me, then so be it. But I am astonished at the duplicity which allows you to still contemplate me as a future son-in-law.' He pointed towards the door. 'Permit me to show you out. Now.'

'My dear sir—'

'Oh, and rest assured, Sir George, that if there are any further meetings between the two of us while I'm in Oxfordshire, they will be purely on matters of business. And I will only tolerate *them* because we happen to be neighbours.'

Sir George's mouth fell open. It was not an attractive look, thought James, whose rage was still boiling inside him. 'Shall we fetch your daughter, sir?'

Walking rapidly, he led the way to the parlour and looked inside.

Dear God, he thought to himself, *let there not be a disaster in here as well.*

It was with considerable relief that he beheld a relatively calm scene, for his housekeeper was sitting beside Belinda and was showing her a book of some kind. On seeing him she rose; Belinda stood also, looking uncertain, frightened even, at the sight of her father at his side. James said, 'Miss Cartwright. I believe your father is ready to take you home.'

Gripping his unfortunate daughter by the arm, Sir George strode without a word towards the main hall, where a footman hurried to open the big front door. Poor Belinda had to almost run to keep up with him and James found his fury matched by his pity for the girl. What a totally obnoxious man.

He turned to his housekeeper, who had closed the book she'd been showing Belinda and was clearly about to depart.

'Miss Bryant!' he said.

She froze, clutching that book tightly. 'My lord?' She was maybe expecting some reprimand, but she met his gaze steadily.

'I wanted to thank you,' he said, 'for taking care of Miss Cartwright.'

'It was no trouble at all. Miss Cartwright was clearly distressed and I was sorry for her.' She was once more about to depart but he blocked her way, he didn't really understand why—perhaps it was because something about her was rather soothing after the bombast of Sir George.

'I noticed,' he said, 'that you were showing her a book that interested her.' He pointed to the volume she held. 'What's in there? Pictures of some kind? Belinda seemed to like them.'

She held it out to him. 'I found this book of drawings when the maids and I were cleaning the library last week, my lord. It contains sketches of the May Day feasts here many years ago and I guessed they might distract Miss Cartwright.'

Those May Day feasts! Suddenly, for James, the memories came flooding back. His father had always played a part in the annual festivities by providing food and ale for the locals and making a thankfully brief speech before ordering them to enjoy themselves. There had been games of all kinds for the children, followed by music and dancing out here in the courtyard. Though after darkness fell.

Yes. He was remembering now. By the time darkness fell, it was a completely different picture.

'I'd like to see the sketches,' he said. 'If I may.'

She handed him the book and after laying it on a nearby table, he opened it with care. On each page were pen-and-ink drawings lightly yet skilfully done, portraying groups of happy families in their Sunday best. He paused at the one of the flower-bedecked maypoles, with children dancing around it, while the Hall stood stately and imposing in the background.

'From what I remember of those May Days,' he told her, 'they used to begin pleasantly enough. Unfortunately, they generally ended in drunkenness and mayhem.'

She looked so crestfallen by his comment that he quickly added, 'But the pictures are beautiful. I wonder who drew them?'

She almost smiled then. 'My father did,' she said softly.

'Your father? So he's a local man, then?'

'He was originally from Oxford, my lord, so he knew this area well. He liked to make notes about the customs and legends of the neighbourhood and on occasions like May Day he always brought his sketchbook. I used to carry his pencils and paper for him.'

He looked at her in surprise. 'You were there, at those feasts? I don't remember you.'

'There's no reason why you should, my lord.'

She said it calmly but he saw a shadow of something—uncertainty, or sadness maybe—flicker across her face. He said, 'You've made no mention of your mother.'

'No. She died, soon after I was born.'

'I'm sorry. Where does your father live now, Miss Bryant?'

'He lives in the village of Hawthorne, my lord.'

He thought, *All the properties in Hawthorne belong to Sir George.*

'That isn't far away. Do you visit him often?'

'As a matter of fact, I usually visit him on a Wednesday afternoon and that's today.' She hurried through her next words. 'But since you have only just arrived, my lord, I have decided to postpone my visit—'

'No!' He shook his head decisively, surprising himself with his speedy reaction. 'There's no need. I shall be busy all afternoon in my study, so you can go as usual. I've already seen that there are plenty of letters and bills awaiting my attention there.'

She nodded, then raised her eyes to his. Yes, he thought. They were brown, but in certain lights there was gold in them too. Odd. He couldn't remember ever seeing eyes quite like them and her lashes were extraordinarily long...

He suddenly realised she was speaking again. 'Thank you, my lord. I can assure you that I'm always back by four. Shall I give orders to Cook regarding your evening meal, my lord?'

Back to reality with a thump.

Those earwigs... 'Since it's your afternoon off, Cook can have some respite as well. Please tell her I'll take supper in my own rooms—cold ham, bread and cheese, that kind of thing. It's what I was used to in the army. As for this afternoon, you enjoy your visit to your father, while I settle at my desk and attend to all the duties that await me.'

Those unusual eyes met his again. 'So you're not going back to London yet, my lord?'

'No. Most certainly not.'

For a moment she looked about to say something more, but she merely nodded. 'With your permission, I shall take my leave.'

He raised his hand. 'Just one thing, Miss Bryant. You seemed rather put out by Sir George's presence. Is there any particular reason for that?'

She shook her head quite firmly. 'None whatsoever, my lord.' But James would swear he'd seen a shadow of something that was almost disgust cross her face at the mention of the man.

Curious, that. Though all he said was, 'Very well. You may go.'

She left and he stayed exactly where he was. Well, he thought, focusing on their recent conversation. May Day. He tried to picture Miss Bryant as a carefree girl, chattering and laughing with all her friends, but he couldn't. It was as if something had silenced her. Something had crushed her.

He sighed, because for the life of him he couldn't work out why she'd taken this job. Surely she could have found a post as a governess or a lady's companion? That would have been more fitting for someone like her and perhaps he should tell her so. Though who the hell was he, to be handing out advice to anyone?

He'd dreamed of military glory, but he'd come home to Grayford Hall not to a hero's welcome but to reports of scurrilous broadsheets in the area—and to arrogant innuendo from that dolt Sir George. He found himself recalling for what could be the hundredth time how everything had gone wrong.

At Waterloo last summer, he'd received injuries that were minor but enough to require that he rest for a while. His brother had suggested he live at the family's mansion in Mayfair to recuperate, but James had stayed instead in another, much smaller property belonging to the estate in nearby Aldford Street while he decided what to do next. And there, last November, he was visited one day by a man from the Home Office.

'Major Brandon,' the man had said. 'We know all about your gallant service in the war. We also know that you speak several languages fluently.'

'And your point is?' James, like any soldier, was wary of shadowy government officials.

'We have an errand for you, Major,' the man replied.

In summary, the man had asked James to travel to Vienna on a diplomatic mission—to visit the Archduke of Austria, who was raising objections to the impact that the latest peace treaty would have on his extensive boundaries. The Archduke had let it be known, however, that he would soften his protests if a precious sixteenth-century book that had belonged to his ancestors was handed over to him without delay. The book had been acquired by the British during some minor European skirmish over a hundred years ago and had been stored since than in St James's Palace. It was indeed a valuable object, bound in fine vellum and its spine embossed in gold lettering.

The book was entitled *Vitas Sanctorum*; it was a history, in Latin, of the lives of the saints written by a famed scholar, Albertus Magnus. It was the only surviving copy and of value throughout the Christian world. James's mission was to deliver it in person, which involved travelling from London to Vienna last winter with the sealed package never leaving his side.

The Archduke had received him eagerly, but as soon as the package was opened it was obvious the book was a fake and the Archduke, furious, had to be compensated with not only an abject apology from the British but also an exceedingly large sum of money in order to secure his agreement to the border treaty.

Because the book had been in James's care, it was he who came under immediate suspicion. On his return to London in February, a government enquiry was set up and James, defending himself, pointed out how sublimely stupid it would have been of him to substitute the book with the fake, since he would be the very first suspect.

But the arguments continued and, though the enquiry ended in March with the conclusion that his guilt could not be proved, neither was there sufficient evidence to completely clear his name. James felt as if his life had been turned upside down, especially as it was during the tortuous enquiry that news was brought to him that his brother, visiting friends in Gloucestershire, had fallen from his horse and broken his neck.

Simon was dead and he, Major James Brandon, was suddenly the Seventh Viscount Grayford. He didn't want the title. He didn't want the estates. Above all, he didn't want the whispers that still circulated everywhere, especially since the whereabouts of the original book remained a mystery.

'Of course,' people murmured, *'that enquiry couldn't declare Major Brandon's guilt, could it? Because he's a viscount now. And we all know that peers of the realm stick together.'*

So there it was. No proof of his guilt, but also no proof of his innocence. A dark shadow had been cast over his name, but damn it all, was it to hang over him for the rest of his life?

He suddenly became aware of a delicate scent in the room. It was Miss Bryant's scent, he realised— lavender, maybe from the soap she used. He frowned, remembering her profile as she'd gazed at those old pictures. She had, he reflected, a charmingly tip-tilted nose and a full, rosy mouth. And if her hair should happen to be long and as striking as her eyes, she could actually be quite pretty...

He quashed his thoughts and set off for his study.

Miss Bryant was definitely a problem. He really had no idea what she was doing here and clearly she didn't either. But…lavender. The scent still lingered stubbornly in his mind.

Chapter Six

That afternoon Emma set off to visit her father, carrying a basket of freshly made scones from Cook's kitchen. The sun made a mockery of her drab winter attire and birds chorused from the blossom-filled blackthorn bushes as if it were high summer rather than mid-April. Normally she loved the way spring was so full of surprises, one day bringing weather as cold and bleak as midwinter but the next pouring out glorious sunshine—though it would take more than sunshine to raise her spirits, she feared.

What a catastrophic start she'd got off to with the Viscount! She'd shown herself to be inept with the servants and a stuttering wreck in the business of the bath—and unfortunately, that wasn't all. There was something about Lord Grayford, not least his extraordinary blue eyes, that made her heart race quite alarmingly, even when he was at his most disdainful.

Thank goodness, she told herself briskly, for this walk in the fresh air to her father's home—which would most certainly remind her of her humble station in life and bring her back to her senses. She marched onwards, resolute.

* * *

It was about two miles from the Hall to the little village of Hawthorne. Biddy, her father's elderly housekeeper, must have been watching from a window for her, because Emma had barely reached the cottage when the door swung open. 'Lord, Miss Emma,' Biddy exclaimed, 'it does me good to see you! But you look quite peaky. Is that big house getting you down?'

In the old days, in their former home in Oxford, her father had several servants but now only Biddy remained. Emma laughed as she stepped into the tiny hallway. 'Biddy, you always ask that! But I'm fine and I've had a lovely walk. Isn't this sunshine a delight?'

Biddy took her cloak and began on the one topic Emma was really hoping she'd avoid. 'We've all heard, Miss Emma, that the Viscount is back. How are you finding him? Will he be spending more time at the Hall than his brother did?'

How very speedily news travelled. 'I don't know, Biddy,' Emma answered honestly. 'You see, he only arrived last night, so I've seen very little of him.'

Very little of him? That was a lie, she thought in horror, since she'd seen the man half-naked. 'But I think he'll certainly stay for a while. And he seems to be…' She hesitated. 'He seems to be a fair man,' she concluded rather weakly.

'Hmm.' Biddy pursed her lips. 'Even so, an army officer like him will have left more than a few broken hearts in his path, so you watch out for him, my dear.'

Emma had to laugh at the thought of the Viscount having illicit thoughts about her. 'I don't think he'd ever be as desperate as that, Biddy. Look, here are some scones Cook gave me. She thought my father might enjoy them.'

Biddy muttered that she hoped Cook didn't think Emma's father was starving to death here and after reassuring her to the contrary, Emma went straight to the little parlour where her father sat in his armchair by the fire. He was reading, but he turned the minute she came in. 'Emma!'

'Dear Papa.' She went to kiss him lightly on the cheek. 'No, don't get up. Cook has sent you some fresh-baked scones and I've left them with Biddy in the kitchen. We can have them with our tea.'

She always tried to bring him some tempting treats, because she worried that in spite of Biddy's care her father, well into his fifties now, was growing thin and anxious-looking. But his smile was warm as he asked the inevitable question. 'How is the Hall?'

She pulled up a chair next to him. 'The Hall,' she replied, 'is rather busy at present because as you'll have heard, the new Viscount has arrived. Will you tell me what you know of him, Papa? There are some rather ugly rumours.'

'Indeed,' said her father. 'And without a doubt, my dear, they are false.'

Just as the Viscount had told her. 'Then why do they persist? It seems so unfair!'

'Indeed it does. The Viscount was an officer, of course, in the British army and decorated more than once for gallantry. Last winter he was sent on a diplomatic mission to Vienna, but there was some kind of blunder. He was accused of stealing a valuable old book that the Archduke of Austria wanted back and despite the lack of real evidence his name hasn't properly been cleared.' Her father shook his head. 'But I do feel he should have stayed in London instead of coming here. He should be defending himself against the scoundrels who've tried to blacken his name.'

Emma listened hard to her father's clear, emphatic words. 'Why does he have these enemies?'

'My dear, men like him might be heroes to the soldiers under their command, but they can attract jealousy. There have been whispers that as a former soldier, the Viscount bears a strong grudge against the Archduke for siding with Napoleon more than once during the long war. Now I don't believe for one minute the Viscount stole the precious book, but I wonder now if he's decided that if people choose not to believe him, then he won't stoop to prove his innocence. He'll be angry and bitter, probably lonely too. I do hope he'll be made welcome in this neighbourhood.'

Emma was silent for a moment. What had she done to make him feel welcome at Grayford Hall? All she'd managed was to present him with a series of blunders and embarrassments. She realised her father was speaking again.

'Tell me,' he said, putting his hand on hers. 'What does the Viscount think of his new housekeeper?'

Emma laughed ruefully. 'Very little, I'm afraid, since he found the place in rather a mess. We weren't expecting him, you see.'

'Does he realise, my dear, that you weren't always—' he was searching for the word '—poor?'

The way her father said it—his sense of shame— wrung Emma's heart. 'No,' she answered steadily. 'He doesn't know anything about me and believe me, I'm

quite happy to keep it that way. Besides, I think he
would find my situation rather difficult to understand.'

'Oh, Emma. I'm so sorry about everything. My stu-
pidity in losing all that money. Your disappointment
over your Season.'

'But I've told you, I didn't really want a Season,
Papa! I didn't like London very much. I never particularly enjoyed the parties or balls.'

Where everyone's trying to outdo each other, she
thought silently. *Where men who've heaped all kinds
of flattery on you turn their backs once they learn
you're no longer wealthy.*

'But you could have found a husband! I feel I ruined your chances of a happy future.'

'And does marriage guarantee a happy future?' She
shook her head stubbornly. 'Not always. I've told you,
I don't particularly want a husband! I'm an independent creature, you know!'

Just then Biddy entered, carrying a tray of tea and
scones. 'You have a visitor, sir,' she announced. 'It's
the Reverend Summers, come all the way over from
Oxford. I told him Miss Emma was here and he said
he'd be delighted to see her.'

Emma's heart sank. Her father was already getting to his feet and while his back was turned Biddy
exchanged expressive looks with Emma. 'I tried to
put him off,' Biddy whispered. 'No luck, I'm afraid.'

Andrew Summers was a clergyman whose wife
had died three years ago, leaving him with two young
boys. Around a year ago he'd made it plain to Emma
that he would be very happy to marry her; chiefly, she
guessed, because he wanted a mother for his children.
She knew he was a good friend to her father, but...

marriage to him? No! She hadn't seen him since refusing his proposal and as he came in she realised he
hadn't changed in the least. Though only in his thir-
ties, his clothes and mannerisms made him look considerably older.

'My dear Miss Bryant!' he exclaimed, bowing eagerly over her hand. 'I wasn't expecting this pleasure.'

Biddy, after glancing at Emma with a look that
conveyed extreme sympathy, quickly made her departure. 'It's always a pleasure to meet with my father's
friends,' Emma replied. 'Please take a seat, Reverend,
while I pour tea.'

But instead he followed her over to the table where
Biddy had left the tray and said in a low voice, 'I can't
tell you how sorry I was, to hear of the sad turn your
life has taken since last we met.'

Emma put down the teapot she'd picked up and
glanced at him swiftly. 'Whatever do you mean?'

'My dear Miss Bryant—you do not deserve to be
reduced to working as a housekeeper!'

She answered very quickly and very firmly 'Actually, it's ideal. I'm able to visit my father at least once a
week and besides, what else would I do with my time?'

'But you once had hopes of such a different life!'

'Times change,' she answered calmly. 'And one
has to adapt.'

Andrew Summers glanced over at her father then
lowered his voice still further. 'Miss Bryant, I have a
respectable job and a small but pleasant house in Oxford. I'm hoping you might have had a change of heart
since we spoke last year. Might you do me the very
great honour of reconsidering my offer of marriage?
You would make me a very happy man.'

Oh, goodness.

'I'm afraid my reply is exactly the same as before. I'm not even thinking of marriage and anyway, I really am quite content to be working at Grayford Hall.'

'You can't be happy, working for—for that man!'

She'd started pouring the tea but now she stopped. 'What do you mean, *that man*?'

'Why, the new Viscount, of course! Everyone knows he's come here to hide. He's had to, because his reputation is ruined!'

Emma found her heart was thudding rather hard. 'I think your information is incorrect, Reverend Summers. I believe the government enquiry found no actual evidence against him.'

'Ah, but now that he's a viscount, how could the case have possibly gone any other way?'

'Emma!' Her father's voice. 'Emma, are you coming with the tea?'

'Of course, Papa.' Swiftly she picked up the tray, saying to the Reverend Summers, 'Would you please bring the plate of scones?'

She put the tea tray on the small table next to her father's chair and soon, thank goodness, the two men were eagerly talking politics. At least it meant Andrew Summers had no more opportunity to pester her further, but she thought again that her father looked tired, broken even by the loss of his social standing and his fortune.

After a while she put down her cup and rose from her chair. 'I'm afraid I must get back to the Hall now,' she announced lightly. 'Duty calls.'

Both men got to their feet, but to her relief only

her father accompanied her to the door. He said anxiously, 'You'll come again soon, Emma, won't you?'

'Of course.' She was already putting on her cloak. 'And Papa, now that I'm being paid a regular salary, you must tell me if you need help in any way. For example, with the rent of this cottage.'

Her father looked puzzled. 'But I'm not paying rent, Emma dear. I haven't paid any for months now.'

'Are you quite sure? No one writes to you, or calls for the money?'

'I'm certain of it. I must admit that I don't understand it myself, but there's no reason for you to worry about it.'

There was, though. She was wondering whether to say more, but then she heard the clock in the parlour strike four. Oh, no, she would be very late back, which would be yet another black mark against her. 'I must go.' She kissed his cheek. 'But I'll see you again, very soon.'

Quickly she made her way back to the path that led across fields to the Hall, but by now yet another worry was coming to the fore. Why, exactly, had she defended the Viscount so strongly to Andrew Summers? Perhaps because she believed, just as her father did, that he'd been wrongly accused over that fateful foreign mission? But on the other hand, why take the side of a man who would probably be dismissing her before too long?

She was also sorely troubled by the news that her father hadn't been asked for his rent, especially as the cottage was owned by Sir George Cartwright. Two years ago, when she and her father had moved in there, Sir George had drawn her to one side and said, 'Well, my dear. You and your father have come upon hard times. But if you should find it difficult at any time to find the rent, I have a word of advice for you.' He'd touched her arm in a way that made her recoil and murmured, 'There are other ways you could pay me, you know.'

Just the memory of it made her feel sick. Speeding her pace as if to distance herself from the man, she hurried along the familiar path until a rustling sound from some nearby bushes caught her attention. Was it a hedgehog? But it sounded larger. Maybe a badger?

She turned and saw a large, extremely scruffy black and white dog hurrying towards her with his long tail wagging frantically.

'Jasper!' Emma crouched down to greet him. 'Oh, Jasper. You poor, poor thing, you look half-starved. Wherever have you *been*?'

Chapter Seven

James slammed down his pen on the desk. All the estate's accounts were in an absolute tangle, which meant he would have to contact his man of business, Joshua Baines, to make sense of them—and Baines was in London. Rising to his feet, he began to pace the room. He'd known that at some point he'd have to go back there, but he'd counted on at least a little respite.

He stopped abruptly at the ominous sound of a carriage coming into the courtyard—hell, if it was Sir George again, he was going to give the man a piece of his mind! Though on looking out of the window, he saw a hired travelling chaise and breathed again. Not Sir George then, but who? The young groom, Gregory, had run to see to the horses, while one of the Hall's footmen was already opening the carriage door.

And a smile spread across James's face, because out stepped Theo Exton.

James headed instantly for the front door, meeting another footman on his way. 'My lord, I was coming to tell you that you have a visitor.'

'Indeed. It's Mr Exton, my cousin, and I believe

he'll be staying for at least a night or two, so arrangements must be made. Tell Miss Bryant to report to me immediately, will you?'

The footman hesitated. 'I would, my lord, but I'm afraid that Miss Bryant has gone to visit her father.'

James frowned. 'I thought she was due back by four.'

'That is true, my lord.' The footman sighed as if to say, *You can see now what we have to put up with here.*

James felt a burst of irritation at her lateness. But Theo was here, so putting his annoyance to one side, he hurried out to greet him. Theo looked tired after his journey. He'd always had a slight limp, but now James could see he was leaning on a stick as he made his way across the courtyard.

James met him before he reached the steps to the main door. 'You made it pretty promptly, then.' He clasped Theo's hand heartily. 'You succeeded in dragging yourself away from the delights of London.'

Theo grinned back. 'Indeed, Cousin—and I don't find the city at all delightful, I can tell you!' He was looking all around. 'I haven't been here for years. I'd almost forgotten how enormous the Hall is.'

'So had I,' said James somewhat wryly.

'Strange, isn't it, how our lives turn out? You never expected to have to take your brother's place. You never wanted to. I know that.' Theo continued to admire the Hall's imposing façade. 'But tell me, what's it like to be back? Are all the old servants still here—Rowley, Mrs Padgett and the rest?'

'Apparently Rowley ran off about a month ago, after having either drunk or sold half my brother's wine cellar. Mrs Padgett's gone to live with her daughter—and as for the butler, he left even before they did.'

'Oh, dear. So who's running the place now?'

'Good question,' said James drily. 'A new housekeeper was appointed in January, but I had no idea till I arrived yesterday. '

A footman holding Theo's portmanteau hovered close to James. 'My lord. Which bedchamber will Mr Exton be using?'

'Take his luggage to the large bedroom in the east wing, will you?' James glanced at the clock above the stables. 'And until Miss Bryant returns, do everything you can to make it comfortable for him.'

The footman bowed and walked smartly into the house. James could see that Theo had been taking all this in.

'So you've acquired a rather unreliable housekeeper, I gather?' He looked amused. 'What's she like? Is she an old harridan who secretly quaffs your sherry?'

James snorted. 'Hardly. But I arrived to find the entire hallway awash with pickles.'

'*Pickles?*'

'I'm not joking. A cask of them had exploded and trust me, the place stank to high heaven. Don't laugh, my friend, because it gets worse. Last night, she burst in on me while I was taking my bath.'

'Your… No!'

'It's true. Believe me, she's a walking catalogue of disasters.'

Theo was chuckling. 'I really can't wait to meet her. Presumably, she's been dismissed from all her previous posts?'

James shook his head. 'She's never actually had previous posts, of any kind. And—' At that point, he broke off, because he heard hurried footsteps behind him and on turning he saw an all too familiar figure almost running from the stables towards the servants' entrance round the side of the house.

Miss Bryant. What the deuce had she been doing in the stables? Why was she looking so furtive?

He said grimly to Theo, 'Your wish to behold my new housekeeper is about to be fulfilled. Because there she is.'

Theo's gaze followed his. 'My God. Is that really her? Somehow she looks familiar. She's young. She's rather pretty, James.'

Pretty?

Part of James's brain—the part he had no control over—was jolted into reluctant agreement, for he'd noticed that the hood of her cloak was down and her hair had fallen from its pins. Hair that was long and silky, of a shade somewhere between blonde and light brown, almost like honey. Not what he'd expected. And somehow it altered her whole face, adding expression to those rather striking eyes...

Stop it.

Concentrating on Theo's other comment, James said, 'I fear she's beginning to look all too familiar to me, Theo. So is that look of dismay on her face.' He guessed she'd been hoping to slip in by the side entrance unnoticed, but he beckoned and she approached him, at the same time trying to push back her hair.

'Miss Bryant,' he said coolly. 'This is Mr Theo Exton, my cousin. He's travelled from London and will be staying here for several nights.'

She curtsied, pink and breathless. 'Mr Exton.'

'It's a pity,' James said, 'that you're rather late. But in your absence I've told one of the footmen to prepare the guest bedroom in the east wing. Now that you're back, perhaps you'll check that everything is in order?'

'I'll do so straight away, my lord. Mr Exton, I offer my sincere apologies.'

James waited for her excuses to come pouring out, but though she still looked hot and bothered, there were none. Perhaps she'd had an assignation with a secret lover? Ha! He remembered how last night she'd looked about to faint on beholding him half-naked and dismissed the thought as absurd. At least she was honest enough not to concoct some lie to account for her absence.

She was speaking again in rather a rush. 'My lord, you did say earlier that you would take a cold supper in your room tonight. But now that your cousin is here, I'm sure Cook would be glad to prepare a full meal for you both.'

James was remembering last night's earwigs. There was also the question of privacy; he rather fancied the idea of a quiet chat with Theo without the servants taking in every word. He said decisively, 'We'll ride over to the Flag tonight and dine there.' He noted that Theo looked rather startled at this announcement and added, 'It belongs to the estate, so I was intending to call in soon anyway. It may as well be tonight.'

Miss Bryant curtsied again and set off once more round to the servants' door, though she took yet another rather anxious look back at the stables.

Then— *'Bloody hell!'*

James couldn't help it. Troopers' language, he

knew, but at that precise moment a great, muddy dog had come charging from the stables and was heading straight for his housekeeper. Lurching to a halt, the dog licked Miss Bryant's hand then saw James. With barely a second's hesitation, the animal came hurtling in his direction and leaped up at him, his muddy paws all over James's chest, his long tail wagging furiously.

Miss Bryant rushed up and was doing her best to tug him away by his scruffy leather collar. 'Jasper, no. Down, Jasper. Oh, dear.' She glanced up at James, clearly mortified. 'I'm so sorry, my lord. I asked Gregory to keep him in the stables, but he must have escaped.'

'Why the deuce should this animal be kept in my stables?' demanded James, trying to brush muddy paw prints from his coat. 'He doesn't actually live here, does he?'

'He did until a short while ago,' said his extremely flustered housekeeper, who'd finally succeeded in calming the creature. The dog was sitting by her side now, his tail thumping furiously on the cobbles. *Jasper.* Good God.

'Mr Rowley brought him here,' Miss Bryant went on hurriedly. 'He said that a dog was needed to catch rats around the outbuildings, but Jasper didn't catch a single one. You see, my lord, he's scared of them.' The dog let out a slight whimper, as if to confirm what she said. Theo, James suspected, was secretly laughing.

'The trouble was,' continued Miss Bryant, 'that poor Jasper used to flee from the sight of a rat or even a mouse, so Mr Rowley beat him often and in the end Jasper ran off. But I found him this afternoon, or rather he found me, when I was on my way back from my father's house. And he looked so hungry, I thought that maybe, if I brought him here, we could feed him and find a new home for him—'

'Feed him at my expense, you mean?'

She looked crestfallen. 'Naturally, my lord, I will pay for his food until he has somewhere else to live. I can ask in Hawthorne village if anyone wants him. He really is sweet-tempered and he'll be no trouble.'

'No trouble? He's enormous! He'll eat his new owner out of house and home! Besides which, it sounds as if he's not much use for anything.'

His tone, he thought, was thoroughly off-putting, but Jasper must have interpreted it differently because he leaped towards James again and was licking his hand as if he'd just offered the creature a guest room in the Hall. Once more Miss Bryant was trying to pull him away and her hair was tumbling all around her face—which was rather distracting to a man's baser senses.

'My lord,' she said, 'I'm so sorry…'

'Take him back to the stables,' James ordered wearily. 'As you said, maybe one of the locals will take him off our hands.'

'Yes, my lord. Jasper, come!'

She headed off to the stables again with the great dog lolloping alongside. For a moment James stood watching, noting once more the rich colour of that hair. Plus her trim waist beneath her hideous gown…

He heard Theo's soft laughter. 'The dog's taken a fancy to you.'

'Heaven forbid…' James spoke wearily.

'Mark my words, you're going to find it difficult

to get rid of him. You always did have a soft spot for waifs and strays.'

'Did I?'

'You certainly did. You took pity on me, for example. Remember our first year at Eton? The bullies made my life a nightmare until you sorted them out.' Theo paused a moment. 'And perhaps, in spite of your harsh words, I think I detect a slight hint of sympathy for your youthful housekeeper.'

James was scowling now. 'She's trouble, Theo. There's some fresh calamity every time I set eyes on her—and I've only been here twenty-four hours.'

'I thought,' said Theo, 'that she seemed rather sweet.'

'Sweet in a *confused* sort of way, do you mean? In a hopeless sort of way?'

'She does have a very pretty face,' said Theo thoughtfully. 'Exceptionally fine eyes. And her figure… Hadn't you noticed?'

'Look,' James began, 'all I want from a housekeeper is a modicum of common sense and capability, so let's forget her, shall we? You'll no doubt see her again soon enough.'

'Very well. But what about the dog?'

'Miss Bryant will have to find him a new home.' He pointed towards the main door. 'Come inside. We can have a drink in my study and you can tell me about your journey while your room is prepared.'

'And,' said Theo, 'I can give you a letter from London.'

James opened it as soon as they were in his study. The notepaper was scented and the handwriting was all too familiar. He was about to put it aside for later, but Theo settled in a chair and said, 'Don't mind me. Read it.'

So James poured them both brandy and read it.

It was from Lady Henrietta Carleon, whom James had first met when he was on leave from the army two years ago. She'd recently been widowed and her husband, much older than she, had left her most comfortably off. From then on James found her the ideal companion for his occasional sojourns in London, since she was amusing and adventurous in bed but made no further demands on him. That had suited James perfectly in those days, since his life was with the army and he was certainly not looking for a wife.

Two months ago Henrietta had welcomed him warmly on his return from Austria and had remained loyal despite the unsatisfactory result of the enquiry. He'd valued that, but hadn't expected her to take the trouble to write. Indeed, the note was certainly brief.

I am missing you already, dearest James. Come back to town, before country life turns you into a dreary yokel.
Yours, Henrietta

Theo raised his eyebrows as James folded it up again. 'Well?'

'Henrietta fears I'll become exceedingly dull if I stay here too long.'

'And will you? Stay here too long, I mean.'

James sighed, turning his brandy glass. 'I really don't know yet. Anyway, I imagine Henrietta will soon find someone else to amuse her.'

'I'm not so sure about that. I hear that she's ready

to scratch the eyes out of anyone who speaks ill of you in her presence, though presumably you're safe from all the crude gossip out here?'

Safe from those broadsheets in Oxford? Safe from Sir George's insulting barbs?

Later, he resolved. *I'll tell Theo all that later, when we can be quite sure we'll not be interrupted.*

As if to reinforce his decision, just at that moment a maid entered and bobbed a curtsy. 'Begging your pardon, my lord, but Miss Bryant says that since it will be a while before you dine this evening, should Mrs Clegg serve some of her fresh-made veal pie in the front parlour?'

Theo made an appreciative sound; James nodded. 'Thank you. We'd like that.'

'So Mrs Clegg's still here?' exclaimed Theo as soon as the maid had left. 'Then all's not lost, James! You have a marvellous cook, so why aren't we eating at the Hall tonight? I know you said the Flag belongs to the estate, but surely we could always just call in for a drink some time!'

'We're eating there,' said James, 'because we always used to go there on the first night of your visits here. Don't you remember? Also, I doubt that you'll find earwigs crawling across the Flag's dining tables. Yes, earwigs. Let me explain…'

Chapter Eight

After depositing Jasper in the stables with Gregory—
'Please look after him Gregory! Don't let him escape
again!'—Emma went to put on her cap and apron then
hurried to the guest bedroom, where three maids were
at work. Thomas was there too, placing fresh candles
in the wall sconces.

'A bit late getting back from your father's, weren't
you, miss?' said Betsey.

'I was.' Emma answered briefly The arrival of poor
Jasper was probably the nail in the coffin of her em-
ployment here, but she was almost past caring and instead concentrated on ensuring there was a good fire
in the hearth, together with fresh bedlinen. She tried
to remember if her *Daily Deeds* manual recommended
anything else, but could recall only one instruction:

> *Do not forget to decorate a guest's bedroom
> with fresh flowers. Nothing is more welcoming.*

She decided to ignore that one.
Suddenly she realised that Moll was asking her a

question. 'Mr Exton's got a limp, hasn't he, miss? Was he a soldier who got hurt in the fighting?'

'No,' Emma replied. 'He suffered an illness as a boy.'

The other maids had gathered round. 'Did you know him back then, miss?'

'Only from a distance. He grew up in this neighbourhood, as I did.'

'Does he ride?' another asked.

'Yes, I believe he does. He avoids long journeys on horseback, but he's happy to go short distances.'

Thomas murmured, 'Like riding to the inn tonight with His Lordship—who doesn't fancy another evening meal here, that's for certain.'

Emma turned on him sharply. 'I don't think there's going to *be* another meal like last night's, Thomas. Do you?'

'No, miss,' said Thomas innocently. Then he glanced at the others and added, 'Is Mr Exton likely to be requiring a bath tonight, I wonder?'

Someone—she thought it was Betsey—stifled a giggle. It was at that very moment that the door burst open and Robert came rushing in. 'Miss,' he exclaimed, 'it's that dog! And you'll never guess where he is!'

Emma's heart bumped to a standstill. 'Jasper's in the stables, of course. I've asked Gregory to look after him.'

'Then he's not done a very good job, miss, because Jasper's in the parlour making short work of the veal pie Cook's just sent through for the Viscount and his friend.'

No. Please, no.

She felt her panic rising. 'Is the Viscount there?'

'Not yet. But I believe he and his friend are on their way.'

'Come with me,' she ordered the two footmen. Then she gathered up her skirts and ran downstairs, aware of Thomas and Robert sauntering after her. She reached the parlour panting and breathless, to see Jasper sitting on the floor, his tail wagging. Indeed there was no sign yet of the Viscount or Mr Exton, but scattered around were the pitiful remnants of what must once have been Cook's pie. Jasper looked rather guilty when he saw Emma, but he was still gazing at her hopefully.

She spun round on Thomas and Robert. 'How did Jasper get in here?'

Robert shrugged. 'How should we know? You said that young fool Gregory was looking after him.'

Emma felt so cross she could have cried. 'But even if Jasper got away from Gregory, *someone* must have let him inside!'

'He was always one to be guided by his nose, miss,' Robert said solemnly. 'If he smelled rats he'd run a mile, but Cook's food he was always after. Oh, His Lordship's going to love this!'

'What,' someone said icily from behind him, 'is His Lordship going to love?'

It was the Viscount. All three whipped round to face him and Emma felt her cheeks grow scarlet. Robert bowed and said, 'Nothing. Nothing at all, Your Lordship.'

'I gather,' the Viscount said, looking at the scraps on the floor, 'that the dog has demolished the food we were promised.' He came further into the room and said to the footmen, 'You two may leave.'

If only I could too, thought Emma.

Jasper had sidled close to her now as if to offer comfort, but she needed more than that to raise her spirits as the Viscount turned his icy blue gaze on her.

'I'm not exactly sure what's been going on here, Miss Bryant,' he said, 'but whatever the dog's been up to, you certainly need to exert more authority over the staff. The servants will never respect you unless you deal with them as your position warrants.'

She felt dizzy with shame. 'My lord, I'm afraid I haven't much experience of managing staff, as you already know. And if you wish me to resign—'

'I do *not* wish you to resign!' He sounded angrier than ever, but then he sighed. 'You can't expect the staff to actually like you. You can't be their friend— that was one of the first lessons I learned as an army officer. You have to make it very clear you're the one in charge. Do you understand?'

'Yes,' she whispered. 'I'm sorry, my lord.'

He looked hard at her. 'Oh, Miss Bryant. Yet another apology? You need to stand up to me as well, you know, if you think I'm being unfair to you. But as I said, you could make your existence here very much easier by taking a firmer line with everyone.'

'Thank you, my lord. May I go now?'

'Yes. And ask Cook if she would mind providing similar refreshment, will you? It could be an hour or more before we head to the inn for our supper and Mr Exton is rather hungry after his journey. Please tell her to deliver the food to my study, where I'll be waiting in person.'

Jasper, the rogue, had somehow sidled over to the Viscount, who was absentmindedly fondling the dog's silken ear. 'I suppose,' His Lordship went on, 'the dog must have been hungry too. He certainly looks as if he needs feeding up.'

'You are too kind to him, my lord,' Emma said rather faintly. 'Jasper, come here.' She curtsied to the Viscount and hastened from the room. The dog followed obediently.

Once more she took Jasper to the stables. 'Oh, Gregory, he got into the house somehow! Please, keep him on his leash at all times!'

Gregory was upset. 'I did, but he chewed through it, miss. See? Then I had to go and get more hay from the barn and he must have run off.'

'Never mind. I'm sure you did your best,' she quickly assured him. But poor Gregory still looked miserable and Jasper too seemed forlorn.

Emma retreated to her own rooms and sat at her desk. She read once more the letter she'd received from Lady Lydia.

Dearest Emma,
When are you coming to visit me? There are several very pleasant gentlemen in this neighbourhood...

She put the letter down and closed her eyes, but found she just couldn't stop thinking of the Viscount's hand as he reached to fondle Jasper's ears. His fingers, so elegant yet so strong...

Out of the blue, she remembered a summer's day when she was twelve and her father had taken her to stay overnight with some friends of his in Witney. Emma had been looking out of the carriage window, half-lost in daydreams, when she caught sight of a wonderful old building through the trees. She had gazed at it, marvelling at its gabled wings and arched windows that glittered like jewels in the sunlight.

'That's Grayford Hall,' her father had told her.

Emma was enthralled. 'How many rooms does it have? A hundred?'

'I doubt anyone's counted them recently,' he'd replied, smiling. 'But I'd guess that if you include the smaller rooms like the attics and storerooms, then yes, there may be a hundred or more.'

From then on, whenever her friends chattered about their dreams of marriage to their ideal man, she'd pictured a Byronic hero returning home from the wars to Grayford Hall. She'd been so young then. So foolish, because on going to London for her Season she'd swiftly realised there were no romantic heroes in real life. Poor Lady Lydia had been bitterly disappointed that Emma had left London still single, but Emma told herself she didn't really care. Surely, many women lived their lives perfectly happily without a man? Besides, it wasn't long afterwards that she'd realised she needed to work and, ridiculous though it sounded now, she'd been truly excited to be offered the job at Grayford Hall.

For she would be actually living in the beautiful old building she'd admired long ago. She'd resolved to be the best housekeeper ever, respected by the staff and valued by her employer.

Oh, dear.

On all fronts, her appointment had been a disaster. Did she look like a housekeeper? Never. She was far too young, for a start. She had neither the experience nor the authority a housekeeper should have. The servants found her a joke and as for Lord Grayford...

A vivid image flashed into her mind of the Viscount when he first arrived, standing in the doorway in his long caped riding coat and boots. She'd felt truly dizzy at the sight, because with his thick black hair and towering figure, he could have stepped out of any of the books she used to love. Then she remembered him fondling the silken ears of Jasper and she realised she'd been imagining those same fingers touching *her*...

Oh, Emma. Just now he'd looked at her in the dining room as if he couldn't believe her foolishness. He was right, she was foolish, because of course the Viscount would never see her as anything other than an incapable underling. She looked into her bedroom mirror, despairing at her drab gown, her wayward hair and unfashionable freckles. Emma the dreamer, forever losing herself in old and fanciful tales of knights and heroes. She guessed that the author of *The Good Housekeeper's Daily Deeds* would have something very firm indeed to say about this state of affairs.

Shaking herself mentally, she resolved to go out to the stables to check that Jasper was still secure and indeed he was, for although he came bounding towards her, he was firmly attached to a long leash. As she patted him Gregory appeared with a broom in his hand. 'His Lordship and Mr Exton have ridden to the inn, miss,' he informed her. He glanced at Jasper a little anxiously. 'I'm keeping a close eye on him. I promise. Is anything wrong?'

'No,' Emma said quickly, 'not at all. But I felt like

some fresh air, so I thought I'd perhaps take Jasper for a short walk around the gardens.'

'It's almost dark, miss!'

'I know. But the moon is full and I'll keep to the paths.'

Jasper was delighted to have her company and though she let him off his leash, he didn't stray far. He did attempt to chase a squirrel but got nowhere near to catching it before running back happily to her side. Emma found that the clear night air refreshed her and the stars twinkling overhead made her think of something her father had once said soon after he'd lost his money. 'The stars remind us how small we are, Emma. How insignificant. They're also a consolation. Life goes on.'

Maybe. But what kind of life was *this*? She was lost and lonely in this job, but her father needed her nearby and he needed her money, especially if there were months of overdue rent to pay to Sir George Cartwright...

The night air felt suddenly chilly. Shivering a little she returned Jasper to Gregory and headed for the house, intending to go in by the servants' door. But she halted when she saw two of the maids standing outside. They hadn't noticed her.

'Did you ever see such a fine figure of a man?' Betsey was saying. 'They used to say Lord Simon was handsome, but something about this one fair sends shivers down my spine.'

'Shivers in all sorts of other places too!' chuckled Moll. 'My, I'd like to get my hands on His Lordship for an hour or two—I'd give him a night to remember. But listen, have you noticed how our Miss Bryant looks all aquiver whenever his name's mentioned?'

Betsey giggled. 'She wouldn't know what to do with a man like that. Oh, what wouldn't I give, to have seen her face when he got out of his bath!'

'What wouldn't I give to have seen His Lordship getting out of his bath myself?'

Still chattering, they headed back inside while Emma, who now felt like fleeing the house for good just as Jasper had some weeks ago, waited a few moments before following. But before she could reach her rooms, something nudged her from behind. She spun round. '*Jasper!*'

Jasper was trailing his leash behind him and was wagging his tail in delight at finding her again. Gregory was running after him. 'I'm sorry, miss! He got away before I could stop him. I'll just take him back and tie him up real tight—'

'No,' she said, surprising herself. 'No, I'll take him, Gregory. He can spend the night with me, just this once, until he gets used to being back at the Hall again.'

I shall be glad of the company, she thought secretly to herself. Taking hold of Jasper's long leash she headed for her rooms, thankful that she met no one on her way, then she settled him down by the fireplace of her tiny parlour.

'Stay there,' she warned him. 'I want no more trouble from you. Do you understand?'

He gave a happy *woof.* Leaving him there, she went through to her bedroom and prepared herself for bed, washing herself with her favourite lavender soap and brushing out her long hair. Yes. She would start thinking about a new job tomorrow. She'd managed to put London behind her, so surely she could do exactly the same with Grayford Hall and all its occupants.

She was just reaching for her usual all-enveloping cotton nightgown, when she changed her mind and walked over to her clothes chest from where she carefully drew out an ivory silk nightgown wrapped in tissue paper. After her father's bankruptcy she'd sold most of her London clothes without regret, but this she'd kept. She held it up against herself, feeling the silk kiss her skin, then she gazed at her image in her mirror.

Why hadn't she got rid of this scandalous garment? Why did she still sometimes bring it out and even try it on? Was it a stupid act of vanity, a relic of past dreams? Or was it to remind her that she could—almost—be beautiful? Some mad impulse made her put it on. It slithered over her head like a caress, then clung to her breasts and softly skimmed her hips. There were no sleeves and the plunging neckline showed how her pale skin gleamed in the light of the flickering candles. Gathering up her long hair she piled it loosely to the top of her head, allowing some curls to trail down her neck.

How the servants would laugh if they could see her like this. *Who does she think she is?* they would scoff. Sighing, she pulled her long woollen dressing gown over the silk nightdress and went to sit at her desk, where she dipped her pen in the inkwell and tried to think of the reminders she must write in her diary for the following day.

One: find out how long the Viscount's guest is staying and check any special requirements of his. Two: discuss next week's menus with Cook.

*Three: find a new home for Jasper, before the
Viscount throws him out...*

But she didn't actually write a word. Instead she
stared at the blank page and she couldn't think of anything—anyone—except Lord Grayford. At last, she
dipped her pen in the inkwell and scribbled,

*Stop these ridiculous fancies. Do you under-
stand? Just—stop.*

And she went to bed, still wearing that sinful nightdress.

Chapter Nine

If he was completely honest, James had to admit that by coming to the Flag tonight with Theo he was hoping to prove that nothing much had changed. Yes, maybe the inn did now belong to him. But he still liked to think of it as the homely refuge where he used to head whenever he was here on leave from the army: to drink with the locals, catch up with the gossip and maybe even answer just a few of their eager questions about the war.

But nothing *was* the same, because the little inn, normally half-empty at this hour, was busy; noisy too, though the public room fell silent when he and Theo entered. Some of the drinkers even jumped to their feet and made awkward little bows. 'My lord! Welcome home.'

But their voices were subdued and clearly the locals weren't nearly as comfortable with a viscount as they were with an easy-going young soldier. Another thing—James reckoned there were strangers in here, people from outside the district. He looked at Theo, who shrugged. Then the landlord, old Joseph Teagle, who'd once thrown James out without ceremony when as a lad he'd got involved in a brawl, came forward.

'My lord,' he said, far too politely for James's liking. 'It's truly an honour to see you here.' And he bowed.

James replied as heartily as he could. 'There's no need to stand on ceremony, Joseph! My friend and I will take supper here, if you please.'

'Of course. But might I suggest you use the private parlour, my lord? As you can see, we're rather busy tonight.'

James hesitated, but Theo nudged him. 'Say yes,' he urged. 'The other drinkers will be uncomfortable while you're in here. Besides, we'll be able to talk more freely if we're alone.'

Something in Theo's voice made James look at him sharply. So his friend had something to tell him, did he? James turned again to the hovering landlord. 'Thank you, Joseph. Yes, we'll use your parlour.'

They were quickly settled in the back room, with a bottle of Joseph's best claret and two plates of his wife Maggie's hearty beef stew. Once they'd made good inroads into their meal, James turned to Theo and said, 'Out with it then. I'm guessing you're longing to tell me something?'

Theo grinned. 'I never was much good at keeping secrets from you, was I? But it's about your housekeeper, Miss Bryant. Ever since you told me her name, I've been puzzling over it, because it seemed familiar.'

James pushed his plate aside and poured them both more wine from the second bottle Joseph had just brought in. 'She's from an Oxfordshire family. That could be why.'

'Yes, but I've realised now exactly who she is. Her father, Pelham Bryant, is a scholar and a historian. He once lived in Oxford, in some comfort I believe. But around two years ago, Bryant lost almost everything.'

'Was he a gambler?'

'In a way, yes. I've heard he indulged in a series of ill-advised investments, which ended in him throwing good money after bad.'

James thought a moment. 'You said this was two years ago. But his daughter has only been the housekeeper at the Hall since January.'

Theo shrugged. 'I don't know the entire story. Maybe her father struggled along for a while then found he couldn't make ends meet. That would explain why she took the housekeeping job, wouldn't it?'

James sighed inwardly. Was there no getting away from Miss Bryant? She was trouble personified: landing him with that enormous dog was only the latest example. And yet... Truth to tell, she was bothering him more than she ought to.

There was something rather brave about her. To accept such a lowly role if she'd once been wealthy took a particular kind of courage. And he was gradually having to admit that she sometimes looked quite fetching, like when she'd raced after Jasper in the courtyard this afternoon. That lovely long hair...

He said, 'A housekeeper's salary is abysmal. Surely she couldn't be so very desperate?'

'I imagine that if you've almost nothing,' Theo said quietly, 'even the smallest addition to your income can make quite a difference.'

James knew that being the poor cousin in a family of rich aristocrats couldn't have been much fun for Theo. Certainly, James's father had been kind enough to him, paying for doctors when Theo was ill as a child and stumping up the fees so he could attend Eton with Simon and James.

Always the poor one, though, Theo. With a lame leg into the bargain after that illness.

He said, 'You're right, of course. The money will make a difference. But she's incompetent, Theo. She allows the staff to run rings round her!'

Theo was silent a moment. Then he said, 'Your staff had no idea I was arriving today. But when Miss Bryant showed me to my room, everything in there was perfect. I'd got a blazing fire, there were crisp sheets on the bed and every other comfort you could think of. Like I said, James—give her a chance. You say last night's meal was bad, but how was your breakfast this morning?'

'Actually, it was rather good.'

'And the general state of the house? Have you anything else to complain about?'

James began counting on his fingers. 'One, the cask of exploding pickles. Two, the earwigs—oh, the devil!' James grinned reluctantly. 'I'm sorry, Theo. You arrived to find me in a filthy mood because I came to Grayford Hall for some peace, but instead it seemed as if I'd landed in Bedlam.'

'You must be missing the army. After all, it was your life for many years.'

'I do miss it, yes.' James reached for his wineglass, his brow furrowing. 'But I was a fool to be tempted into the tangled web of foreign diplomacy. Agreeing to that journey to Vienna was possibly the most foolish mistake I've ever made.'

'Not your fault, James,' Theo said emphatically. 'You took on a vital task in order to safeguard the peace talks. You were doing your duty.'

'Only to have it all thrown back in my face! Even though no one could prove me guilty, I was given a real dressing-down by Lord Liverpool because of the vast sum of money the government had to pay the Archduke as compensation for the lost book. Those smooth-tongued bastards in government—I loathe the lot of them.'

'Don't forget—the enquiry found no evidence to convict you.'

'But no other culprit has ever been found, nor has the original book.' James once more felt the fury grinding away inside him. Some day, someone would pay dearly for what they'd done to him.

Theo was still watching him thoughtfully. 'Perhaps you're right to stay on at the Hall and let the Austrian affair die away in your absence. After all, I doubt if any of your neighbours will have taken notice of the gossip.'

James shook his head. 'You're wrong there. Do you remember Sir George Cartwright?'

'I do. Jumped-up fellow. What about him?'

'He paid me a visit yesterday.'

'To welcome you home?'

'Not a chance. Instead, the damned man spoke to me as if I were a convicted traitor. He also had the nerve to bring his daughter along with him—poor girl, he used to dangle her in front of my brother and yesterday he was hinting quite brazenly that she might be a suitable match for me.'

'Even though he'd openly doubted your innocence? Incredible!'

'Both incredible and stupid. The man actually told me—listen to this, Theo!—that although he found it hard to believe my complete innocence in the Austrian business, he was generously prepared to forgive and forget! I was furious, of course, while poor Belinda was so embarrassed that she was almost in tears.'

'Did you show the fellow the door?'

James shook his head. 'Not straight away. As it happened, Miss Bryant blundered in on us and it turned out to be quite fortunate, because she took Belinda away and soothed her with a glass of cordial. After Sir George's visit, I could have done with some soothing myself.'

Theo said thoughtfully, 'You know, if you'd stayed in London your female admirers would have been only too happy to oblige. Lady Henrietta, for example.' He lifted one eyebrow. 'I don't suppose you'll find much in the way of petticoat distraction here.'

No flirting with the staff now, Henrietta had reminded him when he bade farewell to her in London the night before he left for Oxfordshire.

She could be reassured on that matter. And yet for some annoying reason, James found himself thinking of Miss Bryant again.

He pushed his empty glass aside and rose from his chair. 'I suppose it's time we were heading back to the Hall.' He forced a smile. 'You know, Cousin, if I thought I was coming here for a quiet life, I was sadly mistaken. I'd not realised quite how much my brother had neglected the entire estate.'

There was silence for a moment as Theo buttoned his coat. Then he said, 'Sometimes, James, you speak of your inheritance as if it's a burden.'

James shook his head swiftly. 'Forgive me if I sound ungrateful. I suppose I'd always assumed Simon would have heirs and I'd never have to take responsibility for a damned thing, selfish creature that I am. It's just going to take a certain amount of readjustment, that's all.' He pulled on his coat and was heading for the door when he stopped. 'By the way, I heard talk earlier today that someone's been handing out broadsheets in Oxford claiming I'm in disgrace with the government, that kind of thing. You didn't happen to notice them when you passed through the town earlier, did you?'

Theo shook his head. 'I didn't. Are you sure? It sounds as if someone's gone to a fair bit of trouble.'

Yes, thought James. Yes, it did.

He led the way into the public bar and was once more surprised that there were so many customers. Normally the inn was a sleepy place, patronised by just a few locals for their evening pint: men like Peter Hobday, for instance, whom he could see now over in his usual place by the fire with his sons. But there were outsiders too. Could they be from one of the villages beyond the estate? Though why come to the Flag?

He was heading for the door when he suddenly became aware of the way some of them were turning to look at him.

He tried to dismiss it and pressed on—until he distinctly heard one murmur to another, *'Look who it is. And we've all heard the stories.'*

James felt the slow, cold anger begin to build up in his veins. He could hear Theo hissing behind him: 'James. Let it go. This isn't the time or the place. Come on, best get out to our horses.'

Theo led the way and James followed. Theo was right; he was too ready these days to take offence, too quick to flare up, but his pulse was still hammering with suppressed anger and when they got outside and he realised they were being followed, he felt his whole body tensing.

Yes, several men had pursued them into the yard. All wore scruffy coats with their hats pulled low and they were advancing on him steadily. 'Traitor,' they began to murmur in unison. 'Traitor.'

James rapidly assessed the situation. There were four of them and poor Theo was useless in a fight. They were coming towards him swiftly now, so he clenched his fists and caught the first one right on his jaw, the second in his belly. Both brutes staggered back. Theo had vanished from view and James hoped to God he'd gone for help.

Now another was coming up from behind but James, spinning round, punched him on the nose and saw blood spurt. James thought, *There is actually some blessed relief in being able to thump some of my enemies.* But he froze when he saw the gleam of a blade in one man's fist.

A knife? They would attack a peer of the realm with a *knife*? And where the hell had Theo got to?

Swearing under his breath, James tried to make every punch count, but any moment now he expected to feel the cold kiss of steel. One of the rogues landed a blow to his temple that made him see stars and he thought, *This is it. I'm done for.*

But then—then, he realised his assailants were backing away and the reason was clear. More men were rushing out from the inn to the courtyard led by Peter Hobday and his three strapping sons, who launched themselves at the strangers and kicked them with their hobnail boots as well as using their fists. Very soon a full-scale rout was taking place.

James sank back against the wall and mopped his bruised forehead with his handkerchief. Good God. To think that he'd come to Oxfordshire for some peace. By now old Joseph Teagle was hurrying across to him. 'My lord. I cannot apologise enough. I can't believe something like this could happen here!'

'Me neither.' James was watching his attackers make a hasty exit on horses tethered just beyond the inn's yard while Hobday and his band yelled ripe insults after them.

Where had those men come from? he asked himself. *Who had set them on?*

Then Theo was beside him. 'I went inside to fetch help, James,' he said. 'I realised that was the most useful thing I could do.'

'You have my heartfelt thanks.' James turned to the landlord. 'Joseph, have you any idea who those men were?'

'I've absolutely no notion, my lord!' Teagle was shaking his head. 'You can be sure of one thing, though—they'll never darken my door again. Now, you must come back inside the inn before you set off home. You've had a nasty shock. And my fine brandy is the best remedy I can think of...'

Chapter Ten

Emma was asleep, but it wasn't exactly restful because she was dreaming of Lord Grayford who—*oh, dear*—was walking towards her with a brooding intensity in his blue eyes that sent her senses whirling into a delightful haze of confusion. What was more, he was holding out his arms and letting his mouth curve in a wicked half-smile as he murmured, *'Miss Bryant, I cannot stop thinking about you. I want to kiss you, all over. And for a start, we shall get rid of this.'* He began to remove her cap—yes, she was wearing it in her dream!—so that her hair fell loose and next he was bending his head to kiss her...

Oh, my goodness.

Emma woke in a state of acute consternation.

Thanks to the faint light that the moon cast through the curtains, she could see from the little clock above the fireplace that it was one in the morning. She still felt slightly dazed. A slow, thrumming warmth tingled through her entire body and indeed she dreaded to think what her dream might have offered next.

They say he's a spectacular lover...

What exactly did that mean? She knew the basic facts, of course, but what made a man 'spectacular'?

At that very moment she jumped from her bed because she'd heard a low growling sound. She put her hand to her mouth then almost laughed. Of course, it was Jasper. She'd left him in her parlour, but now he was at the side of her bed pawing at her sheets, maybe because he wanted to go outside. But she tensed again as a noise came from the hallway beyond her door and Jasper looked at her as if to say, *You see?* Emma held her breath as she heard the sound of uneven footsteps and a muttered, very masculine 'Damn it'.

She pulled on her horrid woollen dressing gown, lit a candle and opened her door just an inch or so.

Out in the corridor stood Viscount Grayford, with his back to her. She turned to Jasper and hissed, 'Stay in there.' Then, candlestick in hand, she closed her door and walked towards him. He was dressed in a shirt, breeches and muddy riding boots and she guessed he was a little drunk, because his black hair was all ruffled and he seemed slightly unsteady. He was also staring with an air of puzzlement at some broken shards of pottery lying on the floor.

They were the remains of a small statue of Hebe that had once adorned a nearby side table and most likely the crash had woken Jasper. What was the Viscount doing here, at one in the morning? Of course, it was none of her business what he got up to. He and his cousin must have come back late from the inn. But if any of the servants should come and investigate…

'My lord.' She put her candlestick on the side table where Hebe once stood. 'Is something amiss?'

He whirled round, startled, then recognition

dawned. 'Ah,' he said. 'My youthful housekeeper. I hardly recognised you without your cap.'

She should have covered her hair, she realised. He was staring at it and no wonder—it was loose and a complete mess, but at least she was wearing her all-enveloping dressing gown... 'Your face!' she suddenly blurted out. 'My lord, whatever has happened?'

For she'd realised there was a nasty bruise on his temple and blood was seeping from the wound. He put his hand up to his forehead. 'This? Oh, there was a slight scrap outside the Flag.'

'A scrap?'

'Yes. A fight. So I came down here looking for water to clean myself.' He was still regarding her in puzzlement. 'Why are you up at this hour, Miss Bryant?'

'I was asleep, my lord.' Her voice wavered slightly because vivid images from her dream kept presenting themselves in a most alarming way. 'But then I woke. And here I am, as you see.'

They both gazed at what remained of Hebe on the floor. 'Well,' he said at last, 'I always disliked the thing anyway. And at least it was me rather than you doing the damage this time. But I'm sorry if I disturbed you.'

Yes. He very much *did* disturb her. He towered over her as she stood there and then he was lurching towards the kitchen again, trying to avoid the broken pottery but bumping into a doorpost as he went. He'd been drinking brandy—she could smell it. And that injury to his face...

If he was seen, the Hall would be buzzing with gossip.

She made up her mind quickly. Reaching to touch

his arm she said, 'Please come this way, my lord. You do not want to risk your staff finding you like this. My rooms are just here. If you wait, I'll bring you something to bathe your face.'

His eyes fastened on hers. She saw they were very blue and were fringed by lashes just as black as his hair...

Stop it.

He said, staying exactly where he was, 'So you think it's not good for my reputation to have been in a fight, Miss Bryant? To which my answer is—*what* reputation?'

She pressed her lips together. 'Please go in there.' She pointed firmly to her door. 'I'll be back within moments.'

At last he headed for her rooms—which raised the question, where was her own common sense? To invite him into her sanctuary was rash indeed—some men might take advantage. But almost instantly she remembered the glint of laughter in his eyes as he'd taken in her tousled hair and her shabby nightrobe. Goodness, what a prim, strait-laced creature he must think her. Which, of course, was exactly what a housekeeper was supposed to be—prim and strait-laced.

'Your cap,' he said, suddenly halting at her door. 'I trust you've locked it away for the night? It really is a rather intimidating object, you know.'

'I certainly don't wear it to sleep in, my lord,' she answered firmly. But the corner of his mouth lifted in a smile, just as it had in her dream.

Pull yourself together, Emma.

As he disappeared into her sitting room, she went to the kitchen to collect a cloth and a bowl of water laced with arnica then headed back and found him sitting by the hearth. On his lap rested the volume of Lord Byron's poetry she'd been reading earlier—and at his feet lay a very contented Jasper. She'd forgotten all about Jasper.

The Viscount stood up, putting the book on the mantelshelf. Then he pointed at Jasper. 'I see you've made a friend of him,' he said.

She set down the bowl of water on a nearby table. 'I'll take him back to the stables straight away if you don't want him in the house, my lord.'

'Take him out at this hour? I never said that.' Suddenly he bent to fondle Jasper's neck and ears and oh, no, he was doing it again, kneading the silken fur there with those long fingers of his, making the dog quiver with delight. Making Emma think of things she should definitely not be thinking of at all.

The Viscount looked straight at her and said, 'I had a dog like this, in the army. In Spain.'

Jasper was gazing at him rather stupidly, just like her, really. 'You mean you'd taken him with you? All the way from England?' She stammered a little, still flummoxed by what those fingers were doing.

He shook his head. 'No. This dog just turned up one night when we were setting up camp in the mountains. My men and I called him Perro—that's Spanish for dog. He used to follow me everywhere.'

She noticed there was still a trickle of blood on his forehead that ought to be dabbed away, but she couldn't move. 'What happened to him?'

'I had to leave him behind at the camp, on the day we were ordered to march off to a place called Salamanca.'

Salamanca.

Emma recalled there had been a terrible battle there. Indeed the Viscount was silent a moment and she wondered if he was thinking of the many comrades he must have lost. 'When I got back,' he went on, 'Perro was nowhere to be seen. Someone told me he'd tried to follow me—tried to find me, I fear, right in the thick of the fighting. Most likely he died.'

'I'm sorry,' she blurted out. 'You sound as though you lost a friend.'

'Indeed. Perro was one of the best.' He stroked Jasper one last time then turned his full attention on her. 'Aren't you going to ask me why I got into a fight tonight?'

'No.'

'Why not?'

Oh, his eyes. Those blue, blue eyes...

'I won't ask you, because I don't consider it any of my business, my lord.' She squeezed out the cloth in the bowl of water and arnica. 'Will you hold this against your forehead? It should help to stop the bleeding.'

As he took the cloth their hands touched, only lightly, but she felt a startling jolt and stepped back quickly. What in heaven's name was that? Most likely the shock of having a man as big and tall as him in here, but her heart was pounding quite unnervingly, though he, of course, appeared quite unmoved as he calmly pressed the cloth to his bruised temple. Then he closed his eyes in apparent pleasure at the sensation and she tried, really tried to look away.

But she couldn't. She was transfixed. She found herself suddenly thinking of the time Lady Lydia took her to a grand London house for a party—and in the hallway stood a life-size statue of a naked Greek warrior. 'Close your eyes, Emma,' Lady Lydia had instructed. 'This instant, do you hear?'

The statue had sadly lacked a head, but Emma guessed that Lord Grayford could easily have posed for a replacement. His nose was long and straight; his cheekbones slanted in a decidedly dangerous fashion and his mouth was dangerous in a different way, because it was a beautiful shape with lips that looked soft and inviting...

Suddenly he opened his eyes but fortunately Jasper was dancing around him and trying to lick his hand, which she hoped distracted him from noticing the expression that must have been on her face.

'Miss Bryant,' he said, stooping to coax Jasper away with a pat, 'I must confess that when I arrived yesterday you struck me—to put it kindly—as rather inappropriate for the role you'd taken on.'

Inappropriate?

She almost winced as she remembered the extremely inappropriate garment she was wearing at this very moment beneath her drab dressing gown. Then she realised he was talking again. 'You told me Mr Rowley appointed you,' he was saying. 'Did the man make advances on you on any occasion?'

She remembered with a shiver the insinuations and the leering looks, but kept her voice steady. 'He gave certain hints, my lord. But I made it clear that I would leave straight away if he came anywhere near me.'

'I'm glad to hear you were firm with him.' He nodded approval. 'But I suspect you may have let the other staff here get the better of you a little too often.' He suddenly fixed her with those penetrating eyes. 'Were the footmen responsible for those earwigs on the table last night?'

'My lord, I—'

'Answer me, Miss Bryant.'

She nodded mutely.

'Were they also responsible for the incident of my bath?'

Again she nodded. For a moment there was silence and Jasper looked from one to the other almost anxiously. Then the Viscount said, 'If you wish, I can speak to them on your behalf.'

She spoke up then. 'No. Please, please do not! That would be...*ruinous.* I need to assert my own authority, my lord!' Conscious of his blue eyes boring into hers with a certain amount of scepticism, she stood there, her cheeks flushed with mortification, adding, 'I suspect that the servants were annoyed by the appointment of someone with so little experience. Many of the mishaps here have been due to my own mistakes and believe me, I've made enough of those.'

'Perhaps. But you have some surprising qualities. For instance, here I am stumbling around in the middle of the night, yet you've dealt with it all utterly calmly. Then there was the visit earlier today of Belinda and her father. You did a very good job of soothing the poor girl. What did you think of her?'

'I'm your housekeeper, my lord. I'm not paid to judge your visitors.'

'Maybe not. But neither are you paid to tend to a slightly drunk and somewhat bruised peer of the realm in your private rooms.' He looked straight at her. 'I would genuinely value your opinion.'

'I thought Miss Cartwright was very elegant, my lord. Very...demure.' She remembered Belinda's ravishing outfit and thought with renewed dismay of her own loose hair and ugly nightrobe.

'Belinda's father,' he was saying, 'suggested that I propose marriage to his daughter. I refused, of course. Many would say she's had a lucky escape. Did she strike you as disappointed by my lack of interest, Miss Bryant?'

He was asking *her*? *He's been drinking*, she reminded herself. All this sense of intimacy, of him confiding in her, was a complete illusion because he was intoxicated. She said, as calmly as she could, 'How well does she know you, my lord?'

'Hardly at all. But are you suggesting you need to know someone well, to fall in love with them?'

'I've really no idea, but it would help, I imagine.' Emma squeezed out the cloth in the arnica mixture again as if she was squeezing all nonsensical thoughts such as love out of her body. 'My lord, please hold this to your face a little longer. It will reduce the swelling.' He did so with a slight air of impatience, walking over to peer into the mirror on the wall. Which gave her a fine view of his broad shoulders and—

Oh, goodness. She could see every inch of the way his breeches clung so snugly to his strong thighs and to his...posterior. Whatever you called it, it was a delicious sight.

He turned round, still holding the cloth to his forehead. 'So you don't think Belinda is really in love with me?'

Emma fixed her eyes firmly on the top button of his shirt, which was at her eye level anyway, and said,

'Pray forgive me if I'm speaking too freely. But if she was truly in love with you, then she would have stood up to her father and defended you, wouldn't she?'

He gave a shout of laughter. 'Belinda? Stand up to her father? I can't see that happening in a million years, can you?'

'Not really, my lord.'

He sighed. 'Clearly, Miss Bryant, you overheard something of my conversation with her obnoxious father.'

She took a deep breath. 'Enough to realise that what Sir George said was quite intolerable.'

'You mean, what he said about my reputation? Oh, I've put up with worse than that. It was only my pride that was hurt—my damned pride. Sit down a moment, will you? I'm in no hurry to go back to my room, since I'm pretty sure I won't sleep. And I really can't stand all the exotic stuff in there.'

'No, my lord.'

He looked at her. 'You mean you don't like it either?'

'I find it rather…tiring on the eye.'

'It is indeed.' He sighed. 'What I wanted to tell you was that I was insulted in the Flag tonight. Do you think I was wrong, to get into a fight over it?'

He'd seated himself on a bentwood chair and Emma perched carefully on a chair facing his, noting that Jasper had already sprawled happily at His Lordship's feet. 'I assume somebody cast aspersions on your reputation, my lord?'

'They most certainly did. They made me out to be a rogue and a traitor!'

'Then I hope you gave them exactly what they deserved.'

He laughed. 'Bravo! A woman after my own heart!' His expression suddenly grew more serious. 'I should have had you at my side when I was in London, to calm me down whenever I was in danger of losing my temper. The charges against me are completely unproved, but people talk. They still damned well *talk*. What can I do about it, Miss Bryant?'

He was asking her opinion *again*?

He was tired and bruised and doubtless still a little drunk, but somehow that made him all the more real to her, not a wealthy lord but a living, breathing human being who could be hurt in his mind as well as his body. Once more she felt that short, sharp shock of awareness imploding somewhere inside her, the same shock she'd felt like that in her dream, just before he drew her into his arms and...

Stupid fairy-tale nonsense, Emma!

She said, 'You asked me what you can do about the gossip.'

'Yes? Tell me.'

'My lord, I truly think you should go back to London.'

'No!' He jumped up and began to pace her little sitting room while Jasper watched wide-eyed. 'No, I hate the damned place. And I despise most of the people there!'

Emma stayed exactly where she was. 'You did ask,' she said quietly, 'for my opinion.'

His eyes widened and she wondered for a moment if he was going to roar with rage at her temerity. But instead he threw back his head and laughed. 'By God,' he said, 'you're surprisingly outspoken! But your efforts are in vain, I'm afraid, because I'm going to stay here. I've had enough of polite society and its rewards for my service to my damned country.'

Surprising herself, Emma rose too from her chair and faced him stubbornly. 'Then you must defy polite society! You are guilty of nothing, so show it by going to parties. Be seen in public, as people would expect to see a man of your rank!'

'Is that what you would do... Miss Esmerelda Bryant?'

She reeled. *Esmerelda.* That was her true name, the one she'd been christened with. She whispered. 'How did you know?'

He pointed to her volume of Lord Byron's poetry on the mantelshelf. 'It was inscribed in that book. Inside the front cover.'

'The book was a gift from my mother's aunt. But the name... I never use it now.'

'Why not?'

'Because it's quite inappropriate for a woman of my station! I know my place, my lord, just as I believe you should know yours. Your duty is to go back to London and defend yourself—'

She broke off because he was coming closer, bringing with him the scents of brandy and leather; of arnica too, from the bruise on his temple. He was so powerful, yet the bruise made him look somehow vulnerable and Emma found that the mixture of strength and weakness stirred up a strange, pulsing hunger in all sorts of places. Especially when slowly, very slowly, he began reaching out to her.

Dear God, was he going to *kiss* her?

No. He touched the sleeve of her ugly nightrobe then his hand dropped to his side. She felt stupid to have even imagined it could end in a caress. Then he said, 'I'm sorry you find yourself in straitened circumstances, Miss Bryant. I've learned of your father's misfortune and of yours, in being so suddenly forced into a position you must never have wanted.'

'It was no hardship to come here,' she answered steadily. 'I was grateful to be offered the post, since it meant I could still regularly see my father.'

He nodded but was frowning. 'I would have thought, nevertheless, that you could have looked for alternatives to being a housekeeper.'

'I did consider being perhaps a governess. But that might have meant moving further away.'

'No.' He broke in impatiently, shaking his head. 'No, I meant... Surely you could have married? Even without a dowry, you must have received offers!'

'None that I wished to accept.'

'You mean, you never met a man who tempted you?'

Then, oh, goodness, her heart was pounding again, because he was watching her in a way that did more than unsettle her and he was close again. Too close. 'Lord Grayford,' she began, 'it's really very late. I think that it's time...'

That was the exact moment when Jasper, jealous Jasper, decided to claim His Lordship's attention for himself. He leapt up at the Viscount and Emma tried to pull him away, but Jasper thought it was a game and jumped up at her instead. One of his front paws caught the trailing tie of her nightrobe, with the result that the garment fell open and instantly, her silk nightgown was revealed in all its glory.

She heard the hiss of the Viscount's indrawn breath. Jasper, still jumping around, almost knocked her over and she felt the Viscount's big hands round her waist.

Only to steady her, she reminded herself, but it had the effect of almost stopping her breathing. She could feel the heat of his taut, lean body in every fibre of her being.

'Miss Bryant,' he said softly, arching his black eyebrows. 'My, oh, my.'

Emma felt a melting sensation in her stomach, because his eyes had slid down to where her breasts were only scantily covered by the delicate silk and for one wild moment, beguiled by the scent of him and his nearness, she wanted him to kiss her so badly that it hurt.

He drew back a little, his hands dropping to his sides. 'How full of surprises you are,' he said, his eyes still hooded. 'Do you usually sleep in this garment? With no one but yourself to see it? It really is rather wasted.'

Emma found herself stammering. 'It's years old. I—I bought it in a fit of ridiculous extravagance. To wear it still is foolishly self-indulgent.'

'And more than a little dangerous,' he murmured. 'I imagine that hideous cap you wear would disapprove of it heartily.'

Oh. *Oh*. It must have been her nerves, but she caught the hint of laughter in his voice and suddenly she wanted to laugh too. 'Yes,' she said. 'My cap is completely hideous, isn't it?'

He said solemnly, 'So hideous that it deserves a

formal burial, nothing less,' at which she had to put her hand to her mouth to stifle her giggles.

You are losing your wits, she told herself as she drew together the edges of her nightrobe. But her secret laughter evaporated completely when she glanced up at the Viscount, because what was that new expression on his face?

Surely, it couldn't be that he was looking at her... because he desired her? But there was certainly something different now in the darkening of his eyes and in the set of his firm, strong mouth—something unsettling, even dangerous. He was a man, after all. He was bound to have felt some arousal at the sight of any female clad in scandalous attire. She should step away. Should already have stepped away, because every moment she allowed his gaze to devour her, she was giving him the wrong answer.

But oh, the temptation implied by that truly sinful gaze...

This is not right, she instructed herself. *This is downright madness.*

She tugged tight the cords of her horrid dressing robe and said rather shakily, 'I think that we should not be here like this, my lord.'

Being together. Laughing together. Heading down dangerous paths. And he nodded. 'I'm sorry. You're completely right.' He spoke very quietly, this time with no hint of either laughter or desire. 'I've had too much to drink and I really had better go. Goodnight, Miss Bryant.'

As soon as the door closed behind him, Emma went into her bedroom, sank on to the bed and realised she was trembling with shock and embarrassment and...

And the knowledge that she'd wanted him to kiss her more than anything in the world. Wanted to be cradled in those strong arms and to feel his warm body against hers. Oh, my. Not only was he gorgeous to look at, but he was funny too. That was what really undid her. Funny—and kind also, she suspected, beneath that steely exterior.

Since her time in London, she'd been sure she would never meet anyone she could possibly fall in love with. Well, she was on the verge of something very like it now and was thus proving herself to be a complete and utter idiot. Jasper came to her with soulful eyes and nudged at her leg. 'Oh, Jasper.' She hugged him close for solace. 'This is getting worse and worse, isn't it? What am I to do?'

She had to do what she was paid for, that was the answer. Wearily she went out into the passageway to sweep up the broken pottery, knowing she must never, ever, let anything like this happen again.

On reaching his room, James sat down on the edge of his bed, aware of those two Chinese dogs on the mantelshelf glaring at him accusingly. He glared back then he rested his head in his hands.

You are a fool. Drinking too much. Brawling.

He also knew that every time he saw his housekeeper from now on, he'd be fighting back the image of her in that deliciously naughty nightgown. Dear God, didn't she realise how the garment was guaranteed to have a quite devastating impact on any red-blooded man?

Clearly she didn't. Nor would she have realised that another few minutes of that sore temptation and he'd have been dragging her into his arms and into *very* dangerous territory. Mad, the whole evening. And he was the madman because it had been a stupid idea to go to the Flag. He should have known he would be the centre of attention the minute he arrived, since so many would recognise him from years gone by. Though oddly, the men who attacked him were strangers who had never been seen in the inn before. Could it be Sir George's work? But how could the wretched man have known that James would be in the Flag that night?

Perhaps the broadsheets in Oxford had spread the mischief against him so well that those men, on learning who he was, decided to launch their own kind of justice. Anyway, after they'd fled old Joseph Teagle had persuaded him that the best cure for his very minor wounds was brandy, so he and Theo had gone back inside and James had drunk rather too much. By the time they got home James had stumbled straight up to bed, but the bruise on his forehead had continued to thump like the blazes, so he'd decided to go down to the kitchen to find a damp cloth to clamp to his head. Only to encounter… Miss Bryant.

Miss Bryant. The scent of her. The creaminess of her skin, with that tempting scattering of freckles across her tip-tilted nose. Her thick-lashed gold-brown eyes and her luscious, honey-coloured long hair. As for that nightgown… It was positively indecent. It was the kind of garment worn by London's most sophisticated temptresses—and he was certainly familiar with them, since war heroes were always welcomed with warm embraces by ladies who knew how to both give and take pleasure. Miss Bryant, however—Esmerelda—was innocent. She was vulnerable.

My God, he rebuked himself. *You're wanting to bed your virginal housekeeper? Bad idea, James. Your wits must be addled.*

He shook his head, but his loins were still hot for her.

The note from Henrietta sat on the mantelshelf between the two hideous dogs and, like them, it stared at him reproachfully. Henrietta had sulked when he'd told her he was leaving for Oxfordshire, though James had not felt too much regret on their parting. He'd also resolved that it would do him no harm to be celibate for a while. But little Miss Bryant, with her sweet face and her lovely breasts practically on display thanks to her outrageous nightgown, had almost banished his resolve in an instant.

He'd wanted her all right. He'd wanted to take her in his arms and strip the silky garment from her shoulders and kiss her all over, not to mention the rest…

No. A very definite *no*.

Chapter Eleven

James woke the next morning with the headache he deserved. The junior footman who brought coffee to his bedroom visibly winced at the sight of the bruise on his temple, prompting James to examine his face in the mirror once he was alone. He found that if he brushed his hair forward the bruise could hardly be seen, though it would be too late to stop the news of it spreading among the servants.

His mood wasn't improved by the fact that what sleep he'd managed had been disturbed by dreams of a brown-eyed damsel in an outrageously flimsy silk gown who kept teasing him with her coy smiles, then slipping from his grasp and whispering, *I'm not for you.* The result was, of course, that he'd woken fully aroused.

Lusting after his virginal little housekeeper? What the devil was he thinking of? In future he would stay well away from Miss Bryant and he would not spend another moment pondering her sad past. Her father had lost all his money. Unfortunate, but there it was.

He decided that a day attending to his new responsibilities with his sensible cousin for company was what he needed to restore his equilibrium so, after dressing himself and paying only fleeting attention to the thought that he really ought to get a valet, he headed downstairs.

At the doorway to the breakfast parlour he hesitated, but saw no sign of Miss Bryant. He hoped she hadn't suffered some kind of maidenly collapse after their encounter last night. Maybe she was still in bed, with her long hair spread out on her pillow and that wicked nightgown slipping from her shoulders...

'Good morning, James!'

The hearty greeting came from Theo, who was already settled at the table and tucking into sausage and bacon. But after one glance at his cousin, he shoved the coffee pot in his direction and said sympathetically, 'Feeling a bit rough this morning, are you?'

'I'm all right.' James settled in a chair and poured himself coffee. 'I've a slightly sore head, but Joseph Teagle's brandy is as much to blame as that fight. I suppose I was a little naive to assume that no one here would have heard of the Austrian business. Clearly I was wrong.'

Theo listened with sympathy. 'It certainly sounds as if you have an enemy in the neighbourhood, who might have set on those louts. Maybe someone who's jealous? After all, you've suddenly acquired a title and a good deal of wealth.'

'Which I didn't even want.' James went to help himself to bacon and eggs from the chafing dishes on the sideboard, but as he sat down again his hand went unthinkingly to his forehead.

Theo must have seen the gesture because he said, 'That bruise looks nasty. Does it still hurt?'

James was buttering some toast. 'Not as badly as it might have done. Last night my housekeeper bathed it for me with cold water and arnica.'

His cousin's astonishment was so profound it was almost comical. 'Miss Bryant? You mean, you summoned her in the middle of the night? James, for God's sake…!'

James raised a hand to stem Theo's indignation. 'I didn't summon her. The truth is, she caught me on my way to the kitchen. I had this vague idea of sticking my head in a basin of cold water or something, but she came most efficiently to my aid. Don't worry, though. Full propriety was observed on both sides.'

You liar, James. Your thoughts about her were actually quite wicked.

'Fortunately,' said Theo, 'I can't imagine anything other than full propriety with Miss Bryant. Even so, it's rather odd that she was around at that hour, isn't it? And there was that business of your bath.' He pointed his fork. 'James, has it occurred to you that your housekeeper might have designs on you? Just imagine her situation. She must have had dreams of a good match before her father lost his money. Maybe she's raising her hopes again.'

James regarded him steadily. 'On the contrary, she's trying to send me away.'

'What?'

'It's true. Last night, she scolded me roundly for coming here and hiding from my enemies in London.'

'She actually said that to you? She has no right! I'm rather glad I came up here to keep an eye on you.' Theo took a sip of his coffee. 'And I can stay on for a few days, so let's get on with doing something rather more practical today, shall we? I think yesterday you suggested I take a look with you at the estate's accounts—'

He broke off as the door burst open and Jasper hurtled in, followed by an extremely harassed-looking Miss Bryant pulling on his leash.

'My lord,' she began, still wrestling with the dog, 'Jasper escaped. I'm so sorry...'

Damn it. She looked all sweet and flustered and some of her hair had escaped...

The cap, man. Concentrate on her hideous cap and mud-coloured gown.

James rose to his feet and said to Theo, 'Forget the accounts. This dog is ready for some exercise and so am I. Let him go, Miss Bryant.'

His housekeeper looked bewildered. 'My lord—don't you want me to take Jasper back to the stables?'

'No. As I said, let him go.'

She dropped the leash and Jasper galloped up to him gleefully. James took charge of him and nodded to Theo. 'You and I are going to take a ride round the estate—and Jasper is coming with us.'

He didn't look at Miss Bryant as he left the room.

Keep your distance, he instructed himself, because that was surely the best way to ensure that last night's episode was wiped from both their memories completely.

After they'd gone, Emma began clearing up the trail of disaster Jasper had left in his wake, which included muddy footprints, some woolly remnants of a rug he'd chewed in the hallway and a generous scattering of dog hairs.

She felt as low in spirits as she'd ever been. She had risen early, firstly to get Jasper out to the stables and secondly because she was terrified that the servants would somehow know that the Viscount had been in her rooms last night. She quickly realised they didn't, since they treated her with their usual indifference, but they did know about the bruise the Viscount had acquired, for as Emma gave them all their orders for the day Thomas said, 'I wonder if His Lordship might want a doctor calling out this morning, miss?'

Emma had stiffened. 'Why on earth should he, Thomas?'

'Because he's got an almighty bruise on his forehead. Just wait till you see it.'

Bother.

'Whether he summons a doctor or not is entirely up to him,' she said crisply. 'It's certainly none of our business.'

After that she'd got on with all her usual tasks until Jasper had somehow burst into the house again and found his way straight to the Viscount's breakfast. So much for her vow to avoid the man. He'd looked stern, disapproving even, with no sign of the gentle humour he'd shown last night. Clearly he'd decided to pretend the entire incident had never happened, which was surely for the best. But—her nightgown. Would he tell Mr Exton about it? He'd probably already done so. And when he eventually returned to London, he'd be able to amuse half the *ton* with the tale of his ridiculous young housekeeper who wore clothing as ugly as you could imagine by day, then dressed like a courtesan at night!

Hot with fresh embarrassment, she attempted to restore her composure by taking a basket of household linen to Susan the laundry maid. Susan, who did the household's washing in an outhouse, was sensible and cheery and took little part in the servants' gossip. For a welcome few minutes Emma was able to relax as Susan chattered about the weather and explained how she would be able to get today's washing out in the sun to dry.

But Emma's mind was still far away. She was thinking of the Viscount's expression as he saw what she was wearing beneath her woollen dressing gown. Remembering his voice, as he breathed, *'Miss Bryant. My, oh, my.'*

'Shall I take those sheets from you, miss, before you drop them?'

Susan's voice broke into her reverie. 'Yes. Yes, thank you, Susan.'

'And miss—' this time Susan spoke more hesitantly '—can I ask you something?'

'Of course. What is it?'

'The fact is, miss, quite a few of us from round here have a favour we'd like to ask of His Lordship. And we thought, seeing as how you get the most chance to talk to him, that you might be just the right person to ask him on our behalf.'

The right person? Emma wasn't sure about that at all and her heart sank even further when Susan began to explain. 'The fact is, miss, quite a few of us have been saying that we'd really like to see some of the old ways brought back here. There were always celebrations at Easter and Christmas, at Whitsun and Lammastide too and oh, we used to have lovely times! Though not in Lord Grayford's day—he wasn't interested in such things.' Susan hesitated. 'But we did wonder if the new Viscount might be willing to let us enjoy those special occasions again. And, of course, it will be May Day very soon...'

Susan chattered merrily on, but Emma's spirits sank anew. She'd resolved to keep her distance from Lord Grayford and it was quite clear from his attitude to her this morning that he felt exactly the same. But first Jasper and now Susan had shown her their paths were bound to cross and, as Susan had pointed out, she was the one to speak up for the servants—it was her duty as housekeeper.

But all the time the Viscount's words from yesterday echoed in her mind.

'From what I remember of those May Days, they used to begin pleasantly enough. Unfortunately they generally ended in drunkenness and mayhem...'

Oh, dear.

James had optimistically imagined that a ride around his estate would be a certain cure for a bruised head and a hangover and there was no doubting that Jasper enjoyed the outing hugely—especially his frequent dashes after fast-disappearing rabbits. But James's mood was not improved by the realisation that his ancestors would have regarded the estate's present condition in some horror. Everywhere he looked he saw neglected woodlands, blocked ditches and farm buildings in urgent need of repair. People used to say Simon was the perfect aristocrat, but what the devil had his brother been up to lately? Enjoying himself in London or living it up in his friends' grand country houses, that was what.

Theo's comment as they rode homewards was, 'Things could have been worse. At least your brother didn't bankrupt the estate.'

'It's just as well,' James replied. 'It's going to take a substantial sum to put everything to rights—' He broke off. 'Jasper. Where the deuce is that dog off to now? Jasper!'

They were coming up to the Hall now and Jasper had raced ahead into the courtyard, where James could see Miss Bryant talking to Gregory the stable lad. Jasper danced around her, licking her hand and of course alerting her to the riders' approach. She looked up swiftly and when she saw James she appeared wary.

'Look out,' warned Theo as Miss Bryant began walking towards them. 'Here comes trouble.'

Theo was already dismounting, and James too swung himself from his saddle. 'Miss Bryant,' James said as Gregory led the horses away. 'You appear to be waiting for me.'

'My lord,' she said, meeting his gaze steadily. 'At some point today, would you have time to speak with me about something rather important?'

His first thought was that she had decided to hand in her notice, but before she could say anything more Jasper was leaping around her again, causing her great confusion. With one hand she was trying to pull her cap over her hair again; with the other she endeavoured to fend off Jasper. Theo had a straight face, but James guessed he was secretly laughing his head off.

James said coolly, 'I'll speak with you now, Miss

Bryant, since I'm actually rather busy for the rest of the day. Come into to my study, will you?'

Yes, he was pretty sure she was about to hand in her notice. He wasn't altogether clear what his reaction would be to that and was still pondering it when they reached his study. And there, she told him exactly what it was that she wanted.

A May Day festival.

She spoke politely. Deferentially. They were back where they should be; he was Lord Grayford, she was his housekeeper with no reference at all to last night's incident, just the unspoken agreement to forget it had ever happened.

Right. He should have been relieved and the fact that he wasn't disturbed him considerably.

'I'm not sure about this at all,' he said at last. 'You're telling me that the people on the estate want the old customs restored?'

'May Day in particular, my lord.'

'But the first of May is in less than a week's time! And there hasn't been a May feast for years, for the very good reason that they tend to descend into drunken mischief, as we discussed only the other day.' He glanced sharply at her. 'Miss Bryant, are you quite sure that my staff aren't taking advantage of the fact that I've only just arrived here and might agree to it to make myself popular?'

'I don't think anyone would suspect you of craving popularity, my lord.' Her tone was almost stubborn now. 'But I do think that they maybe see in your arrival some hope for the future.'

'Did you say *hope*?'

'I did, my lord.' She was standing her ground—he'd

grant her that. 'The families who've lived in the district for generations feel very strongly about the old customs. Recently the estate has not, as you'll have seen, been faring well and some think this is partly due to the neglect of the old ways. They are concerned that forgetting to observe age-old traditions leads to bad luck.'

That's superstitious nonsense, was his first reaction, but he didn't say it aloud. Besides, Miss Bryant was talking again, this time all in a rush.

'If you gave your consent, my lord, I could attend to the organisation of the event and I feel sure the older and more responsible villagers would help. All we would ask of you is that you maybe provide some refreshments.' She hesitated then added, 'I thought, from what you said about my father's sketches that you would appreciate restoring the local customs.'

He was remembering more and more of the local customs. Like the King and Queen of May leading a drunken romp into the nearby woods once darkness fell and celebrating the event with several hours of sexual abandon.

Perhaps she was following his thoughts, because she was already pressing onwards. 'As for the problem of too much drinking and—and certain other types of unacceptable behaviour, I think I may have a solution to that too.'

He said dryly, 'Go on, Miss Bryant.'

'My idea,' she went on in a rush, 'is that we could have all the usual events, of course, beginning with the procession led by the King and Queen of May. But here's the difference. The King and the Queen will be children! We'll make the whole event about the chil-

dren! The maypole dances and the games will be for
them—though of course, the adults can join in with
the feast and the general dancing later...' Her voice
faded a little. 'But if you think it's a ridiculous notion, then of course I'll not mention the subject again.'

He said, 'It will make even more work for you and
the staff. Do you realise that?'

'I believe most of the staff will enjoy preparing for
it,' she said quietly. 'Very much.'

He rubbed his head then caught that damned bruise
and winced. 'Well,' he said, 'you may, I suppose, be
right. Go ahead, Miss Bryant. You realise how little
time you have to arrange this?'

'Four and a half days,' she replied promptly.

'Indeed. You may proceed. Only keep me informed,
will you? At every stage!'

Her expression had grown lighter. 'I will, my lord.
And your obligations, truly, will be minimal.'

He rose to his feet. 'I always said I'd have to get
used to country life, since I, unlike my brother, am
planning on living here pretty permanently.'

She hesitated. 'So you're not going back to London
in the near future?'

Once more she was stepping over the boundary
line between master and servant. He kept his voice
cool. Distant even. 'I imagine I'll have to go there at
some point, I suppose, if only to visit my banker and
lawyer. In other words, it will be purely for business.'

She spoke then in another rush. 'You *should* go.
As I said last night, you should return to London and
prove your enemies wrong! Because—'

'Enough!' She broke off as he interrupted in a voice
that really was quite chilly. 'You take too much on

* * *

She found Susan hanging out washing and the laundry maid almost jumped for joy when Emma told her that the Viscount had given his consent to the celebrations. After that Emma headed for the kitchen to announce that the Viscount and his guest would be dining at home and Cook swiftly began her preparations, while Emma went with rather less eagerness to give the maids and the footmen their instructions for the evening.

The footmen listened with such unusual meekness that she suspected mischief and indeed, just as she was about to leave, Robert enquired, 'So what's all this about May Day, Miss Bryant? Who will you be dancing with? Got any beaux you've been hiding from us?'

She was amazed yet again by how swiftly news spread among the staff. 'Of course I haven't,' she answered crisply.

'Well,' said Robert cheerfully, 'some of us reckon you must have hidden talents, persuading His Lordship to hold the celebrations when his older brother wouldn't hear of it. Why, Miss Bryant, you're blushing! Now, you're not setting your sights on the Viscount, are you?'

'Don't be ridiculous, Robert!' This time she almost snapped. 'Isn't it time you started polishing the silverware?'

She went next to the dining room to check that all was in order there. But after leaving Betsey and Moll to attack the mahogany furniture with beeswax polish, she headed back through the main hall and noticed that the post had arrived. Nearly all of it was for the Viscount, including one letter addressed to him in distinctly femi-

yourself, Miss Bryant. Stick to housekeeping and May fairs, will you?'

She bowed her head and said very quietly. 'Yes, my lord.'

She was turning to go when he called out, 'Stop a moment!' She paused and he cleared his throat. 'I believe that I never fully apologised for what happened last night.'

'There is really no need—'

'But there is. I'd had too much to drink and my intrusion into your rooms was inexcusable.' He shook his head slightly. 'I guessed afterwards that you might be starting to feel that even Rowley's unwanted attentions would have been a better alternative.'

She looked up at him with stubborn determination. 'My lord, the steward was a despicable bully and I dealt with him as he deserved.'

'Really?' He found himself intrigued. 'How, exactly?'

She hesitated, then he glimpsed just the faintest of charming dimples in her cheek. She said, 'I discovered by chance that he detested the scent of dried cloves. So I sewed some in a little bag, which I slipped into the top pocket of my apron. From then on, he kept his distance.'

'Do you like the scent of cloves?'

'I detest it, my lord.' She said it quite primly. 'But the cloves served their purpose. I also concealed a hatpin in the brim of my cap, just in case.'

He arched his brows. 'You're a woman of many surprises, Miss Bryant.'

'Not too many, my lord, I hope.' The hint of a smile

had gone. Her face was expressionless as she added, 'May I go now?'

'Yes,' he said. 'Yes, of course. Oh, and by the way, will you tell Cook that Mr Exton and I will be dining here tonight?'

'Very good, my lord.' She headed for the door.

'Miss Bryant,' he called.

She whirled round. 'My lord?'

'Your cap is crooked. I think you frightened it with the mention of that hatpin.'

She looked a little startled then rammed the blasted thing straight over her hair again. James sighed and rubbed his head, wincing as he caught that bruise once more. He decided that if he ever smelled cloves in her presence, he'd better beware.

'It really is a load of superstitious nonsense.' Theo laughed when James explained to him about the May Day feast. 'And do you know the oldest tradition? If a man's caught dancing with a girl after midnight, he's obliged to make her a marriage offer. You must watch yourself.'

'I'll keep well away from the dancing, never fear. But I hope you'll be staying for it, Theo?'

'Me? No, I'm afraid I'll have to leave for London in a day or two. They're expecting me back at work before the end of the week, so I shan't be here to keep an eye on you, my friend. Look out for Miss Bryant, though, won't you? I have a feeling there's more to her than meets the eye.'

James thought, *I am watching her.* And that was the trouble.

* * *

After leaving the Viscount's study Emma headed straight to her room and sat at her desk, her open diary a stark reminder that she ought to start planning for May Day. *A list. You need to make a list.* But for some reason she couldn't think straight, let alone wield a pen.

She'd thought her situation at Grayford Hall was difficult enough when Steward Rowley was here. She'd coped because she had despised him. But with the Viscount, everything was different.

She put her hands to her rather hot cheeks. Did he know how impossibly handsome he'd looked as he rode up to the Hall earlier, with his face all tanned by the sun and his dark hair tousled by the breeze? She'd never felt like this, not ever! He'd been kind to her last night and understandably startled by her attire, though now he must regret those moments of near intimacy most deeply. She was lucky, all in all, that he hadn't dismissed her—yet.

Not so lucky, though, in that he was clearly planning on staying at the Hall—for how long? Long enough, she feared, to encourage her ridiculous fantasies quite alarmingly.

She opened *The Good Housekeeper's Daily Deeds* and some random words blazed out at her.

Avoid at all costs any kind of personal intimacy between yourself and your employer.

A most sensible command. The trouble was that for her, the words *personal intimacy* conjured up a vision she was sure the author never had in mind at all.

nine handwriting. The delicate perfume coming from it made her falter for an instant.

And so? she challenged herself. He was bound to have female friends! Intimate female friends... Shutting her mind to the images the thought provoked, she looked round for a footman to take the mail to His Lordship's study. She noticed only then that there was one letter she'd missed, still on the hall table. It was addressed merely to Grayford Hall and it looked familiar. She opened it and her heart sank because just as she had guessed, there was that sinister drawing of an open-beaked bird together with the message:

Think you'll be welcome here? Think again.

Her instinct was to crumple it up, but instead she looked at it more closely because it suddenly struck her that the way the bird was drawn, in profile, reminded her of the strange creatures she'd marvelled at in her father's books about heraldry: mythical beasts like griffins, dragons and unicorns. And she was due to visit her father this very afternoon. She tore a small sheet of paper from her diary, found a pencil and began to copy it.

James noted over the next few days that the weather looked remarkably promising for the festival that Miss Bryant was so set on. Every time he caught sight of her, she was scurrying around with a list in her hand.

She seemed reluctant to trouble him over the event, consulting him only when his permission was needed: for example over the setting up of the maypole in the courtyard and the ordering of refreshments for the feast. It was rare indeed that she forgot her air of self-defence whenever they talked.

Of course, that was how it had to be. For his sake and hers, he had to dismiss the illusion that there had been some kind of rapport between them that night she'd taken him into her housekeeper's parlour and they'd talked almost like friends.

You also liked the sight of all that flimsy nightgown of hers and what was beneath it, you lecherous rogue.

But he sincerely hoped she hadn't realised it and was fairly confident she hadn't, since after that first night her cap and gown remained very firmly in place.

The day came soon enough when Theo was due to head back to London. James's carriage would convey him to Oxford and Theo would take the mail coach for the remainder of the journey. James was just checking over the two horses Gregory had harnessed to the carriage when Theo appeared from the house, followed by a footman carrying his luggage.

'Well, Cousin,' said Theo cheerfully. 'It's been a brief stay but an eventful one, as ever with you.'

'Eventful?' James laughed. 'In this rural backwater?'

Theo raised an eyebrow. 'I think you're forgetting that on my first night here I witnessed as good a brawl as I've seen in London.' He grinned. 'But from now on, I sincerely hope you have the peaceful time you deserve.'

'It's the May Day festival soon.' James bent down to pat Jasper, who'd followed him out here. 'I doubt that will be peaceful. I don't see how you can possibly go and miss all the fun.'

'Fun?' Theo looked sceptical.

James straightened up and said, 'You'd never believe what Miss Bryant has organised. Hoopla, quoits and something called a hen race. Apparently the children line up their favourite hens and lure them to the finishing post with corn. She assures me it's an old rural custom.'

Theo gave a pretend shudder. 'Oh, James. And to think you were once the catch of the Season.'

'That,' said James quietly, 'was quite some time ago. And I honestly don't miss that kind of thing at all.

'Lady Henrietta misses you. She'll no doubt be telling me so very soon.'

She tells me as well, thought James, thinking of that scented letter and the words she'd used to describe exactly why she missed him.

My dear James,
When you return to London—as I trust you will very soon—we shall have so much fun, of a very intimate kind, I hope.

You, my dear, are thoroughly wasted in Oxfordshire.

There was more. Quite a lot more. But as he'd folded the letter away, he'd found his thoughts straying to a girl with gold-brown eyes and some charming freckles adorning her pretty nose. 'I'd be obliged if you'd fend off Lady Henrietta for now,' said James abruptly. 'And talking of women, Theo—isn't it time you thought of settling down yourself?'

'What—me? With a lame leg and a dull job in the Home Office? I'm in no danger of being pestered by beauties, you can be sure! I wish you joy of your festival. And James, I'll do my utmost, for what it's worth, to defend your name in London.'

They gripped hands and Theo walked to the waiting carriage while James watched. Before long he must return to London himself to see his accountant, but first there was so much to get in order. After Theo's departure he toured the Hall with Jasper at his heels, investigating everything that needed attention—leaking roofs, mould on the walls, windows that wouldn't fasten. Then he went to his study to read through the estate accounts, but once again his thoughts strayed.

Theo had said it would be a waste of time to return to the capital and try to clear his name until the whispering had died down. But he also remembered how Miss Bryant had been adamant that he should go back and prove his enemies wrong. He tried to concentrate again on the paperwork on his desk, but this time was distracted by music coming from outside. Going to his window, he saw Miss Bryant over at the far end of the courtyard, surrounded by a group of children.

She was teaching them some simple dance steps and the music was coming from the fiddler Frank Barnett, who James remembered always used to be in great demand at local events. Old Frank was sawing away at his fiddle with gusto, while Miss Bryant was patiently showing the children how to skip around a large circle she must have chalked out on the flagged courtyard.

Of course, she was preparing them for the maypole dancing. He almost smiled at seeing how some of the little ones clearly had no idea of the steps, but were enjoying themselves immensely. She'd told James that the maypole itself would be erected by willing volunteers the day before the festival, though he could see now that quite a few parents were already present. The mothers watched their offspring with great pride, but the fathers, James noted, were taking rather more interest in Miss Bryant. He couldn't blame them. He thought of Henrietta's letter again and decided that he really did not like her habit of dabbing her wildly expensive perfume on her correspondence.

He preferred the scent of lavender.

Chapter Twelve

It was the first of May. The celebrations were due to start at three o'clock that afternoon and Emma had been ticking off items on her list since early morning.

Make sure the trestle tables are properly set up outside.
Remind the musicians which tunes to play. Take the children one last time through the dance steps they keep forgetting.

Yesterday she'd visited her father to invite him to attend, but he'd declined with a smile. 'Me? Oh, no. I'm a little old for such things. But look, Emma.' He'd pointed to his desk. 'I've been searching in my heraldry books for anything resembling that odd little bird picture you showed me the other day. But it really is a puzzle. I've had no joy so far.'

She'd shown him the sketch she'd made of the bird without, of course, mentioning the ominous message. 'It doesn't matter,' she'd said quickly. It must have been intended to unsettle her, that was all. 'And I'm sorry that you're not coming to the May Day celebrations.'

'I'm quite happy here, my dear.'

Which opened up yet another difficult subject. 'Papa. There's something else. Have you still heard nothing from Sir George or his steward about the payment of your rent?'

'Not a word,' her father said.

'Then I think it might be time for me to look for somewhere else for you to live. Somewhere not owned by Sir George, because I don't think he's a suitable landlord for you.'

Her father looked crestfallen. 'But Emma, this is my home!'

She pressed his hand. 'I know, Papa. I'll find you somewhere just as suitable, I promise!' But she'd left her father looking anxious and alone.

As it happened, someone else was absent from the opening of the ceremonies—Lord Grayford. He'd warned her that he had to go into Oxford for a business meeting, but told her he'd be back in time to give his speech before the feast was served.

'And I promise I won't talk for too long,' he'd said. 'I appreciate all the work you've put into this, Miss Bryant.'

The smile he gave her was possibly the first since the night he'd been in her room. It did something to her. It gave her fluttering heart quite ridiculous ideas…

Stop it.

She told herself that his relaxed manner was merely a confirmation that he'd forgotten the incident completely and certainly her clothing today wouldn't give the man the slightest bit of encouragement. She wore a brown dress buttoned up to the neck as usual and all her hair was pinned firmly beneath her starched cap. *Frightening*, Lord Grayford had called it.

She looked around the courtyard. Already the footmen had set up the big wooden tables for the feast and the King and Queen of May were fidgeting excitedly on thrones made by the local carpenter. Both only eight years old, they looked adorable in their costumes and crowns.

Close by, an assortment of chickens pecked and cackled in a special pen, from where they'd later be freed to amble along the route of the hen race. A cluster of proud parents had gathered to watch the little dancers, who stood round the ribbon-garlanded maypole dressed in their Sunday best while Frank Barnett the fiddler and two of his friends—one with a tin whistle and the other with a tambour to beat out the rhythm—would soon be striking up the first tune.

At least, that was the plan.

It was Susan the laundry maid who came rushing up to her. 'Miss Bryant! Frank Barnett went inside the Hall with Thomas a while ago and he's not out yet!'

At almost the same moment Emma saw Thomas emerging from the Hall with a smirk on his face. *Oh, no.* She had been particularly firm with the servants in the last few days and Thomas and Robert had been sullen, but this morning she'd noticed them looking perky again, even whistling as they went about their work. They were up to something, she was sure, so when Thomas came out she went straight over to him.

'Thomas. Where is Frank?'

'No idea, miss.' Thomas looked around, all innocence. 'Isn't he out here?'

'No, he isn't. And you know something!'

'Maybe I do. Maybe I don't,' he said and strolled away.

'Thomas! Come back...' She broke off. The children were getting noisy and the crowd restless; the other two musicians were scratching their heads. Suddenly Emma saw Frank coming unsteadily through the Hall's main doors with his fiddle and bow dangling from his hands. 'Sorry, Mish Bryant,' he mumbled when she rushed up to him. 'I'm a bit late. Aren't I? And oops...' He broke off because he'd nearly tripped over the steps. Then he pointed with his bow towards the maypole and the waiting children. 'Dance,' he was saying. 'It's time to start the dance.'

Emma, horrified, said, 'You're drunk.'

'I'm meant to be drunk, Mish Bryant, ma'am. The spirit of mish...misrule and all that.' Still standing on the Hall's steps he raised his fiddle and tried to play a few notes, then sat down suddenly in a state of amiable confusion. 'Thomas. Where's my friend Thomas? I want to thank him for giving me lots of brandy. He's a good man, Thomas.'

Is he, indeed? thought Emma grimly. She would be having a word with Thomas. But first—the festival.

The children were still waiting eagerly round the maypole while their parents and everyone else had drawn close in anticipation. Emma felt quite cold. How could they go on without any music? And now—oh, no, the hens were loose! The door of their pen had been opened and they were wandering around, looking rather surprised to find themselves out in the courtyard.

She spotted Gregory setting up the quoits game a

short distance away. 'Gregory!' she called out. 'Gregory, the hens—can you get them back in their pen?'

He rushed immediately to round them up, but what could she do about the music? The tin whistle and the tambour weren't enough! Then Susan was at her side again. 'Miss! My Uncle Harry is here. He used to play the fiddle when he was younger, and I'm sure he can still do it!'

Somehow they coaxed a reluctant Frank to let go of his fiddle and Harry stepped forward. Wielding his bow with the relish of a seasoned entertainer, he led the other two musicians into a medley of country dances familiar to them all and soon the children had grasped the ribbons and were skipping round the maypole to the delighted applause of their parents.

Emma could have hugged Harry, but she didn't watch the children for long because she'd spotted Thomas lounging by the stables with Robert. She went straight over there.

'You've really gone too far this time,' she told Thomas. 'You got Frank drunk, didn't you?'

Thomas looked indignant. 'I didn't! He must have come in and helped himself to the ale meant for the feast!'

'Ale? He told me you gave him brandy!'

Thomas gave a sigh. 'Look, I gave him some of the brandy Cook keeps for her recipes, that's all. I didn't force the man to drink it!'

'You must have encouraged him, because he's almost senseless. Thomas. I warned you there must be no more of your tricks.'

'Miss, this is meant to be a day of fun. Where's

your sense of humour?' Robert, at his side, snorted with amusement.

Emma put her hands on her hips. 'You're saying you did all this to be *funny*? It's the two of you who have lost your sense of humour. In fact, I suspect neither of you has got one because you just like to spoil things for other people, don't you?'

She suddenly realised quite a few of the other servants had gathered round to listen and so had some parents. One of the kitchen maids pushed her way through and pointed her finger at Thomas. 'You offered Frank a full glass of Cook's brandy, Thomas, and you cheered him as he drank it all down. I saw you! And I spotted you too, Robert letting those hens escape. What a mean trick!'

Another said, 'Trying to ruin Miss Bryant's lovely treat for us all, you were, both of you. Shame on you! Miss Bryant's saved the day, though. Thank goodness for the Viscount's housekeeper!'

Others cheered and clapped, and Emma felt quite shaky at this outburst of warmth. But she fought down the stupid lump that had suddenly risen in her throat and lifted her hand for silence. 'Please, everyone, go and enjoy yourselves. It's time for you all to join the dancing now!'

From the corner of her eye she saw Thomas and Robert about to slope off. 'Oh, no.' She pointed at them quickly. 'Not you two. Any more trouble from either of you and I'll tell the Viscount that you helped Mr Rowley to steal that wine from the cellar!'

Both of them turned a little pale. Thomas said at last, 'How did you know that?'

She didn't know it, but she'd guessed—and their

reaction had proved her right. 'Perhaps I'm not quite as naive as you think.'

Robert began to bluster. 'Look, it was old Rowley's idea! He paid us to turn a blind eye to what was going on, that was all. It was him who took the best of the wines into Oxford to sell to a dealer there. We had nothing to do with *that*.'

'Very well. I assume you're happy to explain all this to the Viscount?'

The footmen looked at each other. Thomas muttered, 'Not really. Miss, are you going to tell His Lordship?'

'No. I'm not, but I think both of you should take your responsibilities a good deal more seriously from now on. I may only be the housekeeper, but at present I am the senior member of the staff and I'm here to stay. Do you understand?'

'Yes,' they muttered.

'Yes *what*?'

'Yes, Miss Bryant, ma'am.'

Emma glanced at the big clock over the stables. 'Right. It's nearly time for the food to be served, so I want you two to go into the kitchen and help the maids to bring everything out to the tables here. Make yourself useful for a change.'

They walked off and Emma drew a very deep breath. Oh, goodness, that had been a lucky guess. From her first few days at the Hall she'd realised that Rowley had treated Thomas and Robert with particular favour and she'd always wondered if they'd been Rowley's partners in crime. She hoped she'd acted sensibly in promising not to report them, but only time would tell.

Besides, now no one was taking any more notice of either them or her, because the Viscount was riding into the courtyard and everyone watched as he dismounted and climbed the steps to the Hall then turned to face them all. Dressed in a dark blue coat and cream riding breeches, with his black hair ruffled by the light breeze, he looked calm and relaxed.

'I'll keep my speech very brief,' he announced to the eager crowd. 'All I want to say is that I'm delighted to see you all here for this festival. May you continue to enjoy yourselves, not only today but at all the other celebrations we hope to hold in the future.'

'Hoorah for His Lordship!' someone called. Others echoed the cry until the Viscount held up his hand for silence.

'Don't worry, I'm not about to make another speech. But I see now that the food is being brought out, so all I ask is—make sure there's none left!'

There was another outpouring of approval. 'Now, he looks like a proper viscount!' she heard one woman say. 'Right handsome, he is!' Applause broke out again all round the courtyard but a headache thumped somewhere in Emma's overloaded brain. She was glad for him, so glad, but those feelings she'd had as she watched and listened were like a warning bell.

This cannot go on. You tell yourself you're in control of your feelings, but you are not.

That time he'd spent in her room, when he'd opened up to her almost as if she were his equal, was something he must regret deeply. She was his housekeeper—and to imagine anything else was sheer fantasy.

'Miss!' It was Moll the housemaid. 'Miss, we need

some more milk and butter from the cold store. Do you have the key?'

Emma nodded. 'I do. Come with me and you can take what you need.'

The cold store, which was chilled by ice all the year round, was around the back of the stable block. Moll lifted up one of the smaller milk churns—'This should do, miss!'—and Emma selected a big bowl of creamy butter then locked the door again. But instead of following Moll, she leaned against the wall and closed her eyes, feeling as low as she'd felt since arriving here.

There was dust all over her gown from the shelves of the storeroom. She looked and she felt a mess. She reminded herself of some words she'd underlined yesterday in her manual:

> *The good housekeeper has no time for self-indulgence.*

But she was tired and lonely and she didn't know how much longer she could pretend that everything was all right...

'Miss Bryant?'

She jumped in shock. It was the Viscount, scarcely four feet away. Putting the butter bowl down quickly, she tried without success to brush some dust from her gown. Whatever her shaking heart wanted, it wasn't for him to see her like this.

He said, 'Miss Bryant, I wondered where you'd got to. Are you quite all right?'

From somewhere, goodness knew where, she summoned a bright smile. 'Of course, my lord. The maids needed some items from the storeroom so I unlocked it for them. But now, I must return to my duties…'

Her voice trailed away, because he was reaching out and carefully touching her cheek. For a moment she couldn't breathe for the onslaught of sensation shaking her.

He said, 'I feel sure that Cook and all her minions are quite capable of seeing to all that themselves. And in the meantime, I wished to have a word with you in private. I've heard, you see, something of what went on earlier.'

He was so close that she could feel the warmth of his strong body. She realised she was breathing in the faint but delicious scent of his sandalwood soap and it sent her senses scattering to the four winds. She drew a deep breath. 'I'm not quite sure what you're referring to, my lord.'

'I'm talking,' he said, 'of the way you dealt with those two footmen. Tell me—do you think I should dismiss the rogues?'

She made a small sound of surprise in the back of her throat. He was asking *her*? Yes. He was. And his eyes were bluer than the bluest sky, and she wanted to touch that beautiful mouth of his, those lips, and feel them touching her everywhere…

She said at last, 'No, my lord. I don't actually think you should dismiss them because I'm hoping they'll have learnt their lesson. I'm willing to give them another chance, if you are.'

'Very well, Miss Bryant.' His gaze was still on her and it was so intent that she felt heat swirling in her veins. 'I gather that the festival has been quite a success.'

She nodded, but she was thinking that they shouldn't be here like this. Alone. Together. She tried to say so, but although being alone with him might be utter madness, she felt powerless to tear herself away. She tried her hardest to keep her voice light. 'My lord, everyone was very eager to make it a success.'

He lifted his eyebrows. 'Apart from the two footmen.'

'Apart from them, yes. But the others—the household staff, all your tenants and villagers—have been talking about their delight in the return of the old customs.' She hesitated then went on, softly, 'I think they see this as a sign of better times ahead.'

'There's someone who doesn't quite agree,' he said. 'I met an acquaintance of yours in Oxford today. A vicar called Andrew Summers.'

'Oh.' A harsh slap of reality, that. 'Did he mention our May Day celebration?'

'He certainly did. He told me he'd heard about your plans for today and also told me it wasn't right to revive these old customs. He said they were—' his mouth twisted a little '—an undesirable remnant of wicked heathen rituals.'

'Oh,' she said again a little faintly. Goodness, she could just imagine the Reverend Summers saying it. Then she added, trying to sound nonchalant, 'Did he say anything else?'

'Yes.' He was looking at her quizzically. 'He was a little critical of you. Have you offended him in some way?'

She felt her indignation rise up. 'He once offered to marry me, my lord—in rather a condescending way,

I fear. He's a widower with two children and he told me he needed a wife to look after them. I refused, because...'

'Because?'

She spoke rather more quietly now. 'I believe people should marry for love.'

There was a pause. Then: 'So you told me,' he said, 'when we spoke of Sir George Cartwright's unfortunate daughter.'

Yes. That night, that unforgettable night in her room. Which meant that maybe he, like her, remembered every word they'd spoken. From the courtyard close to the house she could hear the sounds of music and laughter, but here in the silence that hung between them she burned with mortification. Oh, God. Why did she keep saying such totally inappropriate things?

He said suddenly, 'And are you looking for this... true love you speak of?'

She shook her head and forced a smile. 'As you can tell, I've perhaps read too many ridiculously romantic novels.'

'Or poems by Lord Byron, maybe?'

'Yes.' She shrugged. 'Foolish of me, I know.'

She'd tried to sound dismissive, amused even by the topic. He didn't smile, but he never took those distractingly blue eyes from her as he said, 'On the contrary, Miss Bryant, I find you remarkably wise.'

She couldn't think of a word to say. It was torment to be alone with him like this. To have him looking at her in a way that reminded her of those wicked dreams, which even now heated her blood and made her pulse pound. She knew that this was the moment she should offer her excuses—make up something about the food, or tell him she needed to check that the children weren't running riot over their games. But already he was speaking again.

'Do you know,' he said, 'I thought I would hate coming back here, because my memories of the place aren't pleasure-filled.' He looked around. 'Even when my brother and I were home from school, my parents had little to do with either of us. I joined the army to get as far away from here as I could.'

'And to serve your country!' she cried out. 'Don't forget that!'

'Perhaps.' He shrugged. 'Though there's always an element of selfishness in the most noble of actions. Let me tell you something. When I heard that my brother was dead, I was angry with him. Can you believe that? Angry. I thought, *You fool, Simon. You've let me down again.* Tell me, Miss Bryant, what kind of reaction is that to hearing the news of your only brother's death? I don't deserve the title, or the estate, or the loyalty of those good people enjoying the feast.'

Impulsively she said, 'My lord! These people know, as I do, that you're brave and honest and you truly care for your country and for them...'

Her voice trailed away, because he'd picked up her hand and was holding it in his, oh, so gently. 'I think you're too good for me also,' he said.

She could see the dark shadows in his eyes and her whole body ached with something she didn't under-stand. He'd scarcely even touched her, yet she felt... How exactly did she feel?

She felt a desperate emptiness within her, as though

she was within grasping distance of something that would somehow complete her yet was totally beyond her reach. And without it, her life was desolate. 'My lord,' she said haltingly, 'I really must get back to my duties.' And she stepped backwards, but her over-loaded emotions were so muddled by the expression on his face—of sadness, of yearning almost—that she stumbled over an empty milk churn that had been left by the storeroom door.

And he caught her.

His hands were round her waist, his eyes were locked on hers and she felt her heart thumping painfully as he slowly lifted his hand to her hair.

'Your cap's fallen off,' he said.

'Oh.' She looked around, seeing nothing. 'I must find it.'

'You must not.' His fingers were cupping her cheek now. 'You have beautiful hair and it's a crime to cover it. If I find the hideous thing, I shall burn it, Esmerelda.'

She knew from the way his eyes had darkened what would happen next. She also knew she should stop him, but she longed with all her being to feel his lips on her mouth and she trembled with the need to ex-plore his hard body, so dangerously, temptingly close.

He would let her go the instant she told him to, she was sure of that.

Then tell him. Tell him, now.

But his lips touched hers—and her resolve vanished like the mist in the morning sun.

She had been kissed by a man only once before, at a party during her London Season. She'd left the crowded reception room for some fresh air out on the terrace and a drunken admirer had followed her and forced himself on her. His kiss had been hot and messy and she'd pushed him away with a strength she hadn't known she possessed.

The Viscount's kiss was nothing like that. His mouth was firm and warm, and she felt her lips part with a shocking delight as he explored further with the tip of his tongue, probing and caressing while his strong arms enfolded her. Oh, this was so much better than her delicious dream! And she was being truly wicked, because she was loving the hardness of his chest against her yearning breasts and the way his mouth did wonderful things to hers.

He must have kissed dozens of beautiful women, she reminded herself. This would mean nothing to him.

But his warm, firm lips promised so much more and as his strength enveloped her she felt her senses whirl with delight—

He pulled away abruptly. 'Listen,' he said.

She realised now that the music had stopped. She could hear voices too, raised in unison: the voices of the crowds in the courtyard. 'The Viscount! Where is our Viscount?'

He was looking down at her, his expression unreadable. 'You go first,' he said. 'I'll follow in a few moments. They told me they'd like me to present the prizes for the children's games and I think it must be time.'

'Of course.' That haze of delicious torment had swiftly evaporated, leaving her cold and shaken. She bent to pick up the butter bowl but as she straightened he put his hand to her cheek and said, 'We must talk again soon, Esmerelda, you and I. Talk properly, yes?'

She nodded wordlessly then set off for the kitchen with the butter.

One of the maids presented her with her cap. 'It was lying just outside, miss!' She stayed for some time with Cook and the scullery maids, helping to clear up the remains of the feast and scrub the cooking implements. Work was a distraction, of sorts. She knew the Viscount would be busy too, mingling with his employees and tenants. He would doubtless make a fine job of it, just as he could so easily make a fine job of seducing her, if he chose.

The kitchen was still warm from the heat of the big oven, but Emma was shivering inside. She had thought she was sensible, but at the touch of his lips all her resistance had vanished and a tempting devil inside her still whispered, *You realise you could be his mistress? Just imagine all the delights in store!*

She'd never been ignorant of the facts of life. It was just that they'd seemed rather ridiculous in connection with the men who'd courted her in the past, like the Reverend Summers or the man in London. The thought of doing *that* with them almost made her laugh.

But with Lord Grayford? She remembered overhearing the housemaids' talk.

'They used to say Lord Simon was handsome, but something about this one fair sends shivers down my spine.'

'It's lust!' the Reverend Summers would have preached from his pulpit. 'And lust is one of the deadliest sins!' But Emma knew she was awash with it and it wasn't only lust, because her heart was aching for a proud man brought low by gossipmongers. She longed to ease his troubles. To stand by his side and comfort him; yes, to offer him physical solace if that was what he wanted.

But if she allowed him to seduce her, she knew that everything she valued would be compromised: not just her job, but her desperate attempt to maintain her own and her father's independence. She would also have to face the desolation of the affair ending, as it inevitably must.

But, that little voice inside her persisted, *might it not be worth it?*

No. No, it most certainly wouldn't. Such a future offered nothing but peril and not only for her, because if the Viscount took his housekeeper as his mistress, he would be a laughing stock among his peers. So Miss Emma Bryant, housekeeper, fought down her yearnings because she also knew that even though his desire for her had been physically evident, men like Lord Grayford wanted experienced women for their bed sport, not innocents like her who had so little idea of the many ways of pleasing a man.

We must talk, he'd said. But what was there to talk about? *Keep that housekeeper's hat on, Emma.*

She must never let the opportunity for this kind of intimacy arise again. Nor could she continue to see him day after day, so there was only one answer.

Slowly she walked back to the busy courtyard, where she was instantly surrounded by welcoming faces. 'It's been a wonderful day, Miss Bryant! Thank you so much!'

A wonderful day for many, perhaps. She took a

little solace from that. But for her, all the delight had vanished, drifting away into the evening air like the music from that now silent fiddle.

Chapter Thirteen

James rose the next morning to see that a steady drizzle was falling. Even so, he resolved to go for a short ride before breakfast but he was scarcely half a mile from the Hall before it began raining hard. Why on earth had he set out in such a miserable weather? he wondered bitterly as he turned Goliath round. Maybe in hopes of clearing his head?

In hopes of salving his conscience, more like. What kind of rogue was he, to make advances on his young housekeeper? Theo had suggested that Emma Bryant had designs on him, but James knew it was the other way round. He was the villain of the piece, no doubt about it.

It was no more than a kiss, he'd tried to tell himself. A kiss for May Day. But even that was completely over the limit. He could try to fool himself it was light-hearted, but he'd felt his self-control vanish when her lips softened beneath his, for she'd tasted as sweet as honey. He could still recall how she'd melted in his embrace and her small breasts had pressed almost yearningly against him…

You're heading for danger, James.

She might not have realised what she was doing, but he had no such excuse. He had always claimed to be honourable, but no man of honour seduced a servant! From the beginning she'd declared her loyalty to him—yet was this how he repaid her?

Indulging in erotic fantasies about Emma Bryant was nothing short of diabolical. Any more episodes like yesterday's would no doubt result in her leaving and what would she do then? The picture of her labouring at yet another ill-paid job, alone and unprotected, left him feeling responsible and deeply disturbed.

After changing out of his damp riding clothes and taking his breakfast, which he didn't enjoy at all, he strode around the Hall in a mood as black as thunder, pretending he was adding to his list of all the things that needed sorting when really he knew he was hoping to bump into Miss Bryant. But then what? Should he try to apologise for kissing her? Tell her it was a foolish mistake and doubtless trample her feelings all over again?

Every room held memories of his own privileged if cold upbringing. Often Cousin Theo had come to stay; quiet, stoical Theo, taunted by Simon for his limp and fiercely defended by James. He remembered their aristocratic mother who'd always kept herself at a distance from her sons, while what spare time their busy father had was spent on Simon the heir.

There was no affection shown to the children of the Grayford line. Not the kind of affection he'd seen

Emma Bryant offer to the children she'd so patiently coached for their parts in the May festival. He remembered the young ones' faces yesterday, full of innocent delight in the dancing and the games she'd organised. Remembered too the way she'd hugged them close after all their little triumphs. She should have children of her own, he thought. And a husband who loved her. Not like that idiot vicar he'd met yesterday.

James felt a sudden, shocking yearning for her shoot through him. But seducing her would be the ultimate betrayal—and that was why he must keep his hands off her. She deserved better.

Eventually, after he'd eaten his lunch without really registering what was on the plate, James accosted one of the footmen. 'Where is Miss Bryant? I wish to speak to her about some household matters.'

'She's gone to visit her father, sir. It's her afternoon off.'

He should have remembered. 'She's due back at four, I take it?'

'Indeed, my lord.' The footman hesitated. 'Though sometimes, I fear, she can be rather unpunctual—'

'See to your own duties, man,' snapped James, 'and leave Miss Bryant to me. Do you understand?'

The footman bowed his head. 'My lord.'

James carried on with his inventory, striding from one room to the next. But what really struck him was that most of this great house was empty, devoid of life except for those damned portraits. His ancestors' scowling disapproval of the Hall's newest Viscount seemed to increase in severity every time he went by.

Eventually he returned downstairs and as he passed the door to the housekeeper's rooms, he wondered if Miss Bryant was back. He rapped in a business-like fashion at the door but there was no reply, so he opened it and stepped inside.

Her desk, he noticed, was arranged as if for a military campaign with blotting pad, inkwell and pens all set out with care. There was a bundle of household bills all neatly pinned together and there was also some kind of housekeeping diary lying open. He glanced at it.

Remember to check the laundry store today.
Do not forget to be firm with the footmen about their duties...

Something caught in his chest at that. Her evident resolve to do well at a job for which she had no training made him almost ache for her.

Then he noticed a scrap of paper that appeared to have been cut from a local news sheet. He picked it up and saw that it was a list of accommodation available to rent. One particular dwelling—Lowfield Lodge—had been underlined. He remembered Lowfield Lodge; it was the only dwelling at a remote spot called Far Lea, just off the Stepton Road, and last time he saw it it had been a dump, unfit for human habitation. Was she thinking of it for her father? Or for herself? *Damn.* Thanks to his complete crassness, she was probably looking for another job and James knew only one thing—that he must stop her.

Striding out to the stables, he told Gregory to prepare Goliath and paced the courtyard until the big horse was ready. It had stopped raining, but the sunshine of yesterday was a mere memory and as he galloped off his mood was as black as those rainclouds which still lurked over the hills.

Lowfield Lodge lay at the end of a stony track leading up from the road. James drew Goliath to a halt as he approached, because he could see that outside the dilapidated building, a horse was tethered. It was Sir George Cartwright's showy chestnut mare.

What the hell...?

Leaving Goliath's reins looped over a fence post around the side, he walked to the front door and heard Sir George's voice raised in anger.

Instantly he attempted to open the door, but it resisted—bolted from the inside, he guessed. And now he could hear Emma saying, 'I don't know why you followed me here, but I wish to leave, this minute.'

'We have business to discuss, you and I!' Sir George's tone was harsh. 'Your father can stay in his cottage rent free—on certain conditions, which I can't see you objecting to. After all, every woman wants someone to make life easy for her. I'm making you a generous offer.'

'I despise your offer! In fact, I find it insulting and monstrous!'

'So you've set your sights higher? I thought as much!'

'No. No, you cannot mean...'

'I've seen the way you look at the Viscount,' James heard Sir George say. 'Really, you're just a little slut, aren't you?'

With a sudden burst of energy, James slammed his shoulder into the door and the bolt gave way. Inside Sir George was gripping Emma by the wrists, but she was struggling hard.

They both froze as he entered. James said, 'Get your filthy hands off her, you brute.'

Sir George tried to sneer, but let his grasp on her slacken. 'You want her for yourself, do you? Might as well forget the housekeeping and get on with the business of bedding her. Is that it?'

Taking two strides towards him, James punched him in the ribs and as Sir George stumbled James pulled him up and shoved him towards the open door. Sir George clung to the doorpost, gasping for breath. 'Throwing your weight around won't do you any good, Grayford. Neither will hiding away here, when everyone knows you're a traitor to your country—'

He broke off as the younger man advanced on him again, but James stopped when he felt a hand pulling at his arm. 'My lord,' Emma urged. 'Don't lower yourself. Let him go.' Sir George, who'd been cowering in anticipation of the blow, threw them both one last furious look and hurried off towards his horse. 'Let him go,' Emma repeated to James. 'Though I'm afraid he will talk, about you and me.'

Yes, the man surely would talk about how the Viscount had charged in here to Emma's defence. James found himself heaving with rage and self-disgust. Hell's teeth, what a mess he was making of everything. He slumped down on an old wooden bench in a corner of the room and put his head on his hands.

Then he was suddenly aware of a warm touch on his arm, because Emma had sat down next to him.

'It's all right,' she whispered. 'He did me no harm. And you mustn't let this trouble you, my lord. Really.'

He turned to look at her, amazed. A few moments ago that odious brute had tried to assault her! But now she was comforting *him*?

'He deserved a thorough thrashing,' he said flatly. 'How can you be so calm?'

'I've perhaps fared worse. When my father lost his money, many of our so-called friends shunned us instantly. The women talked behind my back and the men—well, when they realised I was facing relative poverty, I received more than one proposition, the nature of which I'm sure you can guess. So you could say that I'm used to defending myself.' She was silent a moment. 'Though there is a particular difficulty with Sir George.'

'Please explain.'

'It's not your concern!'

'I'd like to decide that for myself.'

She sighed. 'Very well. Unfortunately the cottage my father lives in belongs to Sir George, but I discovered only recently that his steward has stopped collecting the rent.' She paused a moment. 'Sir George has propositioned me before and of course I've always refused. But I think he was hoping the issue of the unpaid rent would force my hand rather.'

'You mean—' James found he was clenching his fists '—that he'd already made inappropriate suggestions when he came to the Hall that morning with his daughter?'

She looked even more tense. 'Yes.'

He thought, *Devil take the man.* He barked out, 'Why didn't you tell me?'

'Because I've learned the hard way that people in general tend to blame the woman when something like this occurs. They assume that there must have been some kind of encouragement. Sir George is trying to persuade me to accept his advances in exchange for my father living rent-free. That's why I'm looking for a new place for him to live.'

James said, 'Are you also looking for a new job for yourself?'

She hesitated then said, very softly, 'Yes. I am.'

James looked at her as she sat by his side, so calm, so outwardly self-possessed. But when he thought of what she'd been through… He said, 'I'm sorry. Yesterday at the May feast, I behaved as badly towards you as that damned man just now. I had no right whatsoever to take advantage of you.'

She was suddenly on her feet. 'You did *not* take advantage of me!'

He said slowly, 'What?'

'You are always, always denigrating yourself! It's the same with this "traitor" business—you're simply accepting the blame your enemies have heaped on you, just as you're blaming yourself for that kiss yesterday. It was my fault just as much as yours!'

He stood too, realising he felt a little lightheaded. 'Emma. You mean—you wanted me to kiss you?'

She was suddenly looking very tired. She whispered, so quietly that he barely heard, 'Who wouldn't?'

'What?' He still couldn't believe he'd heard her right.

She drew her cloak around her and said, 'I think I'd best leave now, my lord. My father is expecting me. I shall walk to Hawthorne village.'

* * *

Emma turned to go but she realised that every part of her was crying out in rebellion, because she wanted him to haul her back and take her in his arms, not only to kiss her, but…

She stopped abruptly at the open door. Because she'd seen that where the track to the cottage met the road to Stepton, some labourers had arrived with a horse and cart full of stones and were starting to mend a gap in the wall. At the same moment she felt a strong hand on her shoulder.

'Emma. I'm afraid we'll have to wait until those men have gone.'

She nodded. If the two of them emerged, the labourers would very likely recognise him and speculation would be rife.

Already Lord Grayford was drawing her back and closing the door. 'I'm sorry. They'll be moving on very soon, I imagine.' He looked around, taking in the roughly plastered walls and broken furniture. 'Listen. You can't possibly be thinking of bringing your father to live here.'

'Why not?' she answered defiantly. 'It would all need a thorough clean, of course, but I would see to that. As to furniture, my father could bring his own…'

He pulled her round to face him and something in his expression tore at her. The concern. The hunger. He said, 'Stop it, Emma. Stop thinking such ridiculous thoughts. Your father cannot live here. I won't allow it.'

Slowly her colour retreated then flooded her cheeks again. She said, 'You have no right to issue such a command.'

'I do, because I think you're being stubborn and ridiculous.'

'So you think I'm stupid?'

'No.' His eyes were dark and sad. 'No, as a matter of fact I think you're brave and wonderful and very, very beautiful.'

Her pulse was beginning to pound. She said almost bitterly, 'Those are extravagant compliments, my lord. But I think I'm a fool.'

'Why?' He reached to touch her cheek.

Why? Because she was a nobody with impossible dreams. But oh, those dreams of hers—and at this moment she wanted him so badly that her very heart shook.

In the distance she could hear the noise of the labourers hammering those stones into place. But the sound was soon drowned by the hammering of her pulse, because Lord Grayford had gathered her in his arms and his mouth, his beautiful mouth, was moving gently over hers. She gasped as his tongue caressed the sensitive flesh inside her lip; then he was probing, clasping her closer, and she found herself arching desperately to meet his powerful body.

There was a stirring in her belly and even lower, down *there.* It was like yesterday, only so much more. She was dizzy and agitated, engulfed by a wave of physical longing so fierce that she trembled and maybe he sensed it, because he eased his mouth away.

But he still held her. 'Emma,' he said. 'Emma?'

Her mind whirled. She knew she should pull away, for this was insanity. But he was actually giving her the *option* to pull away and that was what destroyed her resistance. He wasn't forcing her, yet the aching tenderness of his kiss had captivated her heart and soul.

For she wanted to be held captive. She wanted to feel the sweet caress of his tongue and she let out a tiny sigh of longing as he once more possessed her mouth. One of his strong hands was round her waist, pulling her closer—'Esmerelda,' he breathed, 'you'll be the ruin of me.' Then he clasped her close and a sharp but delicious thrill ran through her as she recognised the hard ridge of flesh beneath his breeches that meant he wanted her, badly. It should have shocked her but instead melted her to her core. His hand had moved to cup her breast, stroking it through the fabric of her gown while he kissed her so deeply and slowly that she thought she might die of delight.

Through a haze of desire, she heard the calls of the workmen as they packed their shovels away on their cart and started off down the track below. Lord Grayford must have heard them also, because he eased himself away from her, leaving her body feeling tender and acutely vulnerable and her mind reeling with the knowledge that another few minutes of his caresses and she would have given herself to him completely.

Her heart was still pounding as he rested his hands on her shoulders. 'Emma. Look at me. I know you probably think I'm going to say yet again that I'm sorry. But I'm *not* sorry. I don't want you to leave Grayford Hall. I don't want you to go anywhere. I want *you.* I know it's going to be difficult, but there must be some way we can sort this. Maybe I shouldn't have let things go so far, but I can't regret it. Emma, we need to discuss this properly, you and I. Please?'

She said quietly, 'There's no need to say any more, my lord. I've told you already that I'm looking for a new post. For your sake and mine, please accept my resignation.'

He let his hands fall to his sides. '*No.* You must not punish yourself for what was not your fault!'

'But it was my fault just as much as yours!' She sounded desperate. 'I made the decision some time ago to earn my living in an honourable fashion, and I fully intend to keep it that way. If I stay, this will keep happening—and believe me, your reputation will *not* be enhanced by an association with your housekeeper!'

He was silent a moment. She had felt so right in his arms and her shy but passionate responses had set his body on fire. Even now he had to grit his teeth against the urge to embrace her and more. Oh, yes—much more.

But she was gazing at him with those lovely brown eyes as she said steadfastly, 'My lord, you will quickly find another housekeeper who is far more competent than me. You will also one day find someone who will make you a suitable wife. Someone elegant and beautiful…'

Her voice trailed away as he took her hand and kissed it. 'Find me someone like you, then, Esmerelda,' he said.

That nearly undid her. She drew her hand away with what was possibly the greatest effort of her life and watched as he straightened his coat then went to look out of the window, turning his back on her as she'd commanded. It was as well. It was the only possible option.

'We're free to leave,' he said flatly, facing her once more. 'I think you said you intended to visit your father?'

Her reply was steadfast as she pulled on her plain grey bonnet. 'Yes. I shall tell him that Lowfield Lodge is unsuitable, but I'll soon find somewhere else.'

Lord Grayford said abruptly, 'I'll make quite sure he can stay on where he is. I'll buy that cottage in Hawthorne from Sir George and your father can pay me a nominal rent.'

Her eyes widened. 'No. No, I cannot be under such an obligation to you! Besides, what makes you think Sir George will sell?'

'I know a few things about that man and the various ways he's acquired his money,' the Viscount said grimly. 'I'll make sure he sells.'

'Then I'll make sure my father pays you the full rent, because he won't want your charity, Lord Grayford!'

'Have it your way.' He shrugged then said, 'Emma. Can't I somehow make you reconsider your resignation?'

She found his expression unreadable in the shadows, but something in his voice wrenched her heart. 'I'm sorry, my lord. But no.'

'Very well. I'll come with you to your father's house.'

'There is no need!'

'I want to be sure Sir George isn't prowling around still. Besides, we can both tell your father his home is safe.'

'Yes,' she said. 'And Lord Grayford, I think we should forget what just happened here.'

He'd been heading for the door, but at that he turned. 'I won't,' he said steadily. 'Ever.'

Chapter Fourteen

They walked to her father's house and James led Goliath. It was as well it wasn't far, James reflected, because their conversation was stilted, to say the least. They talked of the weather and the recent harvests; quite ridiculous topics really, when just now they'd almost...

Damn it. There was Miss Bryant, walking primly alongside him acting as if all that hadn't happened. But she still looked extraordinarily desirable, because her bonnet was dangling down her back by its ribbons and her lovely honey-coloured hair had come loose from its pins to distract him mercilessly. She'd left her cloak unfastened and her dress, plain though it was, fitted her so snugly that he couldn't help thinking of her slender but tempting figure beneath.

And she was leaving. If only he could make her change her mind.

By seducing her? You bastard, James.

Now he could see the little village of Hawthorne coming into view and he forced himself to concentrate on the forthcoming encounter. Aloud he said, 'Your father is a well-known scholar, I recall. What, exactly, is his area of expertise?'

He was glad to see her face lighten. 'He loves history,' she said. 'And he's written several books about the genealogy of the royal families of Europe. He's become quite an authority.'

'Really?' He'd certainly become aware during the war of the complexities of the various European dynasties. 'That's rather a vast subject.'

'Indeed.' She lifted her head as if in defiance. 'My father's particularly interested in the minor branches of the Habsburg family. He's also a skilled linguist.' She added, more hesitantly this time, 'He's not been to any of these countries, of course. But you have probably been to many of them.'

'I have,' he answered shortly. 'Including Austria.'

He saw her bite her lip. 'Of course. I'm sorry. I should have remembered.'

That certainly put an end to any further conversation. Fortunately they were entering the village now and more than a few heads turned in surprise at the sight of the imposing Viscount leading Goliath down Hawthorne's cobbled street, with Miss Bryant at his side. Some people curtsied or bowed. Others merely stared in wonder at both him and his big horse.

'Here's my father's cottage,' said Emma, pointing. 'And there's just one more thing, my lord. You might find him rather older than you'd expect. He was thirty-five when he married my mother and the recent years have taken their toll on him.'

James nodded and handed some pence to a couple of loitering lads to watch over Goliath. By the time he joined Emma an elderly housemaid was already opening the cottage door and her eyes widened when she saw him there. 'Oh, my saints,' she breathed, making a curtsy so deep that James feared she might fall over. 'It's Lord Grayford! And Miss Emma. What on earth…'

'It's all right, Biddy,' Emma said quickly. 'Lord Grayford just wished to pay my father a visit.'

'Sir,' Biddy said. 'I mean, my lord… Oh, gracious me!' Then she called back into the cottage, over her shoulder, 'Mr Bryant. We have company!'

She stood there all of a flurry until Emma said gently, 'Perhaps you'd prepare a pot of tea for us, Biddy?'

Biddy went scurrying off into what looked like an extremely tiny kitchen while James followed Emma into the parlour, where a gentleman with greying hair rose from his chair. 'My lord?' he said, peering at him over his spectacles. 'My lord, it is you, isn't it?'

James moved forward to take his hand. 'It is indeed, Mr Bryant, but I want no fuss. I gather there's been some bother over your rent, but I've come to tell you that you'll be able to stay on here for as long as you wish.'

'But this cottage belongs to Sir George Cartwright!'

'That man will no longer be your landlord. I will. You have my word on it.'

Mr Bryant still looked anxious, but James saw Emma take his hand and make him sit before saying quietly, 'It really is quite all right, Papa. Lord Grayford will sort it all out, believe me.'

His face flooded with relief. 'I'm so glad. This place might be modest, but I have everything here that I need—my books, my notes and good neighbours. I'm really most grateful, my lord.'

James smiled and said, looking around the room, 'You're a busy man, I can see.'

'My lord, yes.' He glanced at Emma. 'My daughter might have told you that for years I've studied the royal families of Europe.' He pointed to the big desk cluttered with books and papers. 'There are some of the documents I've been working on...'

But then his voice trailed away, because James had walked over to his desk and was staring, astonished, at just one small piece of paper that lay there a little apart from the others.

James pointed to the paper, on which was a small black drawing. He said, 'What's this?'

Mr Bryant glanced at him anxiously, catching the roughness in his voice. 'That? My lord, it's a small puzzle my daughter set me. Emma wished to know if the picture had any heraldic significance.'

'Why?' James's voice was harsh again. He turned to Emma. 'Why are you interested in this?'

She looked shaken by his expression. 'Two notes— identical notes—recently arrived at the Hall, my lord. They contained unpleasant messages, and both came with the same tiny drawing. I copied the drawing because I was puzzled by its meaning.'

'What did the notes say?'

She spoke carefully. *'"Think you'll be welcome here? Think again."'*

He couldn't utter a word. She went on in a rush, 'I thought the notes were meant for me, since I was a newcomer to the Hall. I would have burned them but the drawings troubled me, so I asked my father if he knew their significance.'

'And do you?' He turned to Emma's father.

The older man spoke hesitantly. 'I was not aware of the notes. But perhaps those words confirm what I suspected—that the black bird in profile, with its sinister eyes, is in fact an eagle—do you see the downward curve to its upper beak? Do you see its large talons?' He pointed. 'And the black eagle is part of the family crest of the Archduke of Austria.'

James turned to Emma. 'I trust you understand now?'

His voice echoed harshly around the little room and she nodded. 'I am so sorry. The note was meant for you. I truly had no idea, I swear.'

Silence filled the air and James, still holding the piece of paper, felt weary resignation. *Austria.* He should have known from the start that those attacks on him were co-ordinated. The strangers at the inn. The broadsheets in Oxford. And now, this.

Think you'll be welcome here? Think again.

He said, 'Miss Bryant, can you think of anyone locally who might want to blacken my name?'

'There's Sir George. But I don't think he's subtle enough to write a note like this.'

'You're right, of course. What about the staff?'

'I think that despite their shortcomings, they're extremely loyal to the family name and to you.'

Her father was still listening anxiously. James said at last, 'This settles it. I need to end this business once and for all. I must go to London.'

'My lord.' Mr Bryant spoke up now, 'I've heard the stories that have circulated about you and I've always believed them to be untrue. I understand that this was a very old and valuable book you were asked to deliver and is the only surviving copy of *Vitas Sanctorum—The Lives of the Saints*—by the scholar Albertus Magnus.'

'That is correct. It dates back to the sixteenth century.'

'Then may I ask—have you searched for it?'

'Mr Bryant,' James replied, 'I'd have no idea where to even start. I imagine it could be anywhere by now.'

'Maybe. But I cannot believe it has been destroyed—it's far too valuable for that. Somebody must either have it in their possession, or have tried to sell it. The latter is most likely, I think. And now I'm wondering if I might be able to help you.'

'How?' said James bitterly. 'How can you help me?'

'When I lived in London, I was familiar with the many libraries and bookshops. My tactic would be to make careful enquiries. The book won't be on display, of course; but people tend to assume I'm old and foolish, so it occurs to me that they wouldn't be alarmed if I started asking about rare books for sale.'

'You would have to come to London for that, sir.'

'I know. And I would do that gladly, my lord. I've followed reports of your service to your country and I feel you've faced a grave injustice over this unproved charge.'

James was aware of Emma looking uncertain, anxious even. He said to her father, 'May I speak with your daughter in private for a moment? Miss Bryant—do you mind?'

In silence she showed him the way to the dining

room that adjoined the parlour and the minute she'd closed the door he said, 'You were right. I must go to London, especially now I see that my reputation is as ruined here as it is there. I think you know what I'm going to say. Your father has offered to come and help me. Please. Will you come too?'

She looked shaken. 'It's impossible! My father and I have no money, nowhere to live!'

'Your father needs you. And as it happens, I own a small property just down the road from my London home.'

'Which is in Mayfair?'

'Yes—Grayford House, in Mount Street. And this other house I mentioned—you and your father are welcome to stay there.'

Her eyes blazed then. 'But we could not possibly afford the rent! And we will not live off your charity, my lord!'

James rubbed his forehead. 'Look. Your father is a renowned historian and should be paid for his work. I shall tell people I've employed him to look into my family's ancestry...'

He let his words tail away because she was still shaking her head. 'I know what London is like! People will realise you're regularly visiting my father and if I'm there too, the gossipmongers will have a field day!'

James wanted to pace the room, but it was too damned small. 'Please,' he urged. 'You've told me often enough that I should go to London and clear my name. It seems to me that my best chance yet lies with your father, but he needs you with him. I've offered you a house and money and I don't see how I can do any more!'

She said, with a stubborn tilt to her chin, 'You are forgetting something, my lord. When my father lost his money and I found myself open to insulting offers from men like Sir George Cartwright, I vowed that I would *always* be independent and earn my own living.'

Damn it. He wanted to take her in his arms and tame her obstinacy with kisses, but she'd told him that she wasn't having any more of that. He said curtly, 'If you want to work, there is a vacancy at Grayford House. The housekeeper is away for a short while, but I don't suppose you'd consider that for one minute.'

She took a step backwards but said, 'Tell me more.'

'The post has not been advertised,' he said, 'because Mrs Riggs will be away for only a matter of weeks. She's gone, I believe to help her daughter, who is expecting her first child. Mr Dantry the butler does an excellent job of running the household, but I could tell Dantry that you will take her place, temporarily. You would certainly have no problems with staff discipline under Dantry's strict regime.'

He kept expecting her to say no. Instead she said, 'There will be talk. People will think it most strange that you've brought me all the way from Oxfordshire.'

He shook his head. 'Miss Bryant, if you're truly worried about the London gossips, I can tell you one sure way to make yourself invisible.'

She still looked suspicious. 'How?'

He let a faint smile twist his mouth. 'Just carry on wearing that truly awful cap and gown of yours.'

He watched the expressions fluttering across her

face. Doubt. Anxiety. He added, quietly, 'You have my word that I will not touch you again. You will be my housekeeper for the duration of Mrs Riggs's absence and that is all—I think it's for six weeks. As I said, you'll find there'll not be a great deal for you to do.'

She nodded. 'That would give my father some time to investigate the whereabouts of the lost book. But you do realise, don't you, that he might not succeed?'

It was then that they heard her father's voice. 'Emma! Emma, my dear, look here—I've already found the names of some dealers in rare books in London!'

And the Viscount said to her, softly, 'Will you come?'

She agreed, of course. What else could she have done?

In her heart Emma knew she should be closing the door on this chapter of her life for good. Looking for a new post and never seeing this man again.

My father has offered the Viscount his help, she told herself. *Therefore, I have to go to London to be with my father. I could have said no if I'd wanted. There is no possibility of me falling in love with the man, let alone him with me. Nor would I want it...*

And she was the world's worst liar.

She replied at last, trying to sound calm and in control. 'Clearly, my lord, my father could be of great help in clearing your name. But there's another thing. If you are planning to entertain or have guests to stay, I prefer to remain very much in the background.'

'Don't worry,' he assured her. 'I shall be holding no parties or balls and there won't, I imagine, be many visitors at the house at all. Which leads me to another subject. I hope you realise that I'm encountering a good deal of hostility in London? Oh, not to my face, not directly. But you might hear things said about me that disturb you rather.'

His blue eyes had grown suddenly bleaker and Emma felt any lingering resistance shatter. Somehow, that simple statement about the terrible injustice he lived with did what no sweet words of seduction could do—it tore at her very heartstrings. She wanted to take this strong, suffering man in her arms and comfort him and oh, so much more.

She suddenly realised she was frightened, because she'd fought so very hard to live her life in a way that meant she could never be hurt by anyone. And if she'd fallen in love, it could lead to nothing but heartbreak for her.

She said at last, 'I don't care what people say, my lord. I've told you. I believe you are innocent.'

He was watching her in silence. 'Thank you,' he said at last. Then he took her hand and pressed a kiss to it; featherlight, but it set her blood pounding so hard that she felt breathless. 'Miss Bryant, may I escort you back to the Hall?'

She shook her head, summoning her last reserves of common sense. 'No. You'll wish to ride Goliath home. I'll spend a little more time with my father, if I may, then I shall walk back on my own.'

An hour and a half later, Emma was indeed back at Grayford Hall. She retired to her rooms and ate her evening meal on her own; she updated the household accounts and prepared for bed early, the prim Miss Bryant, though she did remember to fill in her diary.

London was all she could write.

London. With Lord Grayford.

Biddy had stopped her as she was leaving her father's cottage, her kind face full of concern. 'My dear,' she'd said. 'Are you sure about this? You always said you never wanted to go back to London again.'

Emma had shaken her head. 'This time it will be different, Biddy. No balls or parties for me, thank goodness. I'm to be a housekeeper, that's all.'

Biddy's keen eyes had searched her. 'You're quite sure there's nothing more?'

'Indeed I am. And, Biddy—you will come with us, won't you?'

'Try keeping me away,' Biddy said stoutly, and they hugged one another before Emma set off home.

She looked at her diary again.

There is nothing between Lord Grayford and me, she wanted to add fiercely. *There absolutely must be nothing between us.*

But she didn't write it down. Instead she blew out her candle and climbed into her small bed, and only then did she permit herself to remember the way he'd made love to her in that half-ruined lodge this afternoon. Only it wasn't love—she must remember that. It was lust. But her body had been on fire for him.

Chapter Fifteen

May—London

Four days later James arrived at Grayford House, the family's ancestral home in Mayfair. Everything was in immaculate order and if Dantry was surprised when James told him a new housekeeper was on her way to fill in for Mrs Riggs's temporary absence, he was too well trained to show it.

James took some care to explain Emma's circumstances to the butler. 'Miss Bryant,' he said, 'was working at the Hall and is still learning her craft. But since her father had to come to London for a while, I realised she would like to be close to him. I also thought it might help her improve her skills by working with you, Dantry. I told her that in view of the temporary nature of her post here, she could visit her father every afternoon. He will be staying in the family's house in Aldford Street.'

If Dantry held any suspicions, James hoped the

nearby presence of Emma's father would allay them and indeed it seemed to.

'Very good, sir,' said his butler. 'I shall do my utmost to assist the young lady.'

As James had expected, the paperwork regarding his inheritance was considerable and there were solicitors, accountants and other business people due to visit him shortly. But his first visitor was Cousin Theo, to whom he'd written about his forthcoming arrival. James led him to the grand drawing room, where a maid served coffee.

Theo began by welcoming him warmly to London, but when James told him that Miss Bryant's father would also be coming to town shortly, he almost dropped his cup. 'James. Why on earth…'

'Pelham Bryant,' James said, 'as you told me, is a historian. He also has considerable knowledge of old books.'

'You're not telling me you're setting him on the trail of the Archduke's missing book?'

'He was eager to help and I thought it worth a try. His daughter is coming with him.'

Theo looked even more astonished. 'Staying with her father, you mean?'

'No. When Miss Bryant arrives—which will be in a matter of days—she's going to be my housekeeper.' Jasper, whom James had brought with him, looked up eagerly at the mention of the name *Bryant* as if expecting to see Emma, then lowered his head rather forlornly.

Theo's shock was evident. 'Good God, James. Is this wise?' He paused then added, 'Is something going on that I wasn't aware of?'

'Not at all. She told me she couldn't let her father come to London without her being on hand to care for him. She refused to accept what she saw as my charity, so I suggested she take on the role of housekeeper here. It's only for a matter of weeks, since the regular one is away for a while.'

'You're not worried people will talk?'

'I don't even see what there is to talk about. I shall spread the word that Mr Bryant is working on my family's history, and it was convenient for her to come here to be close to him.'

Theo drank his coffee. 'I see. Well, James, I wish you luck. But as I said, it sounds a forlorn hope to me. Even if you find that book, aren't people going to say that maybe you had it all along? Besides, there's always the danger that if you get too close to whoever has it, then they might destroy it.'

'You're not sounding very hopeful, Cousin.'

Theo gave a rueful smile. 'I'm sorry. But on a more positive note, I've been working on your behalf too.'

'You have?'

'Indeed.' Theo leaned forward in his chair. 'You see, I was thinking that someone in the Home Office must have handled that book before you were sent on your mission. Since it was so valuable, only a few people would have had access to it. So I decided I could try—very subtly, you understand—to discover who might have had the chance to make the substitution.'

'Thank you,' said James. 'But I'll still let Mr Bryant see what he can find out.'

'Your choice, I suppose. And the more chances you have of finding the culprit, the better.' Theo raised his coffee cup in salutation. 'Welcome back to London, Cousin. It's good to have you here.'

James was aware after Theo had gone that really he'd told him very little. He'd not told him, for example, about the messages Emma had opened, with their ominous drawing. And he hadn't told Theo that Emma had not wanted to come to London at all. She'd made her feelings towards him perfectly clear that afternoon at Lowfield Lodge, when she informed him she wanted neither to accept his charity nor to be his mistress.

He received more visitors over the next few days, but not as many as a new peer of the realm might have expected. He was sent a small number of invitations to parties and receptions, all of which he politely declined, saying that he was extremely busy with his new responsibilities. But on the third morning, a sealed letter arrived which stopped him in his tracks—because it contained a message that was adorned with the same drawing of a black bird that he'd last seen on Pelham Bryant's desk in Oxfordshire. The message said,

> *Ask too many questions and someone you care for will get hurt.*

Emma arrived in London with her father and Biddy a week later in the Viscount's travelling chaise. It was with mixed feelings that she gazed out of the window, watching the green fields and market gardens of London's suburbs give way to the ever-more crowded city streets.

She was remembering the time she'd travelled to London two years ago to stay at the house of Lady

Lydia, her great-aunt and godmother. All her friends in Oxford had told her it would be like a dream come true. 'There'll be balls!' they'd exclaimed. 'Parties! And oh, all those handsome gentlemen—Emma, you're so lucky!'

This couldn't be more different. This time she was a housekeeper, at the other end of the social scale. And she had made the fatal mistake of falling for her employer.

Soon the carriage was stopping outside the house in Aldford Street, where her father would stay. Lord Grayford had described the house as small and no doubt it was compared to his family mansion, but to Emma it was exquisite, neatly set in a terrace of white-stuccoed houses not far from the Park. The coachman was already taking her father's luggage up the steps and a housekeeper was opening the door. Emma came in briefly to make sure all was well.

'Emma, my dear,' her father exclaimed, 'all this is wonderful!'

'Too good to be true, if you ask me,' muttered Biddy, who'd been sceptical about the entire trip. But Emma smiled and hugged her father before saying, 'I must go. The carriage is taking me on to the Viscount's home. Though I'll visit you tomorrow, Papa, I promise!'

Grayford House was only around the corner and there she was met with some formality by the butler. 'We understand you've come,' Mr Dantry said solemnly, 'to take the place of our Mrs Riggs, who is temporarily absent. His Lordship informed me that you will be visiting your father every afternoon, which poses no problem. He also said that you are learning the skills of your profession, so may I urge you to ask me if there's anything at all I can help you with?'

Mr Dantry proceeded to outline Mrs Riggs's duties, which as far as Emma could see consisted chiefly of ensuring that the housemaids performed their daily tasks. Then he showed her round the house, pointing out every detail, until at last she asked, 'I gather the Viscount arrived some days ago?'

'Indeed he did, Miss Bryant. At present His Lordship is visiting his bankers in Chancery Lane. You will realise that he is, of course, kept very busy with the matters of the estate.'

She nodded. 'Of course.'

Had she really thought he might be here to welcome her? No—a ridiculous notion. But she had hoped, perhaps, that he would wish to visit her father, so that together they could make plans to clear his name…

All in good time, she told herself. Instead she made herself familiar with the house, which was furnished with statues, antiques and paintings which were just as dazzling on the eye as the ones in the Oxfordshire house. Her own plain rooms—a small parlour and bedroom on the ground floor—were almost a relief in comparison.

She had looked forward to joining in the activities of the household, but when she volunteered to help the maids dust and tidy the vast drawing room on her first morning there, the maids were aghast. 'Oh, no, miss. That's our job.' So she drank tea in her parlour, she read *The Good Housekeeper's Daily Deeds* from cover to cover and every afternoon she visited her father, who kept asking her the same question. 'Have you talked with the Viscount yet? I really want to know, Emma, how I may be of use to him!'

But she'd been at Grayford House for four days before she even saw him and in fact their first encounter was brought about by Jasper, who came rushing up to her one morning in the main hall.

'Jasper!' she cried out in pleasure. 'Why, Jasper, I didn't know you were here!'

It was then that she realised the Viscount was watching her from the open doorway of the front parlour. 'I couldn't leave him behind,' he said. 'I've brought Gregory too. He'll learn a good deal from my grooms here. I trust you are settling in well, Miss Bryant?'

She couldn't reply immediately, because he looked different. Perhaps it was his clothes; yes, indeed, that must be it, for he was wearing the formal attire to be expected of a man of his rank: dark coat, starched white neckcloth, fawn breeches and top boots. He looked devastatingly handsome, a man of power and wealth, making the gulf between them seem even wider and deeper. His expression was unreadable, but it was the formality of his speech that chilled her the most. 'Indeed, my lord,' she said, equally expressionlessly. 'Although I feel I'm not doing nearly enough to justify my role here.'

'I told you. I don't expect you to. You are not here to be a menial. I've explained to Mr Dantry that you have my permission to see your father daily and he quite understands. You are visiting him every afternoon, aren't you? As I suggested?'

'I am.' She paused then pressed on. 'My lord, my

father is concerned that you haven't been to see him yet. I truly think he can help you, and since his time here is limited—'

'Thank you,' he broke in. 'I've every intention of calling on him soon, but my solicitor has presented me with considerable legal problems relating to the inheritance and naturally, settling them has to be my priority.'

'Of course,' she said quietly.

And he left. Jasper cast one last almost sorrowful look at her then trotted after him. Emma stood very still. Something had changed. Something was wrong, she was sure of it. He'd been so distant, so cold. Of course, that had been their agreement—hadn't she herself insisted on it? But hadn't it also been their agreement that her father would help him clear his name? She could not, would not believe he could sweep the matter aside so quickly, so abruptly!

Emma pressed her hands to her cheeks and forced herself into calmness. She knew that the housemaids were repairing some heavy velvet curtains in the sewing room and she went to offer her help. But Mr Dantry was there too and he cut short her offer, saying politely yet firmly, 'The maids are quite capable of finishing the work in here by themselves, Miss Bryant. Although you could, perhaps, tidy the sewing cabinet and check that we have enough thread. After lunch, I assume you will be visiting your father?'

That afternoon she walked as usual to the house round the corner in Aldford Street. 'This morning, Emma,' her father told her, 'I looked around the British Museum. Such a delight! Then I went on to some of my favourite bookshops. It's wonderful to be back here! And the Viscount called on me, just half an hour ago.'

Emma was astonished. 'He did?'

'Yes, but very briefly.' Her father frowned. 'He's told me he wants to proceed cautiously in the matter of the book, because if he's too open in his search then whoever has it might send it far away or perhaps even destroy it. Which would, of course, put an end to his chance of clearing his name.'

'Oh.' Yes, she could see that, but... 'Surely, then, the Viscount's best option is to hurry? Before anyone realises what he's doing and while there's still a chance that the book is in London?' Her father looked anxious and Emma swiftly corrected herself. 'Of course. The Viscount will know what's best.'

Patience, she told herself. It was the Viscount's business, not hers; besides, for all she knew he might be pursuing some other line she'd not even thought of. After a while she left. She guessed Biddy wanted to talk to her, because she'd glanced at Emma rather anxiously as she brought in their tea. But Emma didn't particularly want to answer Biddy's questions, so she made her departure swiftly, setting off on the short walk back to the Viscount's imposing mansion.

After that she saw Lord Grayford most days. He would nod and say 'Good day' pleasantly enough, but she never had a chance to ask him how his quest to clear his name was progressing. Why wasn't he making more use of her father's knowledge, she continued to wonder, which was why she had agreed to come to London in the first place?

His cousin Theo Exton, a frequent visitor to the house, spoke to her more warmly than Lord Grayford. Indeed, he always paused to greet her whenever he spotted her. 'How are you settling in here, Miss Bryant?' he asked her one day.

'The staff are very kind,' she assured him.

'And so they should be. This is a well-run household, which is fortunate, since the Viscount has a good deal on his mind.'

'Mr Exton, I want him to clear his name!' she blurted out. 'He must do it soon, or...'

'Caution is the watchword. Everything must be done in slow, careful steps.'

She went to join the other staff in the servants' hall for dinner, pulling on her cap even more firmly than usual and pushing all her hair under it as if it offended her. Soon, she and her father would be returning to Oxfordshire and then what would she do? She would have to find another job. Build a new life.

You will be no worse off, she reminded herself.

In fact, she would be better off altogether, because the pain she felt inside whenever the Viscount walked past her with scarcely a nod was barely tolerable.

Mr Dantry continued to be most solicitous. From the start he'd explained all her housekeeping duties and handed her a sheaf of lists and rotas so that all she had to do was give the housemaids their instructions each morning.

'Shouldn't I be discussing the household menus with Cook?' she'd once asked.

'Absolutely no need, Miss Bryant! We have a wonderful Cook, who has everything under control. Speak to her by all means, but I think you'll find there's very little to do in that department.'

Mr Dantry was a busy man, but that didn't mean he had no time to address her on other topics. One day after the servants' lunch he escorted her to the door of her rooms and said, more hesitantly than usual, 'Miss Bryant. As it happens, it's my afternoon off and I was wondering—would you allow me to show you some of the city's finest sights? Napoleon's carriage, or Madame Tussaud's fine exhibition, maybe?'

She was completely taken aback. Mr Dantry had to be at least forty and he was extremely proper, yet he was speaking to her as eagerly and as shyly as a young man at his first ball. Oh, goodness. Was he getting ideas about her?

'You are most kind,' she said quickly. 'But I will be visiting my father this afternoon, as usual.'

'Of course.' She thought he looked wistful. 'Your father is fortunate to have such a caring daughter. Duty above pleasure, that's what I always say!'

'Indeed,' Emma said. 'Duty above pleasure.'

Unless the pleasure was with Lord Grayford...
Stop that, Emma.

She closed her door after the butler had left and leaned rather faintly against it. She missed the Viscount. She missed her old conversations with him and his light-hearted teasing. For a moment she had to blink back the unshed tears. Then she tugged off her wretched cap, threw it on the bed and put on her cloak. Time to visit her father.

She was heading through the main hall, intending to leave by the servants' entrance, when she realised that someone had arrived. Theo Exton, maybe? This, however, wasn't Mr Exton and now Mr Dantry had come to hover attendance on the newcomer. 'My lady,' he was saying, 'Lord Grayford is expecting you. Please come this way.'

Lord Grayford's visitor, who had dark curls peeping out from under a pink silk bonnet and wore a pelisse of emerald green, caught sight of Emma, who curtsied. The woman stared at her rather sharply and Emma thought, *I know her from somewhere.*

A footman opened the door to the parlour and Emma heard her saying loudly, 'Darling James, I believe I've just seen your new housekeeper! Poor thing. What a dowd! At least I can be sure she has no designs on you, yet strangely enough, I could swear I recognised her... Now, do you remember you promised to drive me to the Park this afternoon?' The parlour door closed but Emma stayed where she was, because in the air was the scent of the same expensive perfume that had clung to that letter delivered to Grayford Hall.

She remembered then. She had been introduced to this woman once at a ball in London. Her name was Lady Henrietta Carleon and Her Ladyship, surrounded by friends, had used almost exactly the same words about Emma as she'd used then. *'Poor thing. What a dowd.'*

Chapter Sixteen

James was gazing out of the window of the front parlour when Henrietta made her entrance. He'd seen her carriage arrive and was making an effort to mentally prepare himself, but instead he kept thinking of the note he'd received in the post this morning.

It was exactly the same as the other one. There was the same drawing of a black bird with a hooked beak, in profile. The same carefully inscribed message:

Ask too many questions and someone you care for will get hurt.

Someone he cared for. That could only mean Emma, which was why he'd been so damnably cold to her, why he could not continue to use either her or her father in order to clear his name.

And now he was faced with Henrietta, who'd come flouncing in as if she owned the place and was eyeing him archly from beneath the brim of her no doubt vastly expensive bonnet. She thought she'd recognised his housekeeper? Impossible—as if Henrietta would ever notice anyone so much below her in rank!

'My housekeeper is from Oxfordshire,' he told her flatly. 'So you can't possibly have met her. And I haven't forgotten my promise to drive you to the Park, Henrietta.'

On the contrary, he'd made the offer with some determination. She'd been worryingly eager to welcome him back to London, so he'd viewed this outing as the chance to demonstrate that they were merely friends now. But by the time they'd driven past Upper Grosvenor Street and were entering the Park gates, he'd realised Henrietta was clearly seeing the outing as the way to re-establish her claim on him—and the opportunity to invite him to a ball at her house in two nights' time.

'A ball?' He was guiding his curricle and pair down towards the lake when she told him. 'Then I'll apologise in advance. I don't attend balls any more, since I've two left feet when it comes to dancing.' With the reins grasped in one hand, he indicated his muscular frame with the other. 'I'm really not built for it.'

'Nonsense,' said Henrietta. She eyed him appreciatively. 'I suspect you're still concerned about that foreign mission you were sent on, but you're being ridiculously sensitive, James. The very worst thing you can do is to hide.'

Which was just what Emma had told him, of course. *Emma*. Always Emma.

He shook his head. 'I'm not hiding. After all, I'm here, aren't I?' He indicated the leafy acres of the Park, omitting to mention that he'd avoided the most crowded areas. 'The fact is that I don't like balls. I never have.'

She leaned towards him—probably, he suspected, to put her décolletage on full display. 'Do come, James! You know you'll be among friends.'

'I'll think about it,' he said. 'That's all.'

She had talked of other subjects then, rather wisely in his view, until at last they drove back to his house and she departed in her own carriage. Whereupon he almost immediately bumped into Miss Bryant. Literally, because she was hurrying along the hallway holding a pile of linen that almost blocked her view and just as she was about to collide with him he called out, 'Steady there.'

She halted abruptly, shifted her load and said, rather breathlessly, 'My apologies, my lord.' James felt the usual familiar lurch on seeing her. Hideous gown, hideous cap. Beautiful eyes, adorable little nose and oh-so-kissable lips…

It's time to stop all that, you rogue.

He was thinking of the notes. The warning in each one. Maybe it wasn't about her. Maybe it was just some idiotic, aimless threat. But something inside him twisted like a just-healed scar at the thought of any harm coming to her.

She was waiting, he realised, for him to send her on her way. Instead he said, 'Miss Bryant. How are you finding life here?'

If she'd expected him to ask something more personal, she gave no sign of it. She said, 'I find it satisfactory, my lord. The staff are hard-working, and Mr Dantry is very helpful.'

He tried to react as an employer should. 'Good. Mr Dantry is a stickler for routine and I guessed you would have no problems. I trust he allows you to visit your father each afternoon?'

He saw her hesitate before all of a sudden she blurted out, 'My lord, my father has been working very hard on the matter you asked him to investigate. And he's found there's a strong but secret market in books and paintings that disappeared during the war. Many precious items were stolen or smuggled and now they're being sold to rich collectors. He told me he's compiled a list of book dealers he suspects might be involved in the secret trade—he feels this could be relevant for your search, but he is concerned you may be changing your mind about the whole business.'

He cursed inwardly. He'd been beginning to hope, for her sake, that she might be putting the whole damned business aside. He said, 'I thought I'd explained that for the time being, I've decided to take things slowly.'

'But—'

'Miss Bryant, I value your father's efforts. But it has occurred to me that even if I did find the book— what is to stop my enemies from claiming that I've had it all along?'

He saw that she looked utterly shaken. She said, almost in disbelief, 'So you are giving up?'

He made a gesture of impatience. 'No. No, of course not—but I do have other important avenues to follow. For example, I have a contact at the Home Office who is hoping to discover exactly who might have had the opportunity to substitute the book before it was given to me at the start of my journey.'

'You mean your cousin, Mr Exton?'

'Yes. I do.'

He realised that the fire had gone from her extraordinary eyes. She merely said, 'I wish you the very best, my lord.'

He watched her for a moment longer than he should have done. 'You sound rather distant,' he said quietly.

'Of course.' She jutted her chin almost proudly. 'I am your housekeeper. Nothing more.'

Nothing more? Indeed, that had been their agreement. But damn it, they'd kissed, they'd been close—and he'd as good as forced her into this! He had used his quest to bring her here because yes, he wanted to prove his innocence but also, quite honestly, he didn't want her going out of his life!

Though if those threats truly were against her, he was putting her life in great danger.

She was still waiting there with the pile of bedlinen in her arms and he glimpsed something then in her expression that smote him somewhere in the region of his heart. Regret? Longing, even? But whatever for? Surely not for *him*?

That was the very moment when Jasper came trotting down the hall and rushed up to her. 'Jasper is fond of you,' James said. 'He's not forgotten that you gave him a home again, even though I objected strongly at first.'

'He's lovely,' she said, smiling down at Jasper.

He watched then said, 'Do you know, sometimes—quite often, in fact—I find myself wishing I was back in Oxfordshire. Sometimes I even imagine being one of my tenant farmers, with a flock of sheep and a few fields of wheat, free to live as I wanted.'

She looked up at him, her eyes wide and almost distraught. 'Don't give up,' he heard her whisper. 'Please, my lord. You must not give up…'

She spun round, because at that exact moment Mr Dantry came bustling towards them. 'My lord,' he said with a slight bow, 'with your permission, there are some household duties I need to discuss with Miss Bryant.'

'Of course. She's all yours.'

But that, he thought as he left them together, was the wrong phrase because as he glanced back he could see Dantry talking to Miss Bryant and the man was as puffed up and pompous as a courting pigeon. By God, he'd taken a fancy to her! James felt acute frustration boiling in his veins and in other unmentionable places. He wanted to take her in his arms and kiss her, and…

Oh, the devil. He glared at a ridiculous oriental statue his brother had placed on a great pedestal in the centre of the hall. *Emma.* The messages. The threats. Perhaps he should send her home right now, but she would probably refuse and besides, she was only here for a while longer. She would be safe in Oxfordshire and he would be free to follow other trails.

But he would miss his housekeeper more than he'd thought possible, because she'd felt so right, in his arms and in his heart.

After that encounter with Lord Grayford, Emma felt lower than ever. It was plain that he regretted bringing her here and was maybe regretting his decision to search for the lost book. Indeed, he had told her that finding it might prove nothing. But she felt he was dismissing her with half-truths. And as for the Home Office…

He is following the wrong path, she thought. *I know he is.*

The next day Emma was on her way to see Cook for their usual daily meeting, even though both of them were aware these encounters were quite unnecessary since Cook always had everything meticulously planned. Emma was heading for the kitchen when Mr Dantry spotted her. 'Miss Bryant!'

She turned to face him. 'Yes, Mr Dantry?'

'Lady Henrietta Carleon is here. She wishes to speak to you.'

A sense of disbelief came over Emma. 'But I'm on my way to meet with Cook. And surely she came to see the Viscount?'

'His Lordship is not here. She wishes to see you now, in the drawing room. I'll tell Cook you are delayed.'

After straightening her apron and making sure that every scrap of her wayward hair was under her cap, Emma entered the drawing room to see that Lady Henrietta was gazing rather thoughtfully at a portrait of Lord Grayford and his brother that hung above the fireplace.

'My lady.' Emma curtsied. 'I believe you wished to speak to me?'

'Ah, yes,' Her Ladyship turned, taking her time. 'I did, rather.' She glanced once more at the portrait. 'Such an illustrious family. Such a noble heritage. No wonder so many silly, dreaming girls have their eye on Viscount Grayford.' She strolled over to a chair and seated herself, spreading out her full silk skirt. 'Do you know, Miss Bryant, once the news arrived in town that the Viscount was back, quite a few of the gentry were astounded—angry, even—because there are still those who believe his name to be tainted in the matter of that book, you understand me? But there are others—and here I'm talking about women, of course—who still dream of him as a husband. Or, at the very least, as a lover.'

Emma's heart was pounding, but her voice was level as she answered, 'My lady. I don't quite see what any of this has to do with me.'

'Oh, you're good, aren't you?' said Lady Henrietta softly. 'Good at pretending to be a meek little housekeeper.'

Emma stood very still as Lady Henrietta went on, in the same acid tone, 'But I knew from the moment I saw you here that you weren't raised to be a servant. The way you speak. The way you carry yourself. There's pride there, isn't there? There's breeding. And you're—how old? Twenty? Twenty-one? Far, far too young for the position you're holding.'

'I assure you, it is only temporary—'

'I'm quite sure that's what you're hoping. James is a man with strong physical needs, so no doubt you've determined to take advantage of it. Let me guess. You once had ambitions for a good marriage, but then perhaps something went wrong with your dream of landing a rich man. So you've insinuated your way into James's household and you're contriving to work your way into his life, maybe even as his wife.'

Emma would have laughed if she weren't so very angry. 'I don't know quite how to reply, my lady. But since I respect Lord Grayford very much, the best I can say is this. You do the Viscount no favours by insinuating that he cannot make his own decisions on a matter as vital as his marriage!'

Lady Henrietta rose and waved her hand dismissively. 'Well, I've spoken my mind and it's time for me to go. But you'd do well to heed my warning.' She headed for the door then stopped. 'I am quite certain that I've seen you before. Not as a servant, because I never normally notice servants. But it will come to me. You can be sure of that.'

Mr Dantry must have been hovering out in the hallway because Emma heard Lady Henrietta saying to him, 'Tell the Viscount I'm looking forward to seeing him at my ball tonight, will you?'

Emma was unable to move. So he was going to a ball at Lady Henrietta's house, when he'd said he would avoid all society events until his name was cleared.

Hateful, hateful woman.

Lady Henrietta was certain she'd met Emma before and indeed she was right, but she'd not remembered where or when, which was one small mercy. Because the last thing Emma wanted was for the Viscount to know the shame of her London Season.

The kitchen, Emma. That's where you were going.

She steeled herself to carry on as if nothing were wrong, but the Viscount occupied all of her mind. Why wasn't he making use of her father? What could she do, to make him change his mind?

She suddenly remembered the declaration of her housekeeping manual.

Action is better than regret. There are remedies for most domestic disasters and a skilled house-keeper should know them all.

Of course, the author of *Daily Deeds* was thinking of soggy sponge cakes or grubby parquet. Emma was thinking of Lord Grayford's vital quest. For the conviction in her mind was growing that if he wouldn't clear his own name, she would have to do it for him.

James was upstairs in his dressing room that evening, his exasperation mounting as he tried to tie a perfect neckcloth. One after another of the things flew to the floor while the junior footman whom Dantry had volunteered as his valet hesitantly offered a fresh one.

'Hell,' James was muttering to himself. 'Hell.'

How he regretted finally agreeing to go to this damned ball of Henrietta's tonight. He wished he'd stayed in Oxfordshire, as he'd said to Miss Bryant. He wished for another life—not the army, he'd had enough of that—but maybe a rural existence would suit him just fine, with lots of animals and maybe a dozen children running around, filling the Hall with mischief and laughter. Which meant a wife. Sweet, intelligent and determined to believe in his own integrity. And absolutely delicious to kiss...

Like Emma.

Wicked thoughts, James. You promised her that if she came to London, you would not lay a finger on her.

Yet every time he saw her, he was overwhelmed by the longing to strip her of her ridiculous cap and gown and...

'This,' he pronounced grimly to the timid young valet, Jonathan, 'is going to have to do.' He patted his neckcloth, frowning into the mirror.

'Yes, my lord,' said Jonathan.

'Pass me my waistcoat, will you?'

'Yes, my lord.'

'And you don't have to keep saying...'

He bit his lip. Bad-tempered oaf. He felt he'd betrayed Emma by not taking her father's advice and instantly hunting down the dealers he was so keen for James to investigate. But that note. The outright threat...

Should he even be taking it so seriously? He'd always had people who disliked him on account of his refusal to suffer fools gladly, both in the army and in London society. But it was yet more evidence that the Austrian business was refusing to lie down and die and he was furious that after all his war service he could be suspected of fraud. Apprehensive, too, about tonight. Since returning to London he'd met lawyers and bankers aplenty, but he was still wary of polite company; indeed, this ball would be his first formal outing.

As it happened, Henrietta had asked him to bring Theo along too. 'We are rather desperate for men,' she'd told him. 'Too many of them prefer to shut themselves away in the card room, so please, James, do invite your cousin.'

Theo arrived at Grayford House at eight o'clock and like James he'd dressed carefully in a coat of dark blue superfine with cream breeches, but he couldn't hide his limp. There would be no dancing for Theo tonight.

James was finishing off a stiff brandy when Theo came in, which made his cousin laugh. 'Not nervous, are you, James? You're the new Viscount Grayford and you'll be welcomed with open arms. Especially by Lady Henrietta.'

'Perhaps,' said James, adjusting his cuffs. 'But she's going to be disappointed when I tell her my business in London will soon be over and done with.'

Theo glanced at him quickly. 'Will it?'

'I think so.' James looked directly at his cousin. 'I don't suppose you've had any luck tracking down who might have had access to that book at the Home Office, have you?'

'Not yet.' Theo looked concerned. 'I'm sorry.'

As chance would have it, on their way out they caught sight of Emma at the far end of the hallway, no doubt on her way to the servants' quarters. Theo pointed. 'Why, James, there's your housekeeper. Poor girl, I imagine she's as ill suited to her job as ever.'

She looked, thought James, as though she'd not wished to be seen by them at all. Once more he thought of the ball and the women who would be there, dressed in rich gowns and jewels, fluttering their fans and eagerly flirting.

He thought of Emma just then in her cap and brown gown, hurrying away with her eyes lowered. He thought, *She is worth ten, no a hundred, of the women I shall meet tonight.*

With her looks and her innate grace, she should have been a society beauty, decked in silk and diamonds. At his side, damn it—but in a matter of weeks, she would be leaving his life for good.

Chapter Seventeen

When Emma told Mr Dantry she was going to visit her father that evening he raised his eyebrows. 'Really? I thought the arrangement was that you visited him in the afternoons only, Miss Bryant.'

'Did you?' she answered. 'Oh, no! Lord Grayford told me I could visit my father whenever I pleased.'

Mr Dantry looked irritated. But Emma didn't care what he thought, because all she could think of now was—why had the Viscount changed his mind about accepting the help her father could offer him? Something drastic must have happened to make him withdraw so suddenly from his pursuit of the truth.

She put on her cloak and walked swiftly to Aldford Street, trying not to think of where the Viscount was now. What he was doing. For he would be at the ball, he would be among the people with whom he truly belonged; with people who were his equals, as she could never be. He would dance several times, no doubt, with Lady Henrietta; perhaps it was she who'd persuaded him that the shadows cast across his reputation could best be cleared if he acted as though they'd never existed.

But he was mistaken. Emma was convinced that he had a real enemy somewhere and if he wouldn't deal with the situation, then she would.

Of course Biddy was startled to see her, since it was past nine now. So was her father. She quickly reassured him that nothing at all was wrong. 'But, Papa,' she said, 'you know you told me you'd made a list of dealers in London who you suspected might buy and sell stolen books? Please, can you copy it for me? Yes, now if possible.'

It took her father some time to write out the names and addresses in his painstaking way, but she waited patiently. As a result it was gone ten when she set off back to Grayford House with the sheet of paper rolled up in her hand. It was a time of night when Mayfair's genteel streets were strangely quiet, because most people had either travelled to their various social destinations or had settled behind the locked doors of their grand mansions.

The silence meant that she heard the footsteps clearly coming up behind her and though she speeded her pace, whoever was following quickened theirs also. A moment later she felt a sharp blow to the back of her head—and all was blackness.

Emma opened her eyes carefully then shut them again because the light hurt them. In fact she realised her whole head was hurting. She heard a woman say, 'Put out all the candles except one, will you, Maisie? This room is far too bright for her, poor thing.'

Emma opened her eyes again to see Polly, one of

the kindest of the Viscount's housemaids setting down a jug and glass on the chest of drawers by the door. She realised she was lying in her own little bed in Grayford House. But why did her head hurt so? She must have tried to say something aloud because Polly was quickly at her side. 'Miss Bryant. Whatever happened?'

Emma shook her head, but stopped because of the pain. 'I'm not sure. I went to visit my father and I set off home, but...' After she'd said goodbye to her father, she honestly couldn't remember a thing, though she must have got back here somehow. 'Maybe I tripped,' she said.

'We don't think so.' Polly shook her head. 'We think you must have been attacked. Luckily two of our footmen saw you lying in the street and carried you in. It must have been robbers.'

Emma realised for the first time that someone had removed her gown and shoes and wrapped her in her nightrobe. 'No!' She was struggling to sit up. 'I had nothing they would have wanted. No money. I just went to see my father...'

'Of course,' said Polly quickly. 'You rest, now.'

Emma had no real alternative, for she felt as weak as a kitten.

She must have dozed, but she opened her eyes on hearing someone enter. At first she thought she must be imagining it, because Lord Grayford was sitting by her bed. There was no one else in the room.

He was in his evening clothes—blue coat, white shirt, cravat—and his face was taut with concern.

'Emma,' he said in a low voice. 'My God. They told me you were hurt.'

She said, rather stupidly, 'You're home early from the ball.'

She tried to raise herself from her pillows, but he put out one strong hand to stop her. '*No*. Stay as you are.' Then he withdrew his hand and said, 'The ball was a damned disaster so I decided to abandon it. Now tell me. What exactly happened to you tonight?'

As he spoke he was ripping off his cravat and letting it dangle loose from his hand. He looked weary and anxious. She wanted to explain, but her head hurt still, and the words just wouldn't come out properly. 'I'm fine. Really, I am. I can't exactly remember, but I'd been to see my father. I was on my way back here and I must have tripped over a cobblestone in the dark and banged my head.'

He said, 'Who knew you were going to Aldford Street tonight?'

'Only Mr Dantry. He wasn't pleased.'

'But he didn't try to stop you?'

'No.' She shook her head.

'He probably realised you wouldn't take any notice.' She was surprised how grim he looked. 'Do you truly believe, Emma, that what happened tonight was an accident?'

'As I said, I can't remember much but what else could it have been? I had no money on me. No valuables.'

He was silent a moment then he said, 'Should I send for a doctor?'

'No! Please, my lord. I don't want any fuss. In fact I'm feeling better already! Perhaps I should get up...'

'You'll stay exactly where you are,' he said in a voice that brooked no argument. She realised he was looking around her little bedroom. 'One of the maids has left some barley water for you. Would you like a drink?'

All of a sudden the thought of the cooling liquid soothing her dry throat was the most tempting thing on earth. She nodded and before she realised it the Viscount was helping her to sit up, raising the pillows behind her then holding a glass to her lips.

'Better?' he asked.

'Better. Thank you.' She gazed up at him. 'I'm perfectly all right now. I'm only sorry to have caused such trouble.'

'No trouble,' he said. 'None at all.'

But he didn't offer to leave her. Instead he put the glass aside then sat down again, still so close, while she fought to be rational. She had to be imagining that deep concern in his eyes and the tension in the lines around his mouth. He looked almost as if he felt responsible for what had happened. Ridiculous!

She managed to summon a faint smile. 'Tell me, my lord. You said earlier your evening was a disaster. Why, exactly?'

'You really want to know?' He shook his head but smiled back and she was relieved to see a little of the tension vanish from his face. 'It was a ball, Emma. The whole notion of such an event fills me with horror.'

She said, 'I'm sure your dancing isn't *that* bad.'

This time he laughed, and she was so glad to see it, but all too soon the bitterness crept back into his eyes. 'It was the usual kind of affair. You probably can't imagine it, but really the whole evening was about rich, titled folk watching everyone else so they could pull one another down. I should have consulted you first and not gone. Of course, I was an object of great interest, so after around half an hour of being subjected to various interrogations, I went to join Theo in the card room. He hates dancing just as much as I do. Only then Henrietta dragged me back into the ballroom.'

Henrietta.

Emma said, 'I find it hard to imagine anyone dragging a man of your stature anywhere, my lord.'

'Henrietta is a determined lady. After that, she persuaded me to dance with a couple of her friends. But...'

'But what?'

'I missed you,' he said.

Her heart began hammering and she felt the warmth slowly flooding her cheeks. He was probably hardly aware of what he'd said, she told herself. Quite likely he didn't mean it at all, because already he was talking again and his expression was bitter once more. 'Then I heard it. Some high-up government morons were making snide comments. One of them muttered to the other that he didn't know how I dared show my face in town again.'

Emma said, 'I hope you didn't hit him?'

He couldn't resist smiling at that. 'You're thinking of my night at the Flag? No, I remembered your advice and spared the fellow. A shame, really. Hitting people is a damned satisfying way to shut them up. I was a soldier, I wasn't brought up to be a diplomat—or a viscount, for that matter! You don't know how lucky you are, not to have to go through all this society rubbish—'

'But I did,' she said quietly.

His eyes widened as he said slowly. 'What, exactly, are you saying?'

She drew a deep breath. 'I didn't want to tell you, because I thought it irrelevant. But Lady Henrietta—' she saw him frowning '—thought she recognised me the other day when she called here. It's possible that someone else might soon.'

'I don't understand. Why might they recognise you?'

'Because I came to London two years ago, for my Season.'

He still looked bewildered. 'Emma, I knew your father was once quite wealthy. But surely…' He broke off. 'Listen, you've been hurt. You should be resting. Maybe this can wait till tomorrow.'

'No. Please. I want to tell you now. I should have told you from the beginning.' She gazed back at him, defiant in spite of that still lurking headache. 'You see, I have a great-aunt, Lady Lydia Dunstable, who is also my godmother. She used to live in London; she is well connected, and she offered to take me to all the necessary balls and so on. But two months after my arrival in town, my father lost all his money. Lady Lydia offered to help, but neither my father nor I wished to live off her generosity, so we moved back to Oxford and my father had to sell his house.'

He was shaking his head. 'Why didn't you tell me all this at the beginning?'

She met his gaze steadily. 'Because I thought it irrelevant. As I've said, I didn't want anyone's pity, or their charity, so I decided I would work for my living.'

He was silent a moment. Then he said, 'Tell me more about your Season. You must have had admirers. Surely they didn't all desert you?'

She shrugged. 'I wasn't entirely without suitors, but I was rather shy, I suppose. Also, my aunt insisted on choosing my clothes for me.' She smiled a little. 'Dear Aunt Lydia did have remarkably odd tastes.'

'Really?' His eyebrows lifted in query. 'Do tell me. Surely not…caps?'

She couldn't help but smile again. 'No. But my aunt always took me to her own dressmaker, whose customers were on the elderly side. As a result, my first ballgown was of brown taffeta and looked as if it had been designed for a staid dowager—which the other debutantes were not slow to point out. My chance of joining the fashionable set was gone. Not that I really minded,' she added lightly.

'It was their loss,' he said.

Something in the intensity of his expression made her suddenly slightly dizzy.

It's the injury to your head, Emma. Be sensible.

After a moment he went on, 'Tell me. During your time in London did you make any enemies? I don't mean the catty women or snubbed suitors—I mean real enemies, who might harbour a serious grudge against you or maybe your father?'

She was bewildered. 'No! I don't see how we could have done. Why ask, my lord?'

He looked at her directly. 'Because I have reason to believe you were attacked tonight, Emma.'

She stared at him. 'No. I truly think I just fell…'

Though she was starting to remember now. The soft footsteps coming up behind her. The blow, followed by blackness. But she shook her head stubbornly. 'Whether or not I was attacked is open to question. Really, it comes down to my own foolishness, in going out alone after dark.'

'No!' He said it almost fiercely. 'And Emma, I've come to a decision. You must leave London as soon as possible with your father.'

'But…'

He pushed on grimly. 'I forced you into coming here, for which I'll not forgive myself. But I shall do as I promised—I'll guarantee that cottage in Hawthorne is your father's for good. I'll also make sure you never have to endure menial service again—'

'No!' she broke in. She could not believe that he was saying this, because it meant that he was giving up too. 'I've told you, I'm happy to work! As for you, you must fight on, as you always did, surely, in battle! What has *happened* to you?'

The silence that followed was almost terrifying but instead of looking furious, he shook his head and smiled sadly. 'Emma. Emma, if I didn't know you better, I would think you were giving me a thorough scolding.'

'Then I'll scold you again and again. I'll do whatever it takes to make you stay here. You *must* get rid of this stain on your reputation, or your life will always be scarred by your past! My lord, I have resolved that I will stay in London one way or another until you come to your senses and start to defend yourself properly. This investigation into the staff at the Home Office, for instance. Is it getting you anywhere at all?'

'Not yet.' His expression was curiously blank. 'But give it time.'

'Give it time? While your belief in yourself is steadily undermined?' She added more quietly, 'You remember, I hope, that this is the only reason I came to London?'

'I'm sorry,' he said. 'I realise that.' Something shadowed his eyes. 'But it's no good, you see. It really isn't.'

She flared up again. 'You must at least try! Life— *people*—have been so unfair to you!'

'I've punched a few along the way,' he said.

She wanted to cry. Somehow she managed a smile but instead tears welled and before she could do anything about them, he'd reached out to gently cup her chin and turn her face towards his. He was saying in wonder, 'Those are tears. You're crying. Oh, God, Emma. Why feel sorry for a brute like me, who's been so arrogant to you?'

Always keep at a correct distance from your employer.

Well, her housekeeper's manual could go to perdition. She couldn't help it. Could not hide how she felt.

'Oh, my lord,' she said. 'Why do you have to punish yourself so?' And still sitting on her bed, she turned sideways to wrap her arms around his formidable frame and lay her cheek against his chest. She'd meant to comfort him, console him even, but somehow it didn't work out like that at all. He put his hands very carefully on her shoulders and moved her away from him so that for a minute she felt rejected. Humiliated. Then—

'Emma,' he said in a voice she'd not heard him use before. It was rough, it was hoarse even, but so very tender. 'Oh, God, Emma.'

She stopped breathing. And then—then, he kissed her.

His mouth over hers was warm and hungry. He coaxed with his tongue, he slid his lips across hers until she was drowning in the taste of him, all the time loving the feel of his strongly muscled arms enfolding her. She knew, in that moment, that she would let him do anything. *Everything.*

She was suddenly aware that he was easing himself away, though for a moment she swayed against him, already lost, already missing him. She wanted him to hold her and kiss her again and offer her all the wild, sensual pleasure she could scarcely yet imagine. Instead he said, very quietly, 'I meant what I said, Emma. This is not right. I need to send you and your father back to Oxfordshire.'

His expression as dark and as serious as she'd ever seen it. 'We shall talk properly,' he went on, 'when you've rested. But I'm afraid my decision is absolutely final on this.'

She said, 'So you're giving up.'

For a moment he didn't answer, though to her merely his silence was answer enough. Then he said quietly, 'You think I'm a coward. Don't you?'

His words twisted her heart anew. 'Never, oh, never!' she cried out. 'But I just do not *understand*...'

'One thing you should understand,' he said, 'is that

I regret, very much, bringing you to London in the first place.'

She felt quite stunned. For several moments her head throbbed as violently as it had when she first opened her eyes after that blow. She gazed at him, trying but failing to guess what had wrought this terrible change in him.

She whispered at last, 'Very well. But I am still on your side, my lord. Always. Please remember that.'

He nodded, then very slowly he rose and left the room. She sagged back against her pillows, for a moment staring into nothingness.

What she must do was obvious. She would *not* go home but she would find lodgings somewhere so Lord Grayford wouldn't even know she was still in London. And she would visit all the dealers by herself, using the list of her father's. The list. She'd been carrying it on her way home...

Maybe she'd put it in her cloak pocket at some point before she fell? Rather shakily, truly feeling now the aftershock of her ordeal, she rose on wobbly legs and went to where someone had hung up her cloak. She reached deep into the pocket and felt dizzy with dismay—because the list was not there.

James went up to his bedroom, dismissed the young valet who nervously awaited him then he tore off all his elegant attire by himself. After that he went to the window, to thrust the curtains aside and gaze out at the night sky.

It was exactly as he'd feared. Those sinister notes meant that it was indeed Emma who was under threat. She had been attacked as a warning, to him.

He'd lied when he told her tonight that he was giving up his efforts to clear himself. Yet his position was damnable; he couldn't explain all this to her because, knowing her as he did, he guessed that the threat would only make her all the more determined to stay on. So he had to order her home. Cut himself off from her. Remove her from danger.

Because proving his innocence was not worth Emma's life. Someone really wanted him to abandon his search and that same person knew that Emma was the weakness in his armour. Indeed tonight, when he'd got home and was told she'd been injured in the street, he'd wanted to clasp her in his arms and keep her there, safe, for ever.

Yes, for ever. He wanted her badly and had done for weeks. Her courage and her integrity had shaken him to his core. His body still throbbed at the thought of her honey-gold hair, her sweet face and lips and that lovely figure hidden beneath the truly awful clothes she always wore. He found himself almost smiling as he remembered her laughing description of the desperately unfashionable gown she'd worn at her first ball. Hell, she'd probably still managed to look gorgeous, which would be exactly why the other women picked her out for their spiteful comments.

Then he remembered the expression on her face when he'd told her he was sending her away. All the trust had gone from her face. She'd looked as if she'd been betrayed, by him; indeed, pretty soon she might be using dried cloves to ward him off, as she had with Steward Rowley.

Tonight, he'd realised just how badly he'd wanted to protect her from all harm and hold her in his arms.

Whereas the best way he could keep her safe was to get her out of here and out of his life for good.

He had something else to think about. That morning he had gone riding with Theo in the Park and his cousin had said, 'I'm afraid, James, that people are beginning to talk about you and Miss Bryant.'

James had nodded, lips thinned. He said, 'Do you know, I cannot imagine what London society had to discuss before I came along. Sometimes, I think I might run away and sign up as a soldier again.'

'Then make damned sure you come back alive, Cousin!' said Theo with a smile. 'Who knows? By then, all this pernicious talk about the book might be well and truly over.'

Suddenly James had wheeled his horse to face him. 'Theo. I asked you the other day if you'd found anyone at the Home Office who could have replaced that book with the fake before it was parcelled up and handed to me.'

'I'm still working on it,' said Theo earnestly. 'I'll let you know the instant I've any news.'

After that they'd ridden on in silence.

James was lonely again. He hadn't realised how lonely he'd been until his honest and incredibly brave housekeeper had come into his life—and very soon she would be gone. He drew the curtains shut. It was late, but his mind was still racing.

Emma thought he was abandoning the quest to clear his name, but she was wrong. He wasn't sure where the book might be, but as to who his enemy was, he'd harboured suspicions for a while—and it was almost time for him to take action.

* * *

The looks the staff gave Emma the next morning were chilly indeed. They must have realised that Lord Grayford had been in her rooms for far too long last night and it was quite clear on whom they placed the blame. Emma guessed that given the chance, they would have bodily evicted her from Grayford House, with Mr Dantry leading the way.

He was forced to communicate with her briefly about the housemaids' duties for the day, but he looked so disappointed in her that she almost felt sorry for him, except that her heart was grieving too sorely for her to have any emotion to spare. Her only respite from universal disapproval was a chance meeting with Gregory the groom as he entered the house with Jasper at his heels.

'I've just taken him for a good long walk round the park, miss,' Gregory said. 'His Lordship asked me to. Become real fond of him, His Lordship has.'

The mention of the Viscount's name was like a knife through Emma. 'Are you liking it here, Gregory?' she asked, trying to make conversation as if nothing was wrong. 'Are the other grooms kind to you?'

'Not half, miss! I'm having a wonderful time.'

When he'd gone she returned to her rooms. It was almost the servants' lunchtime, but she decided it was worth missing a meal to avoid the hostile looks and the whispers. She'd wanted to tell the Viscount about the list that had been stolen from her last night and let him know that she could easily get those dealers' names again from her father. But she guessed he would be terribly angry that she hadn't abandoned the quest, as he'd ordered her to.

She was still dazed from lack of sleep and from confusion. His kisses last night had been passionate, his words tender, yet he wanted to send her away! But it might take him days to make arrangements for the journey and that was exactly what she needed.

A little more time.

Chapter Eighteen

That afternoon Emma went as usual to see her father at two but made no mention of the attack or the lost list. Indeed, she scarcely got the chance because her father could not wait to tell her of the visit he'd made that morning to the bookshop of a man called Jacob Edgecombe, in Drury Lane.

'Edgecombe is one of the wiliest dealers,' he said, 'and I've always suspected he has criminal connections. That's why I put him at the top of that list I gave you.'

Edgecombe. Yes, she remembered him pointing out the name. Emma's hopes soared. 'Papa, do you think he might know something about the missing book?'

'It's more than that! You see, this morning when I went into Edgecombe's shop, I saw some books set aside in a glass-fronted cabinet behind the counter. They were marked *For collection* and I could just about make out the titles on their spines. Emma, I thought I saw a book called *Vitas Sanctorum.* There could be other old books with the same name, of course, but this one is certainly worth pursuing! By then, Edgecombe was blocking my view and wanted to know what I was after. But my dear, I think you really must tell the Viscount.'

'Leave it with me,' she said.

She returned immediately to Grayford House and went to the stables, where she found Gregory on his own. 'Gregory,' she said, 'I have to make a visit straight away, to Drury Lane.'

'Drury Lane? Miss, you shouldn't be going there all on your own!' Clearly Gregory was growing familiar with the districts of London.

'That's precisely why I want you to come with me. We'll take a hackney cab. Just tell the head groom you're accompanying me on an urgent errand, will you? Say nothing else at all.'

Jacob Edgecombe's shop in Drury Lane was set at the rougher end of the street, close to the noisy fruit market of Covent Garden and opposite a tavern. Emma told Gregory to wait outside then pushed open the door. Somewhere a bell tinkled and as she entered she adjusted her eyes to the candlelit gloom, feeling herself instantly enveloped by the musty smell of the old books set in rows on shelves all around the room.

An elderly man was sitting on a stool behind the counter, examining the pile of books that sat in front of him. She also saw, in a glass cabinet behind him, several volumes marked *For collection*; just as her father had said. Her heart beat faster.

'Yes? What do you want?' The man looked up and addressed her sharply. He was dressed all in black and had grey hair and a wisp of a beard. He was frowning over his spectacles at her.

'Am I speaking to Mr Edgecombe?' Emma greeted him politely.

He nodded but said nothing.

'My name,' Emma went on, 'is Mrs Wilson and I wish to buy a book as a present for an aunt of mine who is coming to visit me in town. She adores history—English history, especially the reign of Queen Anne—and I was told that since you specialise in old books, you might have something suitable.'

'My books are expensive,' he said abruptly. 'And I don't sell anything to women.' He turned his attention back to the book he was studying.

Emma put her hands on his counter. 'But this is meant to be a present to my aunt, from *me*. A surprise. And I assure you, sir, I am willing to spend a considerable amount of money!'

Edgecombe was shaking his head. 'I told you. I want no comeback from an angry husband. It's happened before often enough.'

'But may I not just have a look around before I go? I was told you keep such interesting books here—'

'No!' he snapped. 'Now please leave!'

He stood up and came from behind his counter, preparing to escort her out. Emma turned towards the door but then, with a single swift gesture, she sent that pile of books he'd been studying flying to the floor where they landed around the stool. 'Oh!' she cried. 'I'm so sorry. Please let me pick those up for you—'

'No! Get out of my way, woman!'

But Emma was already stooping to retrieve a fallen book and as she stood upright she gazed at those volumes in the glass cabinet. There it was. Just as her father had said: a book that was clearly very old to judge by its beautiful leather binding, and on its spine she read: *Vitas Sanctorum. Albertus Magnus.*

It was the much-desired and highly valuable *Lives of the Saints* that had caused a diplomatic furore between Britain and the Archduke of Austria. And it had been sold—indeed, it might be collected at any time…

She reached to pick up another book from the floor but Edgecombe barred her way. The man was clearly furious with her. Before she could do or say any more, he was practically bundling her out of the shop, but she was still trying to protest. 'I really, truly think I would find something in here that my aunt would love, Mr Edgecombe!'

He opened the door and pointed to the street. 'I don't want to see you in my shop again, do you hear me? My books are too precious to be thrown around!'

Gregory was waiting outside, looking anxious. 'He sounded in a bit of a temper, miss. What was all that about?'

Emma was already leading the way back along busy Drury Lane, but she paused to put one hand on Gregory's arm. 'Gregory, this is important and it's just between you and me. The Viscount is under suspicion for something he didn't do. Did you know?'

'I'd heard whispers, miss. But I don't believe he did any wrong for one minute.'

'Neither do I. So I'm trying to find a way to clear his name and that's why I had to come here—because although the Viscount came to London to prove his innocence, I fear he's about to give up.'

Gregory nodded. 'You could be right, ma'am. Yesterday, when he returned from his ride with his cousin,

I heard Mr Exton telling him he should go back to Oxfordshire. But he shouldn't. Should he?'

'No,' said Emma quietly. 'No, indeed he shouldn't.'

'Something else, miss. While you were in there, I got chatting with the owner of the tavern opposite—the White Horse. Davey's his name and he doesn't like the bookshop owner one bit. "Guards his shop like a hawk," he told me. "He's there from eight till six and lives in the upstairs rooms. The only time he ever leaves is when he goes out for an hour at five, leaving a lad in charge, who doesn't watch the books nearly as closely as Edgecombe does."'

Emma, taking in every word, led the way swiftly onwards to the hackney cab stand at Long Acre. At least once she had the feeling she was being followed, but on turning round, she saw only the usual bustling crowd and told herself she must have been mistaken.

She met with cold glances from the servants on her return. When she asked if the Viscount was back yet, a footman told her that His Lordship was still out at a meeting with his lawyers and might not return till later.

But the book! The book was awaiting collection and could be gone from that shop any hour, any minute. She headed down the hallway to her rooms and because she was hardly looking where she was going, she almost bumped into Theo Exton.

'I've come to visit Lord Grayford,' he said. 'But I've been told he won't be back for a while.' He looked at her more closely. 'Miss Bryant, you appear a little harassed. Is anything wrong?'

She said, 'I'm concerned about the Viscount. He seems low in spirits.'

'I agree,' he said with a sigh. 'And I know that you, like me, have his best interests at heart. He's concerned about the unfortunate slurs on his name of course, but…' He hesitated. 'Miss Bryant, there is another problem. I'm afraid the servants are whispering about your presence here.' He shook his head. 'You know, once London society gets word of this kind of rumour, then false though it is, his reputation really will be ruined. But I may have a solution.'

'What is it, Mr Exton?'

'I believe that the best course of action is for you to return to Oxfordshire, for my cousin's sake, as soon as possible.'

She nodded. 'You're probably right. But it could take some days to make the necessary arrangements.'

Theo pondered a moment. 'Miss Bryant. I believe I could get you a seat in a carriage to Oxford far earlier. This evening, quite possibly.'

'At such late notice? And the cost! I simply haven't the money available.'

'That's no problem, since I will pay. My job at the Home Office is a good one—James saw to that. Foolish man, he feels guilty about my lameness.' He glanced down at his leg. 'As if it was his fault! Ridiculous!' He laughed. 'Now, listen. I suggest that you go and pack your things.'

'You mean right now?'

'Yes, now. I'll send a carrier to pick them up. And I'll go straight to the coaching inn in Holborn, to book a seat for you, for tonight.'

'What about my father? He would never be ready by then! And there's Biddy—'

'Your father and his maid can follow in a few days' time.' He reached for his pocket watch and examined it. 'I'll be in touch shortly, to let you know what time the coach leaves. And don't worry about the Viscount—I'll explain it all to him.' He sighed a little. 'No doubt he'll bite my head off when he discovers what I've done, but he'll soon realise that both you and I have his best interests at heart.'

'Indeed,' she said, 'we do. Thank you, Mr Exton.'

James returned to the house at six, his head spinning from the figures the lawyers had bombarded him with. One of the older grooms came out to take his horse, which was unusual because Gregory was usually the first to spot his arrival.

'Where's the lad?' he asked the groom.

'Gregory, my lord? He asked for an hour or two off. Something special, he said.'

James felt a stab of unease. When Dantry came to take his coat and hat, James was curt. 'Tell Miss Bryant I'd like to see her in my study, Dantry. Now.'

Dantry said, 'But she's gone, my lord!'

James almost reeled. 'What the hell do you mean, gone?'

'Some carriers' men came an hour ago to pick up her luggage. She'd packed everything, my lord. We thought that maybe you knew…'

'*No.* I had no idea. Why didn't you do something to stop her?'

Dantry looked genuinely shocked. 'My lord, we had no idea she was doing this. When the carriers arrived, I sent the servants all around the house looking for her, but no one could find her. I asked the carriers where they were taking her luggage and they told me they had orders to take it to the Rose Inn at Holborn.'

'But that's a coaching inn!'

'Yes, my lord. They said Miss Bryant is travelling to Oxford by coach this evening.'

James shook his head in sheer disbelief. *No.* This could not be right. He'd told her she needed to leave London and she'd looked disappointed in him, desperately so. But surely, she would consult him before taking such drastic action? Was she really going to Oxford, or did she have something else in mind?

He should have told her everything. All his suspicions... 'Give me back my coat,' he said to Dantry. 'I'm going to go and find her.' Her father might know what she planned. If not, he would go on to the coaching inn and ask questions there.

He was heading for the stables when he saw a familiar figure running along the street, out of breath and clearly distressed. It was Gregory, who called out as soon as he reached him, 'My lord. It's Miss Bryant. I went with her just now to Drury Lane—'

'Drury Lane?'

'Yes. There's a bookseller there. Some men tried to kidnap her, but I shouted for help and some other lads ran up and together we fought them off...'

Oh, no. Oh, dear God.

James summoned two of his sturdiest footmen and told them they were to ride with him to Drury Lane, straight away. On the way his mind was still reeling with what else Gregory had said. *'The bookseller's called Edgecombe, my lord. She went there earlier today. He's got an old book she wants...'*

Gregory had also told him he'd left Emma in the care of a nearby tavern owner. 'Real helpful he was! His lads helped me rescue Miss Bryant and he took her inside the tavern to look after her.'

James drew his horse to a halt as the bookshop on Drury Lane came into view. The footmen on their mounts flanked him silently, awaiting orders. The shop was closed, the shutters down; no lights shone from within. 'Guard that place,' he told the men. 'One of you stand by the front door, and, you, watch the back door and windows. Don't let anyone out.'

As they dismounted James spotted a man standing in the doorway of the tavern opposite who called out, 'Sir. Have you come for the poor young lady? My name's Davey Locke. Her friend told me he was going to fetch you!'

Three lads were standing beside Davey and James guessed these were the ones who'd fought off Emma's attackers. As they took charge of the horses, he drew closer.

'I've come for the young lady, yes. I believe I have you to thank for your assistance. Is she badly hurt?'

'I think not, sir. But I was standing outside at the time and I saw just a little of what happened. The young lady seemed intent on visiting the book dealer over there, run by Edgecombe—he's a shifty one all right. But then, two men rushed up and grabbed her. They looked like they wanted to carry her away and they were rough, but her young friend called out for help and my sons and some others chased them off. Shocking it is, in daylight as well.' He pointed. 'The shop might look shut, but I saw the old devil earlier, at an upstairs window. Do you want to deal with him first, or see the young lady? I've tried to make her comfortable in my back parlour.'

James looked round to check that his footmen were doing their job and guarding the place. There would be no escape from there. 'I'll see her first,' he said.

He realised he'd imagined the most awful things. Imagined her bruised, unconscious even, so when he saw her sitting in the cosy parlour, looking pale but composed, he felt such a rush of relief that he was dizzy.

Emma looked up at him as he entered. She seemed uncertain, defensive even. 'My lord,' she said. 'I'm sorry to have given you this trouble.'

The tavern owner had quietly shut the door, leaving them alone together.

'Emma,' James said. It came out more harshly than he'd meant, perhaps because he saw now that her gown beneath her cloak was torn and muddy. 'What on earth have you been doing?' Oh, God, he was up to his usual tricks—ranting and raving, simply because he cared too much. This brave, headstrong woman—she would be the death of him. 'Are you still searching for that book? But I told you I would deal with it all from now on. I told you to leave the business alone!'

'I couldn't,' she said. 'Because the book is in there. I saw it, but it could disappear again any time. My lord, you must get it!'

'No one is going to leave that shop,' he said, 'with or without a book. Emma, Dantry told me you were leaving for Oxford tonight. He said your bags had been collected.'

'Yes,' she said. 'Mr Exton arranged it for me. I told him I would go but I lied to him. James,' she hesitated, 'I'm afraid your cousin is not your friend. Did you realise?'

He said grimly, 'A little while ago, yes. But now that this has happened to you, I could curse myself for not acting sooner.'

'You must act *now*,' she said urgently. 'The book…'

'I know. But Emma—why didn't you wait for me?'

'I wanted to, of course I did! But you were out, no one knew when you'd be back and I was told Edgecombe wouldn't be here at this hour. I was hoping to use Gregory to cause a distraction.'

'It looks as if Edgecombe was waiting for you.'

She hung her head. 'I know. I realise that.'

He moved over to her and took her hand. 'Emma,' he said. 'It's going to be all right.' Suddenly he realised she was shivering and he wanted to hold her and protect her and punch the daylights out of whoever had done this to her. But first, he had to get her to safety while he did what needed to be done.

At that moment Davey came in and took one look at Emma. 'Sir, the poor lady has had a nasty shock. I think she needs to go home and rest.'

'Indeed,' James said. 'Would one of your lads deliver a message for me?'

He wrote it quickly and penned the address with care.

To Mr Exton
At the Home Office in Whitehall

He pressed coins on Davey in thanks then led Emma outside, noting that his footmen were still there and the place was still locked and shuttered.

'There's definitely someone inside, sir,' one of the men told him. 'An old man—we saw him peeping out of an upstairs window.'

'Then make sure he stays there,' ordered James. 'I'll be back very soon.'

He turned to Emma and said, gently, 'I'm taking you somewhere safe. It might surprise you a little. But trust me, I beg you.'

Chapter Nineteen

The Viscount swiftly found a cab and having given instructions to the driver, he helped Emma inside. She felt ashamed of her weakness. It was the shock, she told herself as the cab rattled along; the outright fear she'd experienced when, outside the bookshop, she'd been grabbed by two men who'd tried to drag her away. She remembered how she'd struggled and screamed until Gregory came rushing up with help. She glanced at Lord Grayford, sitting at her side. He was silent now. Was he angry with her? Quite probably.

She was expecting him to take her back to either his own house or her father's, but instead the hackney pulled up outside a tall terraced house to which he appeared to have the key. There were two flights of stairs to climb and she was glad she was able to tackle them without assistance.

She did, however, step back in shock when the Viscount unlocked the door to the apartment and beckoned her in.

'This belonged to my brother, Simon,' he told her as

he closed the door behind him and gestured around. 'It really seemed the best place for you. It's in the middle of town—we're close to Piccadilly—but hardly anyone knew he owned this place. He kept it very private.'

She looked properly around the large, airy room. There were tall windows at one end with thick velvet curtains. A pair of brocade-covered sofas stood by the hearth and at the far end of the room was a huge four-poster bed. The whole of it was lavishly furnished—there were silk and satin cushions scattered around the sofas and the bed. There were mirrors, large ones, everywhere. And paintings, extremely explicit paintings. They were what had caught her attention in the first place. Oh, goodness...

She saw that the Viscount was smiling a little wryly. 'This was a surprise to me too, when I was investigating my brother's assets after his death. But I had to think quickly just now of somewhere to bring you, if everyone is to believe you've indeed gone to Oxford. You've guessed, I imagine, what my brother used this apartment for. Do you mind?'

She suddenly glimpsed a detailed portrayal of Zeus and his lover Danae, both naked and in a very intimate pose. 'No,' she said, dragging her eyes away quickly. 'No, of course I don't mind.'

He nodded. 'Thank you. I'm afraid I'll have to leave you here, but there's a caretaker called Windham on the ground floor. I've checked him out and he's totally trustworthy should you need him. I'll tell him to let no one in, no matter who they are or what they say. Meanwhile...' He hesitated and glanced at her torn gown. 'I've seen that there are some clothes in that wardrobe over there. Women's clothes, for...'

She supplied the answer. 'For your brother's mistresses?'

'Exactly. See if you can find something suitable.' A half-smile twisted his mouth. 'Believe me, this is all for the best. And, Emma, when I get back—we'll talk. I must go now. The cab is waiting outside.'

She took a step towards him. 'Where are you going?'

His expression hardened. 'Back to Drury Lane. Where else?'

After he'd gone Emma wandered around the rooms, too anxious and disturbed to even sit down in this strange place. So the Viscount knew about Theo. And he'd left her here to wait, while he returned to the bookshop—to do what? How long would he be?

A knock on the door made her jump then a man's voice from outside said, 'I've brought some light refreshment for you, miss. I'm Windham. His Lordship asked me to provide it.'

She swiftly went to open the door. 'Thank you.'

'It's no problem, miss. He told me to look after you. And miss—I've not known His Lordship long, but it's obvious he knows what he's doing. So don't you worry, now.'

His words offered just a little comfort. She managed to eat a small cake and drank a half-glass of the wine, then she explored more of this astounding apartment. The paintings brought a blush to her cheeks. Oh, goodness. Did people really…?

Turning her back on them resolutely, she began to explore the wardrobe but most of the dresses were either extremely low-cut or were made of muslin so sheer that they would show pretty much everything there was to see. They made her gasp, half in amusement and half in shock.

At last she found a gown in dark green silk that wasn't quite as daring as the others and she managed to put it on quite easily. But after that the time hung heavily. She walked to and fro. She watched the road and the passers-by from the window. At last, utterly worn out, she went to lie down on that huge bed and rested her head on the extremely soft pillows.

She wasn't going to sleep. She wasn't…

It was half-past eight when James unlocked the door and came into the apartment. 'Emma,' he called out. 'Emma?'

At first there was no sound and he felt his alarm mount. But then he saw her rising slowly from the bed, and his heart did somersaults.

She looked half-asleep and delicious with it. Even more so because she had found a stunningly beautiful green silk day gown from among the rather audacious garments he knew were in the wardrobe here. She'd probably chosen it thinking it looked respectable compared to what else was in there; indeed, it had a modest neckline and three-quarter-length sleeves, but it fitted her slender figure to perfection. On her feet she wore dainty shoes of cream satin; she'd also brushed out her honey-blonde hair but left it hanging loose and the sunlight gleaming through the tall windows lit her up in an entrancing way.

She looked at him, questioning and anxious. His heart bumped in warning. He didn't need those damned paintings all around to heat his desire for this woman. The blood was surging to his loins already.

She said at last, 'My lord, I hope this gown hasn't startled you? I tried to choose something plain.'

'It's fine,' he said rather gruffly.

She pointed to the bed. 'And I didn't mean to fall asleep. I've been so worried about you. And about your cousin and that book.'

'Then worry no longer,' he said. 'It's sorted.

Her eyes widened. 'How?'

For answer, he reached inside his coat and drew out an old, leather-bound book, holding it towards her so she could see the gold lettering on its spine. '*Vitas Sanctorum,*' he pronounced aloud. 'Or, in English, *The Lives of the Saints*, written by the famous sixteenth-century scholar Albertus Magnus. It's the only copy in existence and worth a small fortune.'

She gazed up at him. 'How?'

'While you slept, I've been back to the bookshop. You see, before I brought you here I'd sent a note to my cousin. I didn't sign it—the note just told Theo that Edgecombe needed to see him urgently. I knew Edgecombe was still on the premises because the footmen I'd left outside would see to that. As soon as Theo arrived, my footmen disappeared because I'd warned them to do so, but I'd also told them to wait nearby in case of trouble. Edgecombe opened up for my cousin and I arrived a few minutes later. As soon as Theo saw me, he realised the game was up and confessed everything. It was, as I suspected, Theo who substituted the original book with the fake last December, just before I set off for Vienna.'

She could see the expression on his face. 'Theo,'

he repeated softly. 'My cousin and my oldest friend.' He rubbed his temples.

She said, 'Was it Theo who attacked me as I came home from my father's last night?'

'It was somebody Theo had hired. He's had you followed for a while now. And last night—you didn't tell me, but you had a list of suspect booksellers in your hand, didn't you? And Theo's hireling grabbed it and passed it to Theo. So Theo warned Edgecombe that he was to be wary if a young woman came in asking odd questions.'

'That was why he was so abrupt with me this afternoon.'

'Indeed,' said James. 'Then Edgecombe hired a couple of ruffians himself, to watch outside his shop in case you came back. God knows what they'd have done to you if young Gregory hadn't raised the alarm.'

Emma was silent a moment. Then she said, 'I suppose Theo was responsible for those warning notes sent to Grayford Hall? And for the attack on you at the Flag on your first night?'

'You're right—he admitted that the Flag business was a gamble, but he'd guessed I would suggest dining there just as we always did on the first night whenever he came to stay. He'd paid those men in advance, though he claimed he hadn't intended them to be quite so vicious. He also paid for those broadsheets in Oxford. I believe he wanted to poison the whole district against me.'

'I'm so dreadfully sorry.'

'He told me exactly why he did it.' His voice was calm, but she could sense the underlying feeling of betrayal. 'Apparently, he's harboured this bitterness towards me for years. "You were always the lucky one, James," he said to me tonight. "Son to a viscount. An army hero. I was always the poor cousin." I tried to say that I'd done my best for him, like finding him his job in the Home Office, but he told me tonight that he hates his job, just as he hates his lame leg. I believe he hates his entire life.'

'What will you do now? What will Theo do? Surely you could have him sent to prison?'

She heard him draw a deep, ragged breath. 'I made him write a letter there and then, declaring his guilt. But then I told him that before I produced it as proof of my innocence, I would give him the chance to leave the country permanently. And do you know what he said, Emma? He said, "Trust you to act generously, James. I suppose that makes you feel good, does it?"'

She felt his pain in every word he spoke, but she knew that until he'd finished, silence was her only option.

'When he arrived at Grayford Hall in April,' James went on, 'I still thought he was my friend. But I soon started to become suspicious, especially as he was insistent I shouldn't bother returning to London. I think you've suspected him for a while too, haven't you?'

'I was beginning to think he was not your friend. Of course, today when he pressed me to go back to Oxford, I knew it for certain then. But you weren't there, so I went back to the bookshop by myself. Like I said, I was worried it might be collected any time soon. And I thought Edgecombe wouldn't be there, but I was wrong. I should have waited for you. What will happen to Edgecombe?'

'He denied all knowledge that the book was stolen,'

he said curtly. 'But as your father guessed, crooked deals like that are his speciality. He was furious with Theo for landing him in this situation and said he would certainly give evidence against him if asked. I think this encouraged Theo to confess all. By God, though, Emma, if you'd been seriously harmed, I'd have dealt with the two of them myself.'

She shivered inside at the power of his feelings for her, but she shook her head and tried to smile. 'Then you would have had yet another scandal to live down. You are not fighting the war any more, James.'

'It's a different kind of war,' he said. 'I've been fighting to reclaim my good name.' He raked his hand through his hair and she realised how very tired he was, even as his blue eyes burned into her. 'I've also been fighting to protect you from danger, Emma. That's why I've behaved so abominably to you since the day you arrived in London, telling you I didn't need your father's help or yours. It's because I received two threats against you. The first came on the day I arrived here.'

She was watching him, her eyes wide. He went on, 'This note had the drawing of the black eagle on it. And it said that unless I stopped searching for the lost book, someone I cared for would get hurt.'

She whispered, 'Someone you cared for?'

'Yes. They meant you.'

Emma had thought she was managing to be both calm and practical but inside, her mind was reeling. If she'd felt lightheaded before, she was quite dizzy now. She said, very quietly, 'So when you saw this threat, you changed your mind completely about using my father's help. You told me to stop. You said you were giving up. But I think you're telling me now that you didn't, really. At all.'

'No,' he said softly. 'I didn't, but I needed to protect you from harm. It was hard, because I knew you would think me a coward or worse. But I told myself, *At least she is safe.*'

'Oh.' Her heart wrenched. 'The notes were Theo's work, of course? Like the ones in Oxfordshire?'

'Yes. Just as it was Theo who warned me against following the book's trail, Theo who tried to fob me off with the lies about his own investigations into an imaginary culprit at the Home Office. And then, when he wrote the notes threatening *you*, in London, I decided to send you home for your safety, hoping I would then be free to uncover the truth on my own.'

'But Theo,' she whispered. 'He's your cousin. How could he have done this to you?'

The Viscount had shifted away from her slightly. 'Like I said, jealousy can do strange things to a man. I thought we were friends, but I suppose I've always had what he wanted. Maybe when he learned of my mission to Austria he saw his chance to get even. He had every opportunity to substitute that book because he worked at the heart of the Home Office.'

He had gone over to the window to gaze out and she glimpsed the expression on his face. It spoke of self-contempt—despair, even—and it tore her heart in two.

She walked slowly towards him. 'My lord. What is it?'

He turned to face her. 'I'm thinking,' he said, 'of what a mess I'm making of all this. Of how my brother Simon would be laughing at me.'

'Laughing at you?' She drew nearer. 'Were you not close, then?'

He shook his head. 'He was the aristocrat—refined, suave, born to life in the drawing room. He didn't like to get his clothes dirty, while I was always hunting for adventure. My father often told me it was a good job I wasn't the heir. He would have been quite horrified that I finally inherited.'

Emma let the silence lie between them for a minute. Then she said, 'My father always told me you were the better of the two of you, by far.'

'What? Me, better than my perfect brother?' His voice was bitter.

'No one would tell you this directly, because they all think that you hero-worshipped Simon. But they were heartily glad when you succeeded to the title.'

He said, 'I don't quite understand what you're saying.'

'I'm trying to tell you that your brother was a harsh man. He was callous in his dealings with men he considered his inferiors—with the local girls too, who didn't dare to refuse him when he... You'll know what I mean.'

His face had become expressionless. Was he concealing his fury at her temerity? He said, 'Go on.'

Go on, indeed, Emma, she told herself. *You're so far in now that nothing you say can be any worse.*

'My lord,' she went on, trying to keep her voice steady, 'you noted almost on your first day how the estate had been neglected. But when you arrived, you gave hope to everyone who lived on the Grayford estate. Your father may have been a clever man in many ways, but he was deluded about his elder son. My father says—do I say that too often?—that it's a common fault among aristocrats, to be blinded to the faults of the heir. You are a worthier successor by far.'

She felt that her heart was truly breaking for this brave man who valued himself so little and had been so gravely wronged by the society he'd served for years. But she was trying to be strong, she *needed* to be strong, both for herself and for him.

She seized his hand almost without realising it. 'What have they done to you, my lord, to make you believe yourself so worthless, when you're the very opposite?'

The distress. The uncertainty, in his dark blue eyes that hid so many secrets. How she longed to comfort and cherish him; to convince him of his self-worth. She stood on tiptoe in those dainty satin shoes and reached to cup his face in her hands, kissing him softly on his cheek. 'You are far, far too harsh on yourself. You are brave and unique and wonderful. All of your true friends must think so—indeed, I'm sure they *do* think so.'

He was still looking at her. His blue eyes were intensifying in their gaze. He took her hands in his. 'Emma,' he whispered.

And James kissed her back. He couldn't help himself. This was no gentle kiss of comfort either—no, it was as if weeks of frustration had built up, it was intense and hot, feverish even, while his arms crushed her against him, crumpling that green silk dress she wore.

Friends? he thought. *Be damned to that.*

After long breathless moments he drew back but

didn't let go of her. Still gazing at her with eyes that burned, he said, 'I thought you couldn't stand the sight of me any more. I realised you'd never truly wanted to come to London. I knew too that your opinion of men was already low and my behaviour must have done nothing to change your mind.'

She was shaking her head adamantly but she didn't pull away from him. 'Let me explain. During my Season, I met no one who affected my feelings in the least and I assumed I was the kind of woman who didn't need a man in her life.' She gazed up at him. 'But with you, I can't pretend to be indifferent any longer. I can't even pretend I only want to be your friend.' Her voice had become little more than a whisper. 'You see, my feelings for you are far stronger than that. And they always will be.'

Still holding her, he was gazing down at her wonderingly. He said at last, 'Out of all the bad things that have happened to me lately, this gift is bestowed on me. You. So sweet, so true, so honest. But Emma, you must realise that I'm far from perfect.'

'And who is?' He could see she was angry with him now. 'You are being indulgent. So you have no time for parties and receptions and all that nonsense? Well, many people will admire you for it—so stand up for yourself! Heaven help me, my lord, I know I'll be going home to Oxfordshire soon, but not until I'm sure that your name has been truly cleared!'

Such a heated, brave little outburst! It moved him more than he could express. He touched her cheek and said, 'I've dealt with my cousin and now I'll deal with you. You are not going anywhere, Emma. Do you understand? You are not leaving me again—*ever*.'

'My lord—'

'Call me James,' he whispered. 'Do you hear me?'

She whispered back, 'James.' And he kissed her.

You're nothing but his housekeeper, Emma reminded herself fiercely. *His incompetent housekeeper, at that. You're not even capable of cooking porridge!*

But everything was different now, because she was a woman in love.

With her senses still reeling from his kiss, she realised he had peeled away the shoulders of the silk gown she was wearing and already his lips were brushing tantalisingly over the curve of her neck and shoulder to her breast.

'Oh…' She let out a low cry as delight sparked through her.

He drew his hand away instantly. 'Do you wish me to stop?'

'No. No, but I don't want…'

'I will make sure,' he said gravely, 'that you are not with child. I promise.'

He carried her to that big bed and lowered her there. Though she was only in her chemise and stockings, she wasn't at all cold because his arms were round her. His caresses began anew and she kissed him back fervently, no longer caring if she seemed a wanton hussy. For so long she had wanted this man and when he lowered his mouth to the peak of her breast and kissed it, her whole being melted in delight. She clutched at him, her fingers raking his back, only to be frustrated by the barrier of his shirt.

'One moment,' he said huskily, smiling down at her, his face in the shadows so beautiful that it hurt.

He stood up and off came his boots, his breeches, his shirt, so that once more she saw that old sword scar that curled under his armpit. Yes indeed, his magnificent body was all hers, his lips were claiming hers once more, his muscled chest was pressed deliciously against her yearning breasts while his fingers moved lower to find that spot at the juncture of her thighs where he gently stroked and teased until an almost agonising pleasure began to shake her senses. Yet oh, her body wanted more, so much more...

He drew back and the sight of his manhood, proud and erect, sent a tidal wave of longing rushing through her veins. She clutched at his shoulders almost desperately. 'James. Please.'

He smiled that wicked smile and kissed her forehead. Then, very gently, he parted her thighs and reached down to...

She felt the hard, solid thickness of him pressing into her. Filling her. Her eyes opened wide.

He said quickly, 'Am I hurting you, Emma?'

'No. No, it's just that... *James.* Please don't stop!'

James truly summoned every ounce of his willpower to restrain the desire that shook his whole body. He coaxed her, he caressed her, he did his best to move only gently within her, though he felt the exquisite tension in every one of his muscles, the longing to let his instincts surge and to make her his completely.

'James,' she whispered, her eyes wide with desire, her cheeks flushed with passion. 'I want you, so badly.'

That finished him. She was so warm and tight around him that his control was gone. He began to move faster, his lips still caressing her while he reached down with his hand to where he knew the core of her pleasure lay. And as he touched her there, in that, oh, so sensitive spot, she cried out and arched her hips wildly to meet his; filled by him, pleasured by him, lost in her world of sensation.

For a few moments he held still, entrapped by her ecstasy. Then, as she collapsed back sated on the pillows, he eased himself out of her and spent his urgent seed.

Emma lay wrapped in his arms and drifted into sleep. When she woke, she realised James wasn't in the bed beside her and for a moment she panicked, but then she saw that he was standing in the doorway fully dressed, bearing a tray full of food and wine. After putting down the tray he found a soft dressing robe for her and then they ate and drank together, sitting on that big bed where they'd made love.

Then they made love again, in new and tender ways, and afterwards as she nestled against him she caught sight of her image in one of those oversized mirrors and thought, 'Can that really be me?'

For she looked transformed. She looked like a woman who'd found her heart's desire. But there was still that deep, deep anxiety for the man who was beside her. He was pulling himself up now and reaching for his wine and she leaned against his shoulder. 'James.'

'Mmm?' His arm came round her waist. 'I love you saying my name.'

That brought a smile. 'James. I've been thinking.'

'I've been thinking of *you*,' he said lazily, holding her close. 'In that delicious silk nightgown you were

wearing that evening I came to your rooms in Grayford Hall. In fact, to be perfectly honest, I've never
stopped thinking about it.'

She felt herself blushing. She also felt secret delight
and she stroked the back of his hand because it made
her feel possessive, it made her think, *He is mine. All
mine, for now at least.*

'I've never stopped thinking about that evening either,' she said almost shyly.

He gave a husky chuckle. 'And what about your
sight of me wrapped in a bath towel?'

'Well,' she said, her tone mischievous, 'I saw only
half of you wrapped in a bath towel, though even that
was something to behold.' Oh, goodness. It must be
the wine talking. He was watching her with laughter
dancing in his eyes and to cover her confusion she
looked around the room, saying brightly, 'What an
incredible place this is. Do you think your brother
used it often?'

He was really laughing now and almost choked on
his wine. 'I imagine so, but as I've said, he and I didn't
really share information about this kind of thing.'

She said slowly, 'It's yours now, of course. Have
you ever brought Lady Henrietta here?'

He took her hand in his. 'No!' he said. 'Now, listen to me. Henrietta is trying to rekindle something
that's already died. I've told her I'm not interested.'
He looked around. 'Most likely I'll sell the place.'

She sighed a little and drank more of her wine.

'Are you feeling better?' he said softly.

'Much. Thank you.'

But she wasn't. She was feeling lost and lonely
again because this was like a dream, this place, this

bed, the way he'd made love to her. But all dreams had to end, didn't they?

She looked up at him and said, 'James. You still realise I want to go back to Oxfordshire?'

All the laughter in his eyes faded. He said, 'No. Emma, I need you. Stay with me. You're the only woman I want. You're the woman I love. Marry me.'

And this—this, perhaps, was the hardest moment of all for her. The bleakest moment of all. Summoning all her inner reserves of strength, she looked at the man she knew she would always love and tried to remember who she was. Nothing but his housekeeper.

Get that cap on, Miss Bryant, she reminded herself fiercely.

'James,' she said, drawing away a little, 'please think for a moment. The most important thing for you now is to get your name cleared once and for all. After that, you must concentrate on fulfilling society's expectations.'

With every word she spoke, she could see the shadows clouding his darkly handsome face. He began, 'I don't give a damn about—'

'Hush!' She reached up to put her finger to his lips. 'You *must* remember your position. You have an important role to play as a landowner and employer. You said yourself that you longed to put the estate back in order, to redress the damage your brother's neglect has caused all the farmers and villagers who now rely on you! If you marry me, you will lower yourself in everyone's eyes. You will lose their respect. You might say you don't care, but James, I do. I could not let people say I lured you into a disastrous marriage!'

He moved away from her and she felt an almost

physical pain squeezing her chest, because it was as if they were already saying goodbye. He said at last, 'What are you going to do, Emma? Back in Oxfordshire?'

'I'm not sure. Though of course, I won't return to my post at Grayford Hall.'

How could I, she thought, *when it would mean being reminded of you, every day and every night?*

The hurt almost choked her. 'I shall find another post quite soon, I'm certain.'

'For God's sake!' His raw emotion broke through as he rose and faced her. 'I could make sure you want for nothing! Haven't I made that quite clear?'

She looked at him steadily. 'I don't want your money, James. I will not be your paid mistress. I realise that some day you will find someone to marry and I don't want to be there when that happens. And I'm safe now, aren't I, from any danger, from either your cousin or Edgecombe?'

'Yes. You are. But…'

'Then I shall stay here overnight if I may, since it's late. But tomorrow morning I will go and stay with my father. Your staff already think I've left for Oxford, so they won't miss me at all.'

He looked almost ashen. 'Is there nothing I can do or say to make you change your mind?'

'No,' she whispered.

He nodded, his face tired and drawn. 'Very well. I shall return to Grayford House. You may, of course, sleep here and in the morning I'll send a carriage to take you to your father. If you need anything at all, remember that Windham is just downstairs. I'll be in touch with you in a few days about your journey home.'

She thought he was going to take her hand, but he didn't. Instead he picked up that precious book as if it was a thing he loathed. And then he left.

The next morning a carriage arrived to take her to Aldford Street. She realised too that James had arranged for her luggage, which had yesterday been delivered to the coaching inn at Holborn, to be transferred to the Aldford Street house. It was there waiting for her. Her father was bemused at first by her arrival, but she quickly explained that the book had been found and the Viscount was well on his way to getting his name cleared. 'And I'm no longer his housekeeper,' she concluded, as lightly as she could.

Her father was delighted about the book, of course. 'So can we go back home now? I've enjoyed London, but I miss my friends.'

'We can go home very soon, Papa. The Viscount is kindly arranging it.'

He suspected nothing of her true feelings, but Biddy did. She came upon Emma sitting by herself and rushed to her. 'Oh, my poor dear. No, don't tell me, I can guess what happened. If that man has let you down, I'll—'

'You will do nothing, Biddy.' Emma almost smiled at the thought of the elderly maid taking on the steely strength of Lord Grayford. 'He asked me to marry him, but I refused.'

Biddy was wide-eyed. 'You *refused*?'

'Yes. Because I would only drag him down, and… and…'

She couldn't say anything else, because her voice had broken. Hugged by Biddy, she wept until she could weep no more.

* * *

The next day a note from the Viscount was delivered to Emma telling her that His Lordship's travelling chaise would take herself, her father and Biddy back to Oxfordshire in one week's time. It also informed her that the Viscount's lawyers had completed the purchase of the cottage in Hawthorne that had belonged to Sir George Cartwright. He wrote:

> *You will oblige me by living in it and taking good care of it. In return, I will not require any rent.*

The tone of the letter was so cold and precise that Emma wanted to instantly rebel. She longed to write back, *We do not want the cottage! We cannot be in your debt!* But for her father's sake, how could she refuse?

Then, two days later, a footman delivered another letter bearing the Grayford crest. She thought it might be further news about their travel arrangements, but it wasn't.

> *To Mr and Miss Bryant*
> *The Viscount is invited to a reunion party in Grosvenor Square tomorrow evening, to welcome the return of his former regiment from America.*
> *Also in attendance will be several officers from the Prussian regiments that fought at Waterloo.*
> *The Viscount is permitted to bring guests and*

*would welcome the company of the renowned
historian Pelham Bryant and his daughter.*
A carriage will be sent at eight o'clock.

Emma wrote a swift note and handed it to the footman. It was a horrified *No.*

His Lordship sent the footman back almost immediately with another note.

This one last favour, Emma. Please.

Chapter Twenty

The regimental reunion was held in the grand house of Lord Carstairs, an old colleague of the Duke of Wellington's and a generous friend to all the men who had fought at Waterloo. There was an orchestra for the dancing, there was food and champagne and even a room set aside for the card players. The ballroom sparkled with the women's jewellery and the gold braid of the officers and James found himself welcomed warmly by men who had been absent from England for almost a year.

He soon realised they'd heard nothing of his recent ordeal. He also guessed they wouldn't have believed the lies about him if they had. Anyway, that was over now, finished. The minister who'd ordered the enquiry had examined Theo's written confession and had issued a formal apology to James, news of which was passed around all government departments and quickly reached the whole town.

The book itself was to be delivered to the Archduke of Austria as a matter of urgency. 'And it won't be taken by me,' James had said with a certain amount of grimness. Theo, he knew, had already left the country, sailing on a ship bound for America. James should have been content, for wasn't this what he'd been fighting for all along? Hadn't a grave injustice been righted at last? Tonight's reunion should be a personal celebration; he should be revelling in the easy companionship of his old soldier friends.

But he drank very little and he hurt like hell, because he missed Emma so badly.

There were certainly plenty of attractive women at this reunion, including some unmarried sisters of his friends who were eagerly introduced to him. 'Here is Lord Grayford, a hero of Salamanca!'

James didn't need the 'hero' bit and he guessed the women were disappointed too, because he paid little attention to any of them. He was too busy hoping that Emma would come, though he truly doubted it now, because he'd received no reply from her to his second appeal.

This one last favour, Emma. Please.

Separating himself from his lively comrades, he stood alone in a corner of the reception hall watching the last guests arrive. He acknowledged that if she didn't come tonight, it was all over. Indeed, he'd almost given up hope when he heard the major domo announcing, 'Mr Pelham Bryant and his daughter, Miss Emma Bryant.'

For a moment James was unable to move, because Emma looked absolutely radiant. That was the only word that could do her justice. Her gown was simple, made of pale turquoise silk with short sleeves and a modest neckline. Her slender arms were clad in long cream gloves while her hair, neatly tied up, was secured by a satin headband. Most of the women here wore clusters of fine emeralds and diamonds; Emma's only jewellery was a necklet of small pearls, but she easily outshone them all. By now other men were staring in open admiration, while the women at their sides eyed this stranger warily.

James strode right up, bowed to her father and took Emma's hand. 'Mr Bryant. Miss Bryant. I'm truly honoured that you accepted my invitation.' He lifted her fingers lightly to his lips and murmured, 'You look beautiful.'

If it hadn't been for Biddy and her father, Emma would not have come. James's simple plea had torn her in two, because she missed him so, but she'd warned herself that this final farewell might haunt her for ever.

But then her father had seen the invitation and he'd been thrilled. 'Once we're back home,' he'd announced, 'I will be able to tell my friends of all those gallant officers who'll be there! The Prussian soldiers too—they were part of Blücher's Field Army of the Lower Rhine, you know, which was so very significant at Waterloo...' Still talking, he'd already set off for his desk to search for some old newspaper articles about the battle.

Biddy had come up to Emma then and said, 'I hope you're going, my dear. For your father's sake and for your own.'

'But Biddy, I will be so out of place! I have no real right to attend!'

'Nonsense,' said Biddy briskly. 'You'll be as lovely

as any of the ladies there, for a start. As for your right
to attend—you've been invited by a viscount, no less!
And do you really think His Lordship would have
asked you if he wasn't madly in love with you?'

'Love!' Emma had tried to laugh, but it came out
shakily. 'He's being kind to Papa and me, that's all.'

Biddy made a comment that sounded something
like *Rubbish* and immediately started planning what
Emma would wear. She headed out to a modiste who
sold second-hand clothes as well as new and came
back with the turquoise gown—'Worn only once, by
a grand lady!' Biddy told Emma with great satisfaction. It was a little large, but Biddy, a skilled seam-
stress, took it in and removed several unnecessary
flounces that cluttered the hem. By seven o'clock, she
had helped Emma into her new finery and brushed her
hair until it gleamed like gold.

Even so, Emma felt quite sick with nerves as she
entered the reception room on her father's arm. As
the silence fell all eyes seemed to turn on them—on
her. What if they'd heard she'd been Lord Grayford's
lowly housekeeper?

I cannot do this. I should not have come.

But then James was striding towards them and he
had that gleam in his eyes—burning, possessive—that
clutched at her very heart. 'You look beautiful,' he
said. And that most dangerous of emotions—hope—
was stirring again in her heart.

The first thing he did was to lead both of them
across the crowded room to where some officers, both
English and Prussian, were seated in deep conversation. But they all rose when James said to them,
'Friends, let me introduce you to this gentleman, Pel-

ham Bryant, who is a renowned historian and linguist. I'm sure he would love to hear your stories of past campaigns.'

With murmurs of interest and several eager glances in Emma's direction also, the officers quickly welcomed Emma's father into their midst while James led Emma into the next dance.

'But you told me you didn't enjoy dancing!' she blurted out.

He leaned close and murmured, 'I don't. Unless it's with you.'

She couldn't resist the spell he inevitably cast over her. Truly, it was a magical evening; the music was entrancing, the dozens of chandeliers cast a glittering light over the whole enchanted scene and as they danced she tried her best to forget her own worries, her own heartbreak that all this would soon be over. Instead she smiled up at him and said, 'You are among friends again, James. I'm so glad.'

'My name is cleared,' he said. 'All thanks to you. Listen, Emma, I—'

At that point the music stopped; the dance was over and whatever he was going to say next went unsaid, because as he led her from the floor, a group of young English officers came hurrying up with their eyes on Emma.

'James,' the first one exclaimed. 'Where have you been hiding this lovely creature?' The officer bowed to her. 'Your servant, ma'am. It's Miss Bryant, isn't it?'

Emma stepped back in surprise. These men knew her name? She could see that James too was puzzled, especially as yet another young officer had come forward. 'It's a pleasure to see you here, ma'am. James, you rogue, we've been puzzling over where we've seen your lovely companion before and then we remembered. She was a debutante two years ago—but then suddenly, she disappeared!' He turned to Emma. 'Isn't that right? We haven't forgotten you. Your mother was niece to the Earl of Sanderby, but what we remember most is that you were so very different from all the other girls, Miss Bryant. You were kind to everyone, even if we tripped over our own feet while we danced with you. I think we were all a little in love with you. But you were only in London a short while then suddenly you vanished! We christened you *The Lost Debutante*, but clearly, you've been found again. James, you're a lucky fellow! Miss Bryant, may I claim the next dance?'

'I'm afraid not,' she heard James reply. 'You see, gentlemen, all of them are already taken. By me.'

As soon as he could guide her away from her eager admirers, James led her into a quiet corner and stood facing her, holding her delicate wrists as lightly as his emotions could allow. He said, 'You told me your Season was a failure. That you received no offers.'

Though she was pale, she returned his gaze. 'That's not exactly true. I told you I *accepted* no offers. And when my father lost his money, all I wanted was to leave London as swiftly as possible.'

'From the sounds of it,' said James, 'quite a few men would have married you anyway, money or no money.'

'Maybe they would. But you see, I wouldn't have married any of them!' She looked almost distraught. 'I just couldn't understand the girls who giggled and flirted with everyone and so desperately wanted a husband. I thought there must be something lacking in me, because I didn't feel like that about any of the men who courted me.'

'Didn't feel like *what*, Emma?'

She whispered at last, 'I felt no desire for them.'

He was silent for a moment, his eyes searching and serious. Then he said softly, 'You can't have forgotten those hours we spent together in my brother's apartment?' He lifted her hand to his lips. 'I don't find there's anything lacking in you *at all*.'

She blushed so delightfully that he wanted to bed her there and then. 'But that was different,' she breathed. 'That was because of you.'

He kissed her hand again because, damn it, that was all he was allowed to do in this crowded room. He said, 'Marry me, Esmerelda.'

'James, I can't! If these friends of yours find out that I've been your housekeeper…'

'If they do, I doubt it will bother them in the least. They'll perhaps think it was some game of ours— especially since your mother was niece to an earl. Not that I care about that in the slightest, but you know it makes all the difference to the old-fashioned members of the *ton*. Why didn't you tell me about your aristocratic relatives?'

'Because the Earl disowned my mother the instant she told him she was marrying my father. You see, the Earl had hired Papa to do some research into his family history, one summer when my mother happened to be staying with her uncle. That was how my parents met and fell in love—she was eighteen, he was thirty. My father was wealthy in his own right, but the Earl thought him not good enough for his niece and as for my mother's parents, they totally agreed with the Earl. *Everyone* agreed with the Earl, on everything and because of her marriage, my mother became estranged from her entire family. Only Lady Lydia, the Earl's sister, stood by her. As for the Earl of Sanderby, he died some years ago.'

'I'm relieved to hear it,' he said. 'That means we won't have to invite him to our wedding.'

'James…'

He held both her hands tightly. 'I love you, Emma. Life isn't worth living without you. Surely, the welcome given you by these friends of mine has convinced you that we'll be accepted everywhere? Marry me. Please don't refuse me again. I love you. I cannot imagine life without you.'

Still she didn't reply. James felt blackness beckoning and tried to suppress the bone-deep longing for her that all but engulfed him. He steadied his voice and said, 'If you need time to think…'

'No,' she said quickly. 'No. I don't. But I was just wondering what my duties would be, as the wife of a viscount.' Something lurked in her eyes then, a hint of laughter. 'And I'm thinking that maybe I *could* manage—as long as I don't have to make pickles.'

He gave a shout of laughter that drew the attention of all around. 'Definitely not,' he declared. Then he pulled her close and murmured, 'But you can interrupt my bath any time at all.' And to the general delight of all there, he kissed her most thoroughly.

Only her father, absorbed in conversation with the English and Prussian officers, seemed oblivious to what was going on. James, concluding the kiss at last and taking Emma resolutely by the hand, marched over to him. 'Mr Bryant,' he said. 'May I ask you for your daughter's hand in marriage?'

Emma's father turned to him calmly. 'Why, I was beginning to think you'd never get round to it. Delighted, my dear Lord Grayford. Delighted. Now listen, this is interesting.' He pointed to his new friends. 'This officer here is explaining to me that his family are connected to a branch of the Habsburgs that I have never, ever heard of. Quite remarkable, wouldn't you say?'

James wanted her. He wanted all of her, body, heart and soul, and in exchange would give her everything he could, because he'd so nearly lost her.

He tried to take her to a quieter part of the ballroom but it was quite impossible to avoid all the people who were eagerly rushing up to offer their congratulations. 'We must find somewhere private to go,' he said to her, his voice hoarse with urgency. 'Emma, I don't want you to leave me tonight.'

She raised her eyes to his, those golden-brown eyes he'd loved from the start, and he realised they were brimming with mischief. 'I can think of somewhere, my lord. There's a certain apartment close to Piccadilly which is very suitably furnished…'

'My brother's so-called love nest?' James grinned. 'You mean it?'

'Yes—' She broke off, suddenly worried. 'But if you and I leave now, how will my father get home to Aldford Street?'

'Your father will want to be here for a while yet, I think, since he's clearly in his element. I'll tell you what. My carriage can take us to Simon's place right now and then the driver can return here and wait for him.'

She looked alight with happiness once more. 'I shall tell him.'

He watched her as she moved gracefully away to speak to her father and the thought that he'd nearly lost her ripped him apart. Why had it taken him so long to acknowledge how very much she meant to him, when he'd known from the start that for the first time in his life, he'd fallen madly in love?

Fate had been against them both, of course. He had gained an unwanted inheritance, while she had been forced to turn her back on the life she might once have expected. He, at first, had stubbornly refused to clear the unwarranted stain on his reputation and she, in her own way, was as obstinate as he.

'I will not let people say, my lord, that I lured you into a disastrous marriage!'

But it was her obstinacy that proved her worth. From the very start, she'd told him he must return to London and fight his cause, though she had hated the idea of coming with him and now he knew why—she'd thought that her brief Season had been a disaster. But clearly that was nothing like the truth and tonight these officer friends of his had proved it to her.

The Lost Debutante, they'd called her. Found by him, though she was the one who had saved him, in a multitude of ways.

Now she was coming back to his side, looking so radiant that all the men she passed by were gazing at her. *She's mine*, he wanted to declare to them and the entire world. *All mine, at last.*

* * *

Once the carriage had driven to Piccadilly and dropped them off in Duke Street, James swiftly unlocked the front door. The caretaker came out briefly from his ground floor rooms. 'My lord. Do you need anything?'

'No, Windham. Everything's fine, thank you.'

The two of them hastened hand in hand up the stairs to Simon's apartment almost like runaway lovers, he thought. Once inside he lit candles, only a few, so the soft light glimmered in the mirrors and cast a sheen over the crimson silk hangings around the big four-poster bed. He saw her glancing at the bed then almost shyly at him, looking uncertain just for moment. But then he took her in his arms.

'Emma,' he said. 'Be in no doubt of it. I love you, very much.'

And he heard her murmur, 'I love you. For always.'

He was already easing off her cloak and then his own coat. Soon enough, all their clothes lay in a heap on the floor and they were naked between the silken sheets of that great bed, her body warm against his. They were both almost laughing in their eagerness as she stroked his shoulders and he kissed his way down her throat to the curve of her breast, tantalising its peak with his tongue until she cried out his name and he felt the hunger burning in his own aroused flesh. He reached with his hand for that little bud of pleasure between her legs, stroking her there tenderly until she was pleading for more; then he coaxed her legs around his so her hips were tilted to greet him. Within moments he was inside her and they were as one.

'Emma,' he breathed. 'Tell me if I'm hurting you.'

'No.' Her voice trembled with passion. 'James. I want more. Please…'

Almost shaking with restrained desire he began to move again, thrusting harder as she clutched at his back and shoulders. He paused, withdrawing just a little to caress her once more, then she arched towards him to clasp him close and he let himself be swept with her into a realm of fierce and tender pleasure.

He held her until her tremors subsided at last. He kissed her face, her eyes, her lips and then, with his arms still wrapped tightly around her, they slept.

He might be a viscount. He might have wealth beyond his dreams. But truly, he had all that he wanted right here in his arms.

Epilogue

One year later—Grayford Hall, Oxfordshire

Emma was sitting on a stone bench in the rose garden when she heard the sound of hoofbeats on the drive. She smiled to herself. Always in a hurry, her husband. How she loved saying that to herself—her husband! She could hear James's voice now as he handed Goliath over to Gregory and Gregory must have told him exactly where she was, because soon James came striding around the corner of the house to where she sat, with Jasper trotting eagerly at his heels.

Her heart always lifted to see him. He was handsome of course—incredibly so, even in the old riding coat and sturdy leather boots he always wore to visit his farms. But he also looked happy. Not carefree, exactly, for he took his duties seriously, but he looked like a man with no secret burden to bear, no hidden bitterness eating at his soul.

He came to sit beside her and put his arm around her. 'How is Clara?'

'She is absolutely fine.' Emma leaned into his strong

shoulder. 'Nurse took her inside for a short rest, but no doubt she'll bring her out again very soon.'

'I've missed her,' he said. 'And you.'

'James! You only been gone for two hours!'

'Too long,' he murmured, kissing her cheek.

They had married a mere month after his proposal at the officers' reunion in Grosvenor Square. Baby Clara had arrived eight months later and the speed of it all could have set tongues wagging, but really that was nothing, thought Emma, compared to the fact that the new Lord Grayford had married his former housekeeper!

For a few weeks, society had been full of it. But the best thing about the *ton* was that there was always some fresh scandal to keep the gossipmongers enthralled. By a great stroke of luck, one of the King's sons had a rather interesting and public break-up with his latest mistress and, since Lord and Lady Grayford were by then back in their Oxfordshire home, their marriage soon became a very dull topic indeed.

As for moving back to Grayford Hall where she had briefly but memorably been the housekeeper, Emma had worried more for James than for herself. 'It will be most strange for the staff,' she'd told him. 'I'm sure they'll be respectful to me for your sake, but...'

'Worry no more,' James had told her. 'I intend to make a few changes on our return.'

He appointed an experienced steward, together with a butler and a housekeeper who between them ruled the household so firmly that before long resignations began to be handed in. Thomas and Robert were the first to leave, but most of the footmen and maids were perfectly happy to stay on; while as for Mrs Clegg the cook, James gave her a pay rise. New staff were promptly brought in to replace those who'd left and, if they'd heard that the new Lady Grayford was once the housekeeper here, they had the good sense to keep quiet about it.

For the staff actually *liked* her, Emma realised, while they also appreciated James's firmness and his fairness. Outwardly, Lord and Lady Grayford were a calm, practical couple, who enjoyed entertaining their friends as well as applying themselves dutifully to all the responsibilities of the estate. But only they knew about the joy they shared together at night in his bedroom, which had been stripped of the Chinese dogs and the pink and yellow counterpane, though within weeks of their arrival, James had put a new statue of Hebe on the mantelshelf.

'It's to remind me,' he told Emma, 'of the evening when I first realised I was falling in love with my housekeeper.'

'I fell in love with you the day you arrived,' Emma answered laughingly. 'Though you were in such a rage with me that I also disliked you, quite abominably! But tell me, James.' Her expression was suddenly serious. 'Do you believe at long last that you are truly worthy of your place here?'

He looked all around, then turned back to her. 'Yes,' he said. 'Yes, I do. Largely thanks to the brave little housekeeper I found here, who despite wearing a ridiculous cap and gown, wouldn't let me *not* believe in myself.'

Since then the winter had passed, baby Clara had arrived and they found themselves busier than ever. Now, in the summer sun, they sat side by side on the garden bench quietly enjoying a rare moment of day-time intimacy until James, glancing across the lawn to the house, rose to his feet. 'Here comes Nurse with Clara,' he announced. Jasper was already rushing off to meet them and James was about to follow, but Emma's hand on his kept him there a moment longer.

'I never thought I could be so happy,' she whispered.

He gazed down at her and tenderly tucked away a lock of stray hair from her forehead. 'I rather think that we have plenty more happiness in store. Don't you?'

She nodded. 'I'm sure of it. Though I could hardly ask for anything else.' They were both silent a moment. Yes, there would be challenges ahead, dark days as well as sunshine—but their love would be enough to see them through.

James was smiling as he pulled her up from the seat. 'Are you sure that you can't imagine anything else to ask for? Then try a little harder. More dogs? More horses? More children?' He pretended to ponder the subject. 'I would suggest more children, most definitely. Another two, perhaps. What do you think?'

'Maybe three more,' she answered teasingly. 'With ponies for each of them, of course, once they're old enough. And...' She hesitated.

'What? What is it?'

'I wish above all for each of them to be blessed in love.' She was reaching up to caress his strong, tender face. 'As I have been.'

'And me,' he murmured, holding her tightly. Then he grinned. 'But as for children... Do you really think four are enough?'

* * * * *